DREAM AGAIN

McIntosh Brothers

Book 1

I0654464

BESTSELLING AUTHOR
Ann Marie Bryan

Victorious By Design
Plymouth, FL

To order copies of this book, please contact:
Victorious By Design, LLC
P.O. Box 638, Plymouth, FL 32768

Email orders@victoriousbydesign.com
Visit our website at www.victoriousbydesign.com

Book cover created by Alerrandre

DEDICATION

I dedicate this book to my six beautiful sisters—Icylin, Beverlyn, Henritta, Ivalyn, Navlet, and Verna—who never stop dreaming. I love you. You are my delight.

CONTENTS

ACKNOWLEDGEMENTS 6
CHAPTER 1 8
CHAPTER 2 13
CHAPTER 3 20
CHAPTER 4 29
CHAPTER 5 34
CHAPTER 6 39
CHAPTER 7 45
CHAPTER 8 53
CHAPTER 9 58
CHAPTER 10 65
CHAPTER 11 68
CHAPTER 12 73
CHAPTER 13 78
CHAPTER 14 84
CHAPTER 15 90
CHAPTER 16 96
CHAPTER 17 103
CHAPTER 18 107
CHAPTER 19 114
CHAPTER 20 118
CHAPTER 21 125
CHAPTER 22 129
CHAPTER 23 137
CHAPTER 24 144
CHAPTER 25 150
CHAPTER 26 154
CHAPTER 27 161
CHAPTER 28 168
CHAPTER 29 177

CHAPTER 30 184
CHAPTER 31 191
CHAPTER 32 199
CHAPTER 33 205
CHAPTER 34 211
CHAPTER 35 216
CHAPTER 36 223
CHAPTER 37 231
CHAPTER 38 239
CHAPTER 39 245
CHAPTER 40 252
CHAPTER 41 257
CHAPTER 42 268
CHAPTER 43 273
CHAPTER 44 281
CHAPTER 45 291
CHAPTER 46 297
CHAPTER 47 309
CHAPTER 48 313
CHAPTER 49 321
CHAPTER 50 326
READING GROUP GUIDE 334
SONGS MENTIONED 336
A NOTE FROM THE AUTHOR 337
ABOUT THE AUTHOR 338
CONNECT WITH THE AUTHOR 339
AVAILABLE TITLES 340
VICTORIOUS BY DESIGN.......................................343

ACKNOWLEDGEMENTS

Thank you to the individuals who contributed to the completion of this book.

My Heavenly Father – All that I am and will be is in You. I'm still amazed by Your love for me. I love You. Thank you for the lessons I have learned with each book.

Orville, my husband, my beloved – I love you. You are my rock. You inspire me daily with your love, support, and prayers.

My siblings – I'm a part of a beautiful family. I'm thankful for the values that Mom instilled in us. She led by example, mirroring the love of Jesus Christ, our Savior. Mom is no longer with us, but I see her priceless love in each of you. Let's charge on, always remembering her in our hearts.

Special thank you to the exceptional members of my Facebook readers' group (Ann Marie Bryan's Readers' Café) for their love, support, laughter, encouragement, and prayers. Thanks to you, I keep churning out story after story. A big thank you to our wonderful admins – Denise Anderson and Paula Hamilton, and our moderators – Tera Kirksey and Ryan Smith, for keeping us inspired and motivated.

Ms. Tina V. Young, proofreader – I love and appreciate you. I value your knowledge, skills, and support. Thanks for ensuring that I have the best possible book before launch. It's a blessing to work with you.

Mrs. Millicent Battick, my-sister-friend and beta reader – thanks for reading my manuscript and for remembering even the minute details to help me stay true to the plot. Thanks, too, for being my enthusiastic cheerleader and a constant source of inspiration. I love you. Your friendship is a gift from the Lord.

I love my awesome chief editor, author M. A. Malcolm. Thank you for going beyond the call of duty, as usual. You have made the entire process a pleasure. Your involvement in my life is a gift for which I will always be grateful. Thanks for using your superb creative and insightful skills to help me bring life-changing books to the world.

A big thank you to my readers. I'm grateful for each of you. I'm inspired by your words of encouragement and reviews of my books. You all rock!

CHAPTER 1

Eyes wide, she stood there gaping at him. He had walked into her life, crushed all her defenses, and held her heart captive. The delicious sensation racing up and down her spine was all the reminder she needed. A decisive "Yes" came from her lips, for she had found the one whom her heart loved.

Gianna Barrett let out a loud sigh of relief as she closed the manuscript from international bestselling author ReTrac. She was thrilled to know the heroine's response to the hero's proposal. It was touch-and-go for a moment with them, so she was glad happily-ever-after was happening... at least, in the make-believe world of books.

She used to dream of a moment like this, but not anymore.

Still, she loved reading romance stories. She was a big fan. There was nothing wrong with chiseled jawlines, gorgeous smiles, rock-hard pecs, and promises of tomorrow. Even if they only helped to create the perfect daydream.

In the next breath, Gianna switched off the ignition of her silver Acura ILX, grabbed her black purse from the passenger seat, and dropped her MacBook Pro in it. She exited the vehicle and felt the cool April breeze whipping around her as she headed towards the impressive state-of-the-art glass building with bronze exterior—a feat of modern architecture in downtown Orlando, Florida. Huge gold letters embedded in a black rectangular plate announced its name—Brooklyn Morris Publishing House.

Gianna mounted the broad steps in the shadow cast by a typical high-rise building and moved through the double doors to enter the glitzy lobby. Designed to give a cinematic experience, it was adorned with murals, crystal chandeliers, kelly-green leather sofas, and lush plants.

Backlit honey onyx panels elevated the overall level of sophistication.

Smiling, Gianna waved at Mark Gallon and Trevon Marwick, the two security officers who were on duty, and they gave her the usual salute. Her three-inch black open-toe shoes click-clacked as she walked across the gold-toned limestone flooring of the aesthetic delight. Just as she made her way past the green onyx circular reception desk to access the elevators, someone called her name. Gianna swung her head to locate the voice.

Familiarity dawned, and she smiled. "Hey, Chrissy!"

Christina Martin unhinged her lanky body from a limestone column nearby and walked towards Gianna. Her tousled brunette hair gave her a free-spirited look, as it fell around her shoulders. "Gigi, great to see you," she said, giving Gianna a brief hug.

Gianna looked at her like a proud mom. "Congrats! New York Times Best Sellers List. Way to go!"

"I'm ecstatic. My first novel and it was like my baby." Christina's light-gray eyes danced with joy. "Thanks for your help. I couldn't have done it without you."

"You're welcome."

"I'm disappointed though. I've been reassigned to another editor."

"Don't worry. Kimberly Dawson will make sure your work shines."

"So I gathered. I just had a meeting with her." Christina's lips blossomed into a huge smile, and Gianna waited for the good news. "I met someone."

"Congratulations!" Gianna touched her shoulder. "I told you it would happen sooner or later."

"You sure did. I'm waiting on him. Er, he went to use the bathroom."

Gianna whipped up a smile. "Good for you. I'm glad you're happy. I've got to run, though; I have a meeting."

"Thanks. See you around."

"You sure will. Bye."

Gianna was moving towards the elevators when Christina spoke.

"You took your time."

Interest piqued, Gianna turned her head and felt her temperature soaring. *Oh no. It can't be.* She cringed, something akin to panic rising in her throat. Cocky, egotistical Caleb Porter was smiling and strutting purposefully towards Christina. He was always on the cutting edge of fashion, and today was no different. His tall, bronze athletic body was in a slate-gray slim-fit suit.

Gianna turned and rushed to press the elevator call button nearest to her.

"G?" Caleb's astounded voice reached her ear.

Mentally, everything in her was protesting about the nickname he'd given her. She held back glaring daggers as she turned to face him. "Hi." *Ugh!* He was dropping wet kisses on Christina's cheek.

Christina was grinning like a fool, patting his chest. "Stop, honey. We're in public."

Gianna's brows crushed together. He was so predictable it was sad.

Caleb flicked his hand dismissively. "That's okay, babes."

He flashed Gianna a dazzling smile. "Hey, G. I forgot you work here."

"Really?" *How convenient.* Gianna wished he would vanish in a puff of smoke. She hadn't seen him in two years, but nothing had changed. He was still acting like he was holding the universe together.

"How do you two know each other?" Christina asked hesitantly.

"We…" Gianna began slowly, thinking of words that would not crush the kind-hearted soul.

"We met at a social event," Caleb pitched in.

Gianna's world ground to a screeching halt. *Barefaced lie.* Now he had her spoiling for a fight. Her hands twitched to grab him by the throat. She restrained herself, for she wished she could rewrite their history, too. Thanks to him, she had built walls—sky-high walls—around her heart.

"Oh, okay," Christina remarked, oblivious to the undercurrents. "I thought you dated in college or something."

"Nooo, babes." Caleb gave up a blank expression like he had no idea how Christina could have jumped to that conclusion.

Mistruths. Deception. Misdirection. Gianna wanted to slap his face. "Got to go," she said, looking at Christina. "Meeting."

"Alright, talk soon," Christina said.

"Take care, G," Caleb dared to say.

It was Gianna's turn to give up a blank expression, but immediately she regretted looking at him. He had the man-you-let-get-away look in his eyes.

Psycho. Gianna clutched her purse with both hands to prevent herself from beating him with it. *I'm holding my peace. I'm holding my peace.* Without another word, she turned and moved to punch the call button. When the elevator door opened, she stepped in, touched the button to the fourteenth floor, and watched the doors close.

She exhaled loudly, then squeezed her eyes shut.

Uuuggghhh!

Meeting Caleb like that took more out of her than she was willing to admit. A part of her had always wondered how in the world she had gotten in a relationship with him. Subtly, Caleb had scaled the high wall and entered her home, her inner circle, and her heart. And almost her bed. Well, she'd been planning to break the rule just to keep him by her side.

Hate rose in her heart, but she dumbed it down.

She'd never believed in fairy tales, and even if she'd had any chance of changing her mind, Caleb Porter had killed it. Determined to move forward, she pushed the painful memories to the back of her mind.

CHAPTER 2

Once the elevator doors opened, Gianna marched through the waiting area and down a passageway to her office. The gold-toned limestone flooring and the shades of green color scheme continued through the interior of the publishing house.

She paused near the slightly opened door of her office to fix her expression before entering. The nameplate on the door—Gianna Giva Barrett, Chief Editor—seemed to pull her eyes as a reminder of her accomplishments. She looked toward the corner office two doors down from hers and made a step in that direction.

"Gigi, don't do it," warned the familiar voice of Maya Harrington, her executive assistant.

Gianna chuckled as she pushed the door and entered the foyer to her office. The smiling face of Maya greeted her.

"Boss lady, you do not need to see Ms. Morris right now," Maya said, leaning back in the army-green leather chair at her L-shaped mahogany desk.

The thirty-five-year-old dark-skinned woman was always in a great mood. Gianna was happy for that, because Maya was the critical bridge between her and her co-workers in a company that at times seemed to demand her soul.

"Well, unless Ms. Morris has ReTrac with her," Maya said smugly.

Gianna beamed. "Now, there's someone who could brighten my day."

"The day you meet ReTrac..." Maya paused, cracking up at Gianna's expression. "Oh, I forgot that will never happen. Thanks to you, we'll never meet him. Ever!"

"Well, if he would stop sending me crappy drafts, I wouldn't have to tell him to rewrite."

"Well, you could have finished reading it; especially when he had sent it the second time."

Gianna held back laughter. "He'll be alright. Anyway, I just finished reading his manuscript, and it was good but still not up to his abilities."

Maya flipped her wavy black hair behind her back. "That's why you're chief editor."

"What do I have after I meet with Brook? I'm thinking of heading home early."

"Early? Before seven o'clock?" Maya inspected Gianna's face. "I suppose I should be happy. I'm impressed, too, you're doing this on a Monday."

"Yes, Mother," Gianna retorted.

Maya chuckled. "I'm a happy camper. You took time for lunch, away from the office at that."

"That's an improvement, right?"

"For sure, and I liked it." Maya smiled at her. "Ms. Morris changed the time of your meeting to an hour later. Not to worry, though, I made the changes to the five-year strategic plan so you can review it while you wait. After you meet with Ms. Morris, you're free."

"Okay, let me get to it."

Gianna moved in the direction of her office.

"Kamala is trying to reach you," Maya mentioned. "She called four times while you were out for lunch."

Gianna kept walking. "Why?"

Long pause.

"You know why."

Gianna stopped and turned to look at Maya. "I already told Kam I couldn't go to New York next weekend."

"Maybe she didn't quite get it."

Gianna flicked a glance at the ceiling. "Oh, boy! I can't wait for this wedding to happen."

Maya sent her an eyebrow lift. "You love your best friend."

"For sure," Gianna grumbled. "Three months to her wedding, and I'm already feeling the freedom."

"At least you're not the maid of honor."

"For that, I'm grateful."

Gianna walked into her glorious office. No stones were left unturned when it came to giving her a sharp, professional image. The high ceiling, perfect lighting, pastel green walls, and mahogany furniture were all geared towards productivity perfection.

She moved past the pair of army-green visitors' chairs, dropped her purse on the executive desk, and took out her cell phone. Taking a seat at the desk, she video-conferenced Kamala.

"Hey, Gigi! Are you okay?" Kamala asked, concern etched in her expression.

"Yes, Kam, I'm fine. I went to lunch away from the building."

"I thought you ran off with ReTrac." Kamala gave a little laugh. "You didn't answer your cell phone."

Gianna smiled at her. "I needed a moment. What's so urgent?"

"I was finalizing the trip to New York and wondered if you had changed your mind."

"No, Kam, I can't. My plate is full. I need to slow down and rest. My body is talking to me."

"Is it because my sisters are taking their husbands? We can share a suite if you like."

"No, you girls will be fine. Plus, your aunt will be there to make sure your fitting goes well."

"There are many fine men in New York, and what if ReTrac turns up?"

"Still a no, Kam," Gianna groaned. "After my debacle with Caleb, my next Mr. Right needs to be properly

15

investigated. Plus, I'm fine with my quiet evenings at home alone."

Kamala rolled her eyes. "He was ignorance at its finest. I'm getting mad just thinking about him. The planet does not revolve around him. Anyway, thank God, he's out of your life."

A burst of air left Gianna. "I just saw him in the lobby downstairs."

Kamala sucked in her breath. "Are you kidding?"

"No. I'll tell you about that later. What else is up?"

"I'm sorry, Gigi." Kamala's assessing gaze ran across Gianna's face. "You're only thirty-two, and I know Mr. Right is around the next bend. And when you meet him, your connection will be electric."

Gianna's forehead scrunched. "If you say so. I will not be going into any relationship with stars in my eyes."

Kamala smiled at her. "You'll find a husband like the ones ReTrac writes about, *and* you'll get married in the spring, just like his Spring Brides series."

Gianna humored her. "And I bet he'll smell of Tom Ford Oud Wood cologne."

"Just like the men in the series. Didn't you say you went to the men's section in Macy's to check it out?"

Gianna cringed. "I told you that in confidence."

Kamala laughed at her expression, then zipped her lips. "Your secret is safe with me, and Maya, and Brooklyn."

"I can see that." Gianna gave up a disbelieving expression.

"It's been two years since Caleb. It's time to give love another chance."

Before Gianna could respond, her intercom buzzed.

"Hold a moment, Kam," Gianna said, and then answered the intercom.

"Maya?"

"Gigi, Ms. Morris would like to see you in half an hour."

"Thanks. Please tell her I'll be there."

"Sure will," Maya said, then disconnected the call.

"Kam, I've got to go."

"Er, you might want to smooth your hair, you look a bit windswept."

"Oh gosh, thanks. Talk with you soon."

"Okie dokie, and if you change your—"

"No, Kam, I won't. Bye."

"Bye."

Gianna let out a long-suffering sigh and headed to the half-bathroom in her office. She washed her face and then dabbed it with the small white towel that hung over the sink. *Time to tame the mane.* She opened the drawer on the sink's cabinet, located a brush, and smoothed her crimped black tresses. Pleased that her thick hair was in some semblance of order, Gianna returned the brush to the drawer and applied lip gloss.

She took a moment to assess her appearance.

A little over five-foot-five-inch frame with not so generous curves.

Heart-shaped face with full lips.

Large dark-brown eyes.

Her Irish heritage was evident, even though she considered herself African American.

Gianna straightened her body, mentally preparing to do battle with Brooklyn Morris, CEO of Brooklyn Morris Publishing House.

For over forty years, her place of employment had been representing writers in all genres, if you could get in. BMP, one of the oldest literary organizations in the United States of America, ranked number one among the Big Five Trade Publishers. With its headquarters in Orlando, Florida, BMP had been attracting and representing world-renowned

17

authors, and having a significant track record of book adaptations to film and television. If you were lucky enough to be a part of the Brooklyn Morris family, it was a given that you would achieve some sort of commercial success.

It had always been Gianna's dream to one day work at BMP. The opportunity for a summer internship with the company presented itself while she was working towards her bachelor's degree in English Language, specializing in creative writing. It was during that time, some twelve years ago, that she'd met Brooklyn, who had taken her under her wings and catapulted her career to the highest level in the editing world.

Somewhere through the years, after her protégé shot to stardom, Brooklyn, the heartbeat of the empire, began filling the role of confidant in Gianna's life. To date, Gianna was the only one who could refer to Brooklyn as Brook. As Brooklyn had done at the helm of the company, as the years progressed, Gianna had inadvertently become the workhorse of the editorial department, pledging her freedom and life to her job.

After taking a cursory glance down the front of her pink long-sleeved blouse, which flowed over a pair of black pants, Gianna walked out of the bathroom. She returned to the chair at her desk and powered on the computer. Fifteen minutes later, she had browsed the changes she'd made to the strategic plan and emailed it back to Maya.

Gianna found herself staring at the row of ReTrac's Spring Brides book covers that lined the wall in front of her. *Now, there's a man with the gift of writing.* Lately, he'd been a bit of a mess, sending her sloppy drafts. She wondered whether he was tired of writing or something else was happening in his life.

"ReTrac," she said softly. That was his pseudonym.

An author extraordinaire, he was ranked highly among the one-named celebrities. His meteoric rise had taken the publishing industry by storm in the approximately five years since he had begun writing Christian Fiction novels. The final of the seven books in the Spring Brides series was just released, and like his other books, the story was in the process of being adapted to film.

For a while now, the elusive ReTrac had been the internet's imaginary boyfriend. Many in the literary world recognized his awesomeness in the writing arena. Of course, there were women forever calling him out of anonymity with spiritual platitudes and words of encouragement, some even offering themselves with tender longings or unfettered lusts.

It had taken a lot of arm-twisting on her part, but Brooklyn had finally divulged that ReTrac was indeed a man.

I'm alive in the ReTracuissance era, Gianna mused. Smiling, she stood and took her tablet from the desk.

CHAPTER 3

Brooklyn Morris gripped the handles of her chair before pushing away from her desk and rising. She was in a teleconference with Allison Ashworth, ReTrac's literary agent, and there was nothing she hated more. Allison was one of the best in her field—a seriously reputable literary representative with an extensive network of contacts and relationships—but her domineering personality often overshadowed her brilliance. Allison had brought many great authors to the Brooklyn Morris family, but Brooklyn's patience was wearing thin with her shenanigans.

Brooklyn glared at the phone on her desk. "You cannot do that," she insisted, trying to maintain some semblance of calm. "Gigi already told me she wants to try her hand at something new, and she's moving to our magazine department. She works hard, so I owe her that much."

"We can understand if Gigi wants to explore other avenues. All we're asking is that she continues to be ReTrac's editor. Don't force us to break ReTrac's contract," Allison said coolly.

Brooklyn ignored the veiled threat and instead held on to the back of her chair. "ReTrac is making it hard for me to convince Gigi otherwise. She said that he didn't make most of the changes she recommended in his new series, and the lack of research is obvious in his work."

Allison chuckled, not in a pleasant way. "Is he supposed to make all the changes she suggests? I know she's *all kinds of awesome*, but she needs to lighten up."

Brooklyn climbed on her soapbox. "As you know, Gigi is highly sought-after nationwide because of her expertise in editing, which, I will hasten to add, spans several genres."

"She did not have to be so brutally honest in her comments," Allison fussed. "I quote, 'the plot is vague and unconvincing, with no surprises. The only surprise is that you wrote something like this. The storyline is—'"

"Okay, so Gigi was honest, but I'm sure she did that because there was no other way to get to ReTrac. She told me that she had emailed him to let him know the storyline was not good. He made minor adjustments to the manuscript and sent it back to her."

"ReTrac is a great storyteller. Gigi is nitpicking," Allison scoffed.

"I promise you she's not nitpicking, especially when ReTrac is writing about pregnancy, and she tells him that it's too early in the pregnancy for this woman to feel baby movements. That is a fact."

"Fine," Allison relented. "She also told ReTrac to visit Tallahassee since that's the setting for the story. I'm encouraging him to do that."

"Best to do that, or he should stick to writing what he knows."

"He has been to Tallahassee."

"So has Gigi. She pursued her bachelor's degree at Florida A & M University."

Allison pretended to stifle a snicker. "Isn't that a while back?"

Brooklyn shook her head. "Not that far back. She's still young."

"If you say so," Allison responded. "Please give me a minute."

Brooklyn heard murmurs in the background before Allison placed the phone on mute. She returned to her chair behind the massive oak desk, wishing her mother was still alive. Her eyes roamed the private office she'd inherited from her mother—it looked more like a posh suite, maintaining the shades of green color scheme shared by all the offices in the building.

"Sorry about that," Allison said. "Nora just walked into my office."

Brooklyn said nothing, but she dropped her head on her desk. She was not in the mood to negotiate with these high society women who were protective of all things ReTrac.

"Brooklyn, are you there?" Allison asked.

"Yes, I'm here. Hi, Nora!"

"Brooklyn," was all the greeting Nora offered.

"Nora has a suggestion." Allison sounded penitent. "She thinks ReTrac needs a break. He has other work stresses. Nora is asking if Gigi can visit Tallahassee, all expenses paid by us, just to help him out with the story. I'm sure you could persuade her to do that."

"That's not a part of Gigi's job."

"I know, but what if he's willing to announce himself to the world with this series?"

"Now, you're talking. That could give me some leverage with Gigi. She always wanted to meet him. That's only fair. She has edited all of his books."

"Yes, that I understand." Allison laughed softly. "On behalf of ReTrac, thanks for everything. The Spring Brides series launch ended with a bang. ReTrac loved it, so you have a pleased client." She paused. "Brooklyn, please do everything you can to keep Gigi as ReTrac's editor. He won't take no for an answer. In his words, 'Fix it. I don't want another editor.'"

"I'll do all I can, but I make no promises."

"I understand."

"Make sure ReTrac goes to Tallahassee, too."

"He cares about his work so I'm sure he'll go there. As a backup, I have clients in Tallahassee so when I'm there, I could take a few shots of the settings for him. Either way, it will be done."

"That's all I'm asking. Enjoy the rest of your day."

"I will. You too. Bye."

"Bye." Brooklyn gritted her teeth as she disconnected the call.

Turning her chair away from the desk, she reclined towards the bank of windows. She gazed at the skyscrapers in the distance before closing her eyes and whispering a prayer for God's guidance.

She was not a particularly soft and feminine woman. Her position in the empire had ensured that. Neither was she a particularly big woman—five-eight and built like a runner, even though she did not exercise regularly. She was fierce in the boardroom and had little patience for stupidity. True, too, she'd gone through several hard knocks in life, and had learned those lessons well.

Brooklyn swiveled the chair back to her desk and reached for her coffee mug. She sipped, but her mind was on Gianna. She would hate to lose ReTrac, but Gianna's happiness was her priority.

A firm knock on her door caused Brooklyn to come out of her relaxed state.

"Come in," she said, knowing it was Gianna, for only she could get past Julia Mortry, her executive assistant.

Gianna entered, tablet in hand. "Brook, are you ready for our meeting?"

"Yes. But this meeting is not really about work, so you can put away your tablet."

Gianna's eyebrows climbed. "Since when?"

Brooklyn eyed her. "Keep up that smart talk and see where it gets you."

"Smart is good, right?"

"I'm too tired to take you on," Brooklyn replied, pushing a small gift bag on her desk towards Gianna. "Got something for you."

Gianna eyed her suspiciously while taking up the bag. "Peace offering?"

Brooklyn waved her off. "Yesterday, I went to get a few things at Sam's Club. Not that I should be encouraging this madness, but clearly, I have a soft spot for you."

Gianna inspected the contents, and joy lit her face. Two bags of Jolly Ranchers. It was well-known that she was a fan of the fruit-flavored hard candies—blue raspberry, cherry, green apple, and watermelon.

"Thanks, Second Mom," Gianna raced around the desk and hugged her, but Brooklyn's hands were still at her side.

"Okay, glad you're grateful. Let's sit in the lounge area."

Gianna released her, and they moved to the hunter-green leather sofas. Gianna was about to take up her usual seat on the small couch across from Brooklyn, but Brooklyn motioned by hand for her to sit on the large sofa with her. Gianna sat at the end of the sofa and turned her body towards Brooklyn.

"This looks serious," Gianna remarked.

"Not at all. I wanted to catch up. How was your trip to Chicago?"

"It was okay."

Brooklyn knew that Gianna was hoping that she wouldn't pry further into the trip she made annually, but that did not deter her. "How's your aunt? Did she do the usual?"

"Aunt Dorette is good," Gianna said. "Yes, she purchased the usual two dozen red roses for me."

The silence stretched between them, each decoding the situation.

Brooklyn wanted to hear more but she let it go.

"Gigi, I need you to take a break from work before you start your next gig."

Gianna let out a long, drawn-out breath. "Yes, I was planning on doing that since the brides series launch already happened. I'm thinking of taking a week."

"A week? Take five weeks and get away from the office. Rest and allow that man to find you—the man that loves books as you do. Grab your happily-ever-after while you're young."

Gianna laughed loudly. "Have you been talking to Elder Richardson? You better stop that."

Brooklyn looked to the ceiling. "The wife of our dear pastor only wants the best for you."

"I enjoy talking with her, but oh boy, I can't stand it when she climbs on her soapbox to tell me how wonderful it is to be married."

"But it is."

"So you say. I'm sorry I never got to meet your dearly departed husband, but I see someone patiently waiting in the wings."

Brooklyn gave a little laugh and changed the subject. "I'm almost sixty years old. I would like to smile at my grandchildren with teeth. Please take a long vacation so that man can find you."

Gianna doubled over. "Okay, I'll think about it."

"I'm giving you five weeks, and if you need more, take it. You can work from anywhere in the world. Call in for your meetings. Take it now while I'm in a giving mood."

"Definitely taking it."

"Good. And while you're out there, go easy on the emotional shielding. It's self-sabotaging. Relax and let someone in."

"Emotional shielding? Self-sabotaging? Tell me how you feel."

"You know me."

"Okay, vacation here I come."

"Great." Brooklyn watched her for a few seconds before speaking again. "I'm asking a favor while you're at it."

Gianna pushed out a loud sigh. "I know that look."

"Don't sound like that. It's a little favor for your favorite author."

Gianna perked up. "What does he want? Is he coming out of hiding?"

Brooklyn smiled at her. "That's on the table. I was hoping you could go to Tallahassee—" Brooklyn paused, holding her hand up as Gianna opened her mouth to speak, "—all expenses paid. You can survey the settings that ReTrac is using for his next series."

"You know that's not right," Gianna accused. "Did Allison call you?"

"Yes, but for the sake of the business, I'm asking you to do it."

Gianna gave her a pointed look. "Did you tell her I went to college in Tallahassee?"

"Yes, but that was quite a while ago. I'm sure some things have changed."

"I'm glad to be a part of ReTrac's journey, but he's spoiled."

"I know. Allison promised that he would visit Tallahassee, too. I'm not sure when he'll be there though." Brooklyn grinned at her. "Maybe he'll be there when you are there. Ooooh, you two might finally meet."

"I know you're buttering me up, but it would be great to meet him."

"It sure would." Brooklyn smiled at her. "Allison said that he's thinking of coming out with this new series, so that's a plus."

"He should. It's very selfish of him to keep everyone in suspense. I hope you've informed him that he'll soon be assigned a new editor."

"Oh, stop that. You know he's singing 'where you go, I go.'"

Gianna had to laugh. "I'm going to Tallahassee only because of you. I'll get that trip out of the way next week and start my vacation after that."

"Okay, Julia is booking me for Seattle, so I'll ask her to make the arrangements for you."

"Are you sure? Maya could do it."

"No worries, Julia won't mind. I'll tell her to give Maya the details."

"Sounds good, but five days in Seattle sounds better."

"I know, right? You could join us. It's all about the work."

"And be a third wheel? No, thank you. Phil would beat his head against a wall. That's if bumping me off doesn't pan out."

"Phil Collier is my employee, and that's that," Brooklyn said, rising.

Gianna stood. "Whatever you say, boss."

Brooklyn ignored Gianna's comment and they made their way across the room.

"I'm leaving early," Gianna mentioned.

"Early? You mean before seven o'clock?"

"Yes."

Near the door, Gianna paused and turned to look at Brooklyn. "Why do you sound like Maya?"

"We know you." Brooklyn rounded her desk and pulled out her chair. "I suppose I should be happy, it being Monday and all. Take care."

"Thanks. I will."

"By the way, the nineties called, they want back their hairstyle."

Gianna snorted. "You don't have to be so harsh. Is my crimped hairstyle losing its pizzazz?"

"Yes."

Gianna laughed a little. "A makeover is in order then."

CHAPTER 4

"Kam is here; she's letting herself in." Her cell phone near her ear, Gianna walked down the passageway towards her bedroom at home. She listened, then smiled. "Yes, Brook, I will do something new. But you know I didn't need to spend so many days in Tallahassee? I'm only checking out two settings." Gianna paused and then laughed loudly. "I should have known that was your plan. You're bent on me finding a husband." She paused then added. "Don't deny it. Anyway, got to run. Enjoy your trip, too. Bye."

After disconnecting the call, Gianna walked to the dresser mirror and took a moment to look at her appearance. Immediately, her pearly whites displayed. She loved the highlights in her hair—center part with tight curls cascading. Her French manicure and pedicure were pleasing. Tugging on the hem of her pastel yellow blouse, she set it correctly over the pair of navy-blue jeans.

Next, she moved the clothes that were on her king-size bed to the black suitcase on the bed bench. Gianna looked towards the door when she heard clanging sounds of shoes on the beige porcelain tiles. The noise stopped.

"May I come in?" Kamala asked.

"Sure," Gianna responded.

In waltzed Kamala, bubbly and oozing confidence. Her sculpted earth-toned body was dressed in a pair of sky-blue jeans and a white blouse. As she sashayed her curvaceous figure towards Gianna, her thick, chemically processed hair danced around her face. Her makeup heightened the glow of her beautiful complexion. With all the finesse that Kamala exhibited, there was still something "street" about her. Truth be told, Kamala would be the first to testify of God's goodness in her life. She had fought many battles to achieve a stable life.

Kamala's pencil-thin eyebrows climbed high over her dark-brown eyes. "You're still packing? Aren't you going to be late?"

"Nope. I had to make sure you're on time. I will not be running to catch the airplane."

Kamala pouted. "See how you do me? You have me rushing to your house thinking that I was late. Shameful."

"And you were late. I asked you to be here at ten o'clock, and you arrived at ten past ten."

"Okay, if you want to point out the—"

"Fact."

Kamala's pout gave way to a full smile, revealing even white teeth. She took a seat on the bed bench and tilted her head. "I admit it. I was late."

Gianna looked at her and then moved to drop her word search puzzle book in her black purse, which was resting on her bed. "I was trying to save both of us, and this friendship."

"That's a good thing."

"I hope so," Gianna teased.

Kamala chuckled softly. "You look great, bestie. I love your outfit. And your makeup is on point—light but enough. And look at your hair. Who knew my best friend was a knockout?"

Gianna took a twirl. "I'm glad you approve, fashionista."

"Oh, stop. Now, my advice is…." Kamala laughed aloud. "You are too funny; I literally saw that eyeroll before it happened."

"Not that it ever stopped you," Gianna remarked, zipping her suitcase and placing it on the floor.

"Oh, good, so here goes. Enjoy our alma mater and say hello to any of our friends that you meet up with."

"I'm not seeing anyone. No one knows I'm coming."

Kamala gave her a blank look, and Gianna cracked up.

"Are you kidding me?" Kamala asked. "Go visit the university. I'm sure you'll see some of our professors and staff that you know."

"This trip is not about that."

"Right. Please, God, let ReTrac turn up in Tallahassee. And if he doesn't, please let Mr. Right be there."

Gianna watched her like she'd lost her mind.

Kamala grinned at her. "But one wedding at a time. Let's get mine out of the way so we can focus on yours."

Gianna grimaced. "Okay."

"Oh, absolutely no pressure. I hope you'll find a husband with a great heart like my Reyon."

"What a nice thing to say." Gianna smiled at her. "Thanks, bestie."

Kamala returned her smile. "God did that for me, so I know He's perfecting that which concerns you."

"Thanks, Kam." Misty-eyed at the kindness in her friend's words, Gianna reached for her purse and hung it on her shoulder. She gripped the extended handle of her suitcase with her other hand and rolled it towards the door.

In the silence, Kamala rose and followed Gianna to the living room.

They had been friends since their college days, and having shared life stories, Kamala was as fiercely protective of her friend as Gianna was of her.

In the living room, Gianna left her suitcase on the colorful, plush rug near the round glass coffee table. She used a remote from the coffee table to close the pastel blue and yellow drapes that were over arch-topped windows with built-in window seats. The open floor plan of her home allowed her to access the kitchen, which was beyond the living room. She checked the kitchen to make sure everything was in order. As she made her exit, she flipped a switch near the nook table to turn off the crystal chandelier that acted as the focal point in the living room.

"Let's roll," Kamala called out. "I don't want to have to speed."

Gianna walked to get her suitcase. "Yes, ma'am. No need to speed, though, you have plenty of time."

Kamala looked to the ceiling. "Don't say a word, Kamala!"

"Alright, let's roll, bestie."

A hint of a smile covered Kamala's face as she moved towards the front door.

Rolling her suitcase along, Gianna followed her.

Kamala stopped and turned towards her. "Oh, and one other thing."

"What?"

"Try and get some fun in. Live a little."

"Oh, okay," Gianna said, eyeing her with pursed lips.

Kamala pushed out a gentle sigh. "You know what, most times, the best cure for heartache lies in the unforeseen."

"Heartache?"

"From our conversations about Caleb, I can tell you're still carrying the heartache."

Gianna exhaled. "I remember the pain, but I wouldn't say I'm carrying it."

"That's good. It's time to look out for the scent of Tom Ford Oud Wood cologne."

"Got it."

They both laughed loudly.

"Why do I buy into your foolishness?" Gianna asked, still cracking up.

Kamala tucked her arm in the crook of Gianna's elbow as they moved forward. "Because you love your bestie."

Gianna looked at Kamala's profile and couldn't help the smile that creased her lips. "So that's what that is."

CHAPTER 5

On the airplane, Gianna slipped into her aisle seat in first class and nodded at the woman who was sitting at the window seat. Kindle in hand, Gianna stored her purse under the seat before her. She was strapping herself in when she noticed the woman observing her with a smile. Instinctively, Gianna returned it.

Soon they were in flight, conversation ebbing and flowing around them.

Gianna tried to focus on reading but constantly felt the woman's gaze. Unable to bear the scrutiny any longer, she turned to introduce herself. The woman beat her to it.

"Hi! I'm Nora McIntosh." Her voice was cultured and soft.

"Nice to meet you, Nora. I'm Gianna Barrett."

Gianna shook Nora's hand and got a chance to take her in. Everything about her appearance screamed elegance. Her tailored green pants suit highlighted her flawless pale skin. She looked to be in her late fifties with delicate features reminding her of the American film actress, Gwyneth Paltrow. Sophisticated. Self-assured. Her cinnamon-brown hair was in a chignon, drawing attention to her graceful neck and square-shaped face. She appeared to be someone who should be traveling with an entourage.

"Short flight," Nora mentioned conversationally.

"Sure is."

"I love flying, though." Nora's light-brown eyes lit up. "Back in the day, I used to drive the four-hour trip from Orlando to Tallahassee, but now I just fly. Well, unless my husband will do the driving."

"That's nice. I attended college in Tallahassee. Florida A & M University."

"Your first degree?"

"Yes. Bachelor's degree in English Language, specializing in creative writing. A few years later, I did a master's degree in mass communications in a joint program that's offered by the University of Central Florida and the University of Florida."

"Well, look at that. I have a bachelor's degree in English Language, too."

Gianna smiled at her. "Good for you."

Nora was about to speak when the flight attendant asked if they would like a snack. They both declined.

Gianna reached for her purse, put her Kindle in it, and pulled out her word search book.

"I see we have something else in common," Nora said, eyeing the book in Gianna's hand.

"You like unscrambling words, too? It's a fave of mine, other than reading."

"I love reading. Oh my, this is too much." Nora let out delicate laughter. "Do you have any favorite authors?"

"Honestly, no, I just read. I like reading romance. If I had to choose a favorite author, I'd say ReTrac."

"I love him so much." Nora winked conspiratorially. "But who doesn't? What do you do for a living? Are you secretly an author?"

Gianna chuckled softly at her expectant expression. "Noooo, not an author. That's hard work. I'm an editor with Brooklyn Morris Publishing House."

"That makes sense," Nora said. "I wrote my memoirs and started on a novel I'm struggling to finish."

"I can help you. I know the publishing industry."

"Oh, no." Nora shook her head, timidly. "I haven't made up my mind about this writing thing. It's a passion, though, and I feel like I can't rest if I don't get this story out of my head."

"Sounds like a writer to me. I'll give you my cell number, and when you're ready, give me a call."

"I'm glad you said when I'm ready."

They exchanged phone numbers.

"Now, if I don't hear from you in a while, I will call you," Gianna teased.

Nora grinned at her. "Please, I need the encouragement. I'm going to shut up now. I can't have you telling your friends about a passenger and her endless chatter."

Gianna laughed a little. "Not a chance."

As Nora relaxed in her seat, Gianna opened her book, took out the pencil she had stashed in it earlier, and went to work.

Companionable silence.

Gianna liked that.

Twenty minutes later, her thoughts were disturbed when she heard Nora muttering.

"Everything okay?" Gianna asked.

"Oh, isn't he adorable!" Nora exclaimed, showing Gianna a photo of a young boy on her tablet. He looked to be no more than three years old and was smiling at the camera.

"Adorable indeed. Is he your—"

"My grandchild? I wish. Don't get me started down that road."

"Uh-oh."

"This is my friend Karen's third grandchild. I don't have any grandchildren, and it's not for lack of grumbling. My boys, grown men…." Nora shook her head. "Let me not burden you with my mundane issues."

"It will happen."

Nora exhaled loudly. "I have three sons. I was going for child number four, hoping it would be a girl, but my body would have none of it. Now, all I do is pray for wonderful daughters-in-law and grandchildren."

Gianna smiled at her. "That's the best thing to do."

"I'd like it to happen in my lifetime when I can at least hold my grandchildren. My sons are all in their thirties. I hope they settle down soon." Nora rolled her eyes. "I've tried to set them up, but they're against all my matchmaking efforts. I dare not go there again."

"That I understand. It gets a bit exhausting."

"Been there, huh?"

"One too many times."

"Alright, I get it."

After the airplane landed, Gianna waved goodbye to Nora, who remained seated.

Soon, Gianna collected her suitcase and climbed into the hotel's bus. As she waited for the other passengers to embark, she noticed Nora walking with a man who was carrying her suitcase. Shortly after, he opened the door of a black limousine and Nora climbed in. Intrigued, Gianna watched as the limo moved out of the line of vehicles and into the lineup to leave the airport.

Forty-five minutes later, Gianna got off the bus at the Grand Orvann Hotel, the latest five-star oasis of tranquility in north Florida. The twenty-story Roman-style venue had become known for its breathtaking ambiance and superb hospitality.

Gianna stepped out of the bus and collected her suitcase.

"Good evening, ma'am. Do you need assistance?" a bellhop asked, dressed in the typical black pants and a white Polo shirt with the logo and name of the hotel embroidered in gold. His badge indicated that his name was Gio Malone.

"Thank you, but I'm good."

The man nodded politely and left.

Gianna moved forward, wheeling her suitcase with her. The sliding door of the hotel opened, ushering her arrival. The circular, expansive lobby was magnificent—

glazed brown and beige porcelain tiles, beautiful chandelier, plush chairs, oil paintings, and gold accents.

Gianna approached the reception desk and checked in. Swipe key in hand, she made her way towards the bank of elevators. She pressed the button and waited.

"Gianna?" someone called out.

Gianna turned and saw a smiling Nora approaching her.

"Hi, Nora!"

"So glad to see you here."

"I'm glad you're here, too."

The elevator doors opened, and they stepped aside for a couple to exit before walking into the elevator.

"What floor are you on?" Gianna asked, getting ready to touch the button.

"Eighth floor, please. Thank you. I see you're on the tenth."

"Yes, that's where I'm hanging out for a few days. Are you here on vacation?" Gianna asked curiously.

"No. I'm here on business until early next week. We should do breakfast or dinner."

"I would love that." Gianna smiled at her.

The elevator stopped on the eighth floor, and Nora stepped out. "Okay, great. I'll text you later to check your availability. Bye."

"Sure. Bye."

CHAPTER 6

"Carter!" Nora screamed with joy. "You made it!"

"Hi, Mom!" Carter smiled, wrapping his mother in a warm embrace.

She hugged him and then stepped away so he could enter her suite. "I didn't know if you were going to make it."

Carter pulled in his small suitcase and closed the door. "I didn't want to disappoint my one and only mother. And, you said that I should get here, urgently."

Nora feigned surprise. "Did I use the word urgently?"

"Yes, Mom."

"It can't be urgent because you drove here instead of flying. And, you would have come yesterday instead of today." Nora waved him over to the burgundy sofas. "Anyway, I'm glad you're here. You work too hard. Time to kick back, even for a minute."

"I was planning to relax at home," he told her, taking a seat across from her.

"We know what that means—work from home."

Carter smiled at her. "No, it's a do-nothing weekend. But, since I'm here, I'm taking the opportunity to meet with the home site team." He chuckled a little. "Thanks for booking my suite. Allena didn't understand why you felt the need to do it, but since you wear the title of mother, she forgave me."

"I can just see the look on your assistant's face." Nora blew air through her teeth. "A do-nothing weekend? That I have to see. How about dinner at six o'clock?"

"Sure, Mom. I'm heading to my room to rest. I'll see you at dinner." Carter stood. "The usual spot?"

"Yes."

"And I guess I'll finally hear why you had me racing here."

"Oh, stop that. I can't remember using the word urgently."

Carter shook his head.

Nora rose and accompanied him to the door.

"You look happy," Carter mentioned, pausing near the door. "Is Dad heading here?"

His mother smiled. "No, he's not. I just feel a great season coming on."

"That's a good thing." Carter returned her smile and then collected his suitcase. "I will see you in a bit."

His mother nodded and closed the door behind him.

Carter walked towards the elevators and took one up to the tenth floor.

In his utterly over-the-top suite, he left his suitcase on the bed bench and scanned the environment—top-of-the-line furnishings and gold touches everywhere. He walked towards the lounge area, paused to take the remote from the glass coffee table, and opened the floor-to-ceiling burgundy drapes. Again, he was floored by the unparalleled view of the flourishing plant life on this perfect getaway. *Beautiful day out*, he thought. *I should go for a walk.*

He rubbed his hand across the back of his neck, attempting to relax the muscles. *Yes, a walk is in order.* Opening his suitcase, he took out a pair of navy-blue and white sneakers and dropped them on the floor. Next, he pulled out a navy-blue and white Armani sweat suit and placed them on the king-size bed. He unbuttoned his purple shirt, exposing ripped abs, and made his way to the bathroom. When he returned, he donned his walking gear. He retrieved the swipe key that was lying on the bed and pocketed it before making his way to the elevators.

He knew the five-star hotel well, having stayed there more than a few times. He made his way towards the gym on the ground floor, but he did not stop. Through the glass walls, he saw a couple of patrons working out. He continued down the passageway and accessed the door leading to a walkway made of brown and beige pavers with flecks of gold. From the long walkway, a guest could move in several directions to enjoy the scenery. He walked straight ahead, as usual, away from the building, through thriving greenery, and into a garden.

He was looking at the Japanese Magnolia beginning to bloom in shades of white and pink when hearty laughter permeated the atmosphere. His pulse ticked up a notch, and instinctively, he smiled. He didn't see anyone, but the sound of laughter continued, followed by clapping.

Moving along the path, he rounded a bend and came upon a white gazebo.

The object of his attention was seated at a table in the gazebo, staring excitedly at the screen of a silver laptop.

He halted his six-foot-three-inch athletic body, feeling unfettered joy springing from his eyes as he took her in. He edged closer, sensing an inevitable pull towards her, and before he knew it, his eyes were traveling her body, taking in her wavy black hair, which cascaded down her back and framed her heart-shaped face. Every synapse in his brain stirred with glee, and he couldn't help the smile that lit his face. She lifted a hand to swipe tresses from her forehead, but her eyes were glued to her laptop.

Curious, he moved in for a closer view.

He stopped and smiled at her.

Suddenly, she lifted her head and smiled back at him.

His heart skipped a beat just as his full lips widened into a grin.

They both started laughing, and he witnessed a series of expressions running across her face. Her laughter, soft and girly, made him want to join in. *Delightfully feminine.* He took in her long floral print sweater dress and leggings.

She recovered first, staring at him. Puzzled. Trying to see what she was working with. And as if she had found her bearings, she hiked up her chin, pinning him with a stare. "May I help you?" she asked.

A forced show of strength. Carter tried not to crack a smile at the sound of her voice. *Throaty. No-nonsense.* He held up his hands in mock surrender. "Hi. My curiosity got the better of me. I heard your laughter and came to investigate."

He climbed the steps of the gazebo, but her eyes warned him not to come closer, so he stopped on the last level.

"I was reading," she said. "It was so good; I couldn't help myself."

"Reading, huh?" His lips gathered in a smile.

She smirked. "I know, right? Probably boring for you. Carry on."

Prickly! "On the contrary, no. I like reading. I enjoy a good book. Let me rephrase: books have been a part of my life for as long as I can remember. A good book will leave a mark on your life."

She arched a brow. "Is that so? What genre do you like?"

A slight smile creased his lips, for he knew she was testing him. "I read a wide range, but by far, romance would be my favorite. Christian Fiction, preferably."

She shot him an incredulous expression. "Right."

His smile widened. "You can take my word for it. By the way, I'm Carter…." He paused at the narrowing of her large dark-brown eyes. "I promise, I'm not an axe murderer."

"Like you would tell me if you were." She gave a short laugh, and her eyes seemed to glow. "Nice meeting you."

"Great meeting you, even though you refuse to give me your name." When she still wouldn't budge, he added, "I like Jolly Ranchers, too."

She looked at the candies next to her laptop. "Small world, huh? You like reading and Jolly Ranchers, and so do I." It was hard to miss the sarcasm in her tone.

He didn't react to her taunt. "Your laughter made my afternoon."

She sent him an eyebrow lift. "Oookay. I must get back to work. Have a good walk or run or whatever you were about to do."

"Are you trying to get rid of me, no-name lady?"

"Gosh, no!" She all but rolled her eyes. "Feel free to use the hotel property like all the other guests, but I must get back to work."

"What kind of work do you do?" he asked, sincerely interested.

"I'm an editor," she said coolly.

Her tone told him he was working her nerves, and he almost laughed out. *That's a first.* He held up his hand for a second time. "Alright, happy editing."

"Thanks," she responded with a slightly creased forehead. Her nostrils flared like she was sniffing, then her expression changed to something he couldn't quite read.

Thinking that was his cue, he turned and descended one step, but he couldn't leave, not without trying to engage her again. He looked at her. "Will you have dinner with me later?"

She opened her mouth, but nothing came out.

"In a public place," he added.

She looked away then back at him, probably drumming up a way to brush him off. Somehow, he admired that.

"Thanks for the invitation, but I already have a date for dinner."

"Does that mean you'll have dinner with me another evening?"

"No. I mean, I don't know you, but thanks for asking."

He made a face at her. "I promise I'm not an axe murderer."

"I doubt you are, but even so, I have a schedule that I need to stick to. Thanks for asking, though."

"Somehow, I feel that we will have dinner together one day."

Her eyes froze him in place. "Okay, if you want to keep holding on to that twisted hope."

He was momentarily stunned. "I'll see you around," he said quietly, and continued descending the steps.

When he'd moved away from the gazebo, he looked back to find her staring at him. He smiled at her, but she avoided his gaze, looking instead at her laptop.

CHAPTER 7

Gianna couldn't wait until the tall, powerfully built man was no longer in sight. Just weird. *Like I'm going to go out with a stranger! And why was he wearing Tom Ford Oud Wood?* The masculine cologne had an outdoorsy scent that suited his bold personality. *His smile was gorgeous. Oh gosh, I'm thinking about him.* Yup, her eyes did the wandering thing without her consent. That very thought gave her reason to vacate the spot.

She quickly powered off her laptop, threw all her stuff into her purse, and escaped like someone was chasing her. Following the pavers, she made her way quickly towards the hotel's main entrance. Soon, she accessed the hallway to the main lobby and took the elevator to her suite.

After closing the door, she held on to the knob, and her shoulders began to quiver from laughter at her foolishness. Shaking her head, she moved towards a desk near the lounge area and placed her laptop on it. She dropped her purse on the burgundy sofa nearby and then sat at the desk to resume her editorial work.

After all, ReTrac deserved her undivided attention.

Yesterday, he'd emailed her the third rewrite of the first novel in the new series and, she noticed, he had filled in more of the information she'd requested. He indicated that he was planning to add more regarding the settings as soon as he made the trip to Tallahassee. In that same email, he'd written a brief note apologizing for not sending her his best work. He also said that he hoped the rewrite was better and not merely hobbling along.

She squeezed back a smile because she had told him that the storyline was becoming increasingly far-fetched as it hobbled along.

As usual, he'd copied his literary agent, Allison Ashworth, on the email to keep her in the loop.

The rewrite is so much better. It was more in line with what she'd come to expect of him. After she'd finished reading another chapter, she felt compelled to click on new comment. Her smile widened as she typed—*Great job! Loved it!*

Momentarily, Gianna wondered if ReTrac was in Tallahassee. Yesterday, when she was in the dining area, she had scanned the patrons before deciding that her efforts were in vain. She had no idea whom she was looking for. *Oh well!*

Gianna cupped her chin in her hands, her elbows resting on the desk as she continued to read. A few minutes later, she jerked upright, realizing that she'd been reading the same paragraph repeatedly. Her mind was on a pair of dreamy, deep-set, light-brown eyes on a beautifully sculptured face, from which emanated a raspy voice. His tapered sideburns were on angular cheekbones that sloped sweetly towards a prominent chin, covered with a low beard. His even white teeth—the kind you see on movie stars—added to his appeal. But wow, his wavy black hair showed off the coolest fade faux hawk haircut she'd ever seen. It suited his slightly rugged features.

Gianna surmised he was in his mid-thirties. Even in his sweats, she could see his well-defined muscles. He appeared to be ready for anything. His light sun-kissed skin-tone told her he worked outdoors. Now, she wondered what he was doing at the hotel. He didn't appear to be on staff, but he seemed comfortable in the environment, and….

Her thoughts all over the place, Gianna began to rein them in. *No time to indulge in fantasy.*

Glancing at the time on her laptop, it indicated five o'clock. She powered off her computer, deciding it was time to get dressed for dinner with Nora. Just then, her cell phone vibrated, and it was a message from Nora telling her to indicate who she was to the maître d', Pamela Peters, and Pamela would escort her to their table in one of the hotel's restaurants. Smiling, Gianna texted her back: *Noted. See you soon. [Smiley face emoji]. Thanks!*

Forty-five minutes later, Gianna was looking sharp in a red knee-length halter dress that showed off her toned arms. Her strappy red evening sandals added that extra pizzazz. In the dresser mirror, she admired her hair, which was in a loose chignon, with tendrils framing her cheeks. She wanted to dress up because Nora was bound to look her awesome self.

With a small black purse in hand, Gianna exited her room. She had begun to make her way down the hallway towards the elevators when a whiff of Tom Ford Oud Wood cologne engulfed her. She desperately wanted to look behind her without making it evident to whosoever was there. A door closed, but she could discern no movements. Unable to help herself, she stopped mid-step and turned. Her eyes bulged, and she all but jumped. *Wait. Is that...?*

Carter was staring her down.

Her breath caught in her throat. Then, just like that, she was breathless. Hot.

Time slowed to a crawl, and for a moment, neither of them moved. Then they both started laughing.

She stole a glance—more than a glance—at him. He cut an imposing figure—fitted navy-blue suit and baby blue shirt that opened at the top to reveal his strong neck. His fade faux hawk haircut was on fleek.

Slowly and with precision, he made his way toward her. She held her breath. Held back a smile, too. His extraordinary athleticism and grace were bringing pure joy to her soul.

"See anything you like?" he asked, smiling as he stood before her.

She stared up at him, the deep rumble of his voice stirring long-forgotten feelings in her core. She looked away, and when she looked back at him, he was still smiling, his light-brown eyes locked on her. Her eyes drifted to the long dimples that bracketed his smile. *Designed to melt the heart.*

Gianna cleared her throat, which was suddenly dry. "Is stalking your job?"

His smile widened, creating a spike in her adrenalin. "I promise I'm not stalking you. It just so happens I live next door."

She quickly reined herself in by pursing her lips. "Interesting," she said.

"Interesting?" he mimicked her, laughter in his eyes. "Isn't that what people say when the situation is less than desirable?"

She flushed, her mind reeling from a sudden loss of words.

"Shall we?" he said. "I would hate for you to be late for your all-important date."

"Sure," she said, turning and moving forward.

He fell in lockstep with her.

Oh gosh! Now she was sorry she'd made it sound like she had a date with a man. She hoped he was on his way to somewhere else and not the dining room she would be in.

They came out of the hallway, rounded a corner, and made it down a second hallway towards the elevators.

"You look nice," Carter said as he punched the call button.

"Thanks."

She looked towards him, only to find him watching her curiously. She stared back at him, a smile tugging at her lips. "You cleaned up nicely, too." *Beautifully groomed.*

"A compliment. I'm lit right now."

"Oh, stop."

He gave a sharp intake of breath, then dramatically asked, "Can you repeat that? I just broke the replay button."

A gurgle popped from Gianna. "Are you going to stop?"

"I could."

"You better. I see you've found yourself a dinner date, after all." It was out before she could prevent it.

"I had no choice, since you told me not to hold on to that *twisted hope.*"

She winced inwardly. "Well, good for you."

"I could take you along if you've changed your mind."

A soft gasp left her. "That would be a negative."

He chuckled under his breath. "You're full of good news today, aren't you?"

She flushed. "You caught me at a bad time."

"Is that so?"

"Yes, that's so."

She walked into the elevator, and he stepped in behind her. Space shrank, as did everything else.

"The ground floor, please," Gianna said.

"That I can do."

She stepped away from him just as he pressed the button.

"Thank you," she said, noticing that he too was heading to the ground floor.

Gianna kept her eyes on the double doors of the elevator, knowing he was staring at her. She couldn't wait for the elevator to reach its destination. Jumping out and running away from this man were her thoughts the entire ride down.

"I'm not sure I caught you at a bad time, Gianna." Her name rolled off his tongue as if he'd found a treasure.

"You did."

Something about the way he said her name made her heartbeat spike. She tried not to think about that and looked at him questioningly. She didn't recall telling him her name.

"It's on your necklace." There was a hint of a smile in his voice.

Immediately, her hand went to the delicate gold chain at her neck. It was a gift from her parents. "Oh, I see," was all she could come up with.

"That's a beautiful name."

"Thank you."

"So, Gianna, since you won't have dinner with me, can you go for a jog with me in the morning, say seven o'clock?"

"Carter, I don't think so, and trust me, I'm not playing hard to get."

He wriggled his eyebrows. "You're not?"

"No, I'm not."

His sudden playfulness was unexpected, and she laughed a little.

The doors of the elevator opened, and she stepped out, bidding him a quick goodbye. She didn't wait for a response but swiftly moved right and then around a corner to make her way to the entrance of the huge dining area. She was about to speak to the maître d', whose badge indicated Pamela, when she sensed Carter nearby. Gianna was about to address him when an older man greeted him.

"Good to see you, Mr. Miller," she heard Carter respond.

Gianna quickly gave Pamela her name and told her she was with Nora McIntosh.

"Yes, I was told to expect you." Pamela looked beyond her. "Would you like to wait for...?"

"No, but thank you," Gianna said hastily, hoping the young woman had insights into her escape plan.

Pamela looked puzzled before asking Gianna to follow her.

She did.

Soft music was playing in the background, and people were seated, enjoying their meals, and having inaudible conversations. Gianna followed Pamela as she meandered through the restaurant until they came to a cozy semi-private area.

"Thank you," Gianna said to Pamela.

"Enjoy," Pamela responded before taking her leave.

"Hi, Nora." Gianna reached down to hug her.

Nora hugged her back. "Hello, my dear."

"You look wonderful," Gianna complimented her.

Nora was decked out in a chic royal-blue cap-sleeve sheath dress, with her hair wrapped in an elegant, sleek updo.

"So do you."

"Thanks."

"Hi, Mom."

Gianna saw Nora's face blossom into a huge smile. "Carter!"

What...? A quiet gasp left Gianna's lips. She turned. Nope, her mind was not playing tricks on her. She was looking at an equally stunned Carter.

"Are you following me?" he teased.

"Of course not," Gianna said, a little too sharply. She smiled self-consciously. "No, sirree."

"I see you two already met," Nora chipped in, smiling.

"We did, Mom." Carter moved past Gianna and hugged his mother. "We met earlier today."

Gianna was glad he omitted certain facts about their short meet and greet. Deep in thought, she heard Carter's voice in the distance. "Wha-what?" she asked.

She hadn't realized he had moved to stand next to her. The woodsy scent of his cologne filled her nostrils. She glanced up at him and observed the edge of his mouth quirked up in a half-smile. *Gosh, he's tall.* Her head barely made it to his shoulder.

"I was asking if you wanted to sit where you are," Carter said.

"Yes, thanks," she replied, her attention riveted on his chest. *Dear God, why am I looking at this man's chest?* She felt off-kilter.

He reached for the chair, and inadvertently, their hands collided. She snatched hers away as if she had been scorched.

She heard him suck in a breath as he pulled the chair away from the table and waited for her to be seated.

Her heart rate increasing, she gripped the table for support.

Carter waited until she was comfortable before taking a seat across from her.

CHAPTER 8

Shoot. Gianna had noticed him gawking.

Carter hoped his face did not betray his feelings. He could hardly believe his good fortune as he stared at her across the table. The excitement spiked his energy. It surprised him that she knew his mother and he couldn't wait to hear how they had met, but the ladies seemed tight-lipped when he tried to find out. He would drag it out of his mother sooner or later. They were almost finished eating, and he hoped Gianna was not planning to run off to her room. She only had eyes for his mother, and that was alright because it gave him a chance to observe her. Though she was self-conscious under his gaze, that did not stop him. She intrigued him.

What are you doing, Carter? He mused. *A woman toppled your equilibrium… by the brush of her hand.*

A chuckle rose in his throat at the ridiculousness of the situation.

Am I feeling again?

I'm feeling?

What in the world?

Gianna's touch—warm and feathery—had set off sparks between them.

She gasped at our contact.

Wait.

I gasped, too.

What. In. The. World?

The weirdness of it all hit him hard.

He glanced at the subject of his thoughts and felt an adrenalin rush like he'd run a marathon.

What. In. The. World?

He had to fix this problem.

Fast.

But first, he had to calm down.

Think.

He worked to bring his heartbeat to normalcy, thankful that his mother and Gianna were still having a happy banter.

He surmised that she was in her early thirties and a little over five-feet-five because in her heels, her head was nearing his shoulder. Her complexion was fairer than he'd recalled, which indicated she was mixed race, just as he was. *Soft-spoken.* Now that's a shocker. He was still trying to reconcile this refined, delicate Gianna with the feisty person he'd met in the gazebo. *A puzzling blend of deception—fragile but strong.* He made a mental note because he knew either personality could surface during their future interactions. He intended to put a window in that wall she had erected.

He watched as Gianna smiled when his mother spoke about her sons as if he wasn't there. *Ah, a broad smile.* He'd observed that Gianna's pouty full lips tended to border on the edge of a smile. That one smile—exposing the gap in her upper front teeth and the slight dimples in her cheeks—lit her entire face and made his heart glad. Her expressive, large dark-brown eyes with slightly upturned outer corners, exuded an exotic aura, but each time she'd glanced his way, they held a hint of shyness.

Pregnant silence.

It was his turn to join their conversation, and he wouldn't disappoint them. He finished chewing on the piece of grilled chicken then sent his mother a quizzical glance. "Mom, you know I'm sitting right here?"

His mother smiled at him. "It's the truth—you're my good son."

"Pax and Ry would be shaking their heads right now." He looked at Gianna. "She says that about the three of us."

"You'll meet my other two sons, I'm sure."

"Are they coming here, as well?" Gianna asked.

Nora smiled. "No. I was hoping you would stay in touch." She threw a glance towards the ceiling. "You know, keep this old lady around. I happen to enjoy your company."

"If I remember, Mom," Carter chimed in, "you couldn't wait to get us out of the house so you and Dad could have it all to yourselves."

Gianna shot an appreciative glance in Carter's direction.

His slight smile told her, *You owe me one.*

He swore she almost smiled.

Nora chuckled. "It seemed like a good idea at the time. Three rambunctious boys were running around the house."

"I can only imagine," Gianna remarked.

Nora flashed her a horrified glance. "You have no idea. The three of them and their father would gang up on me and still do. All I've been asking the good Lord for these days are three wonderful daughters-in-law."

Carter deliberately began drinking his strawberry lemonade.

"Don't think I don't see you're avoiding the subject," his mother accused him.

Gianna laughed softly. "I'm sure any day now."

"It's so good to hear you say that." Nora sipped her fruit juice, her expression indicating that at last, someone was on her side.

"How did you meet?" Carter asked, looking from his mother to Gianna.

Gianna had food in her mouth, so his mother responded. "We met on the plane coming here. She looked like the daughter I never had, so I immediately thought about adopting her."

Both Carter and Gianna chuckled.

"Mom, you do have a flair for drama."

"I like her, too," Gianna confessed, "and wanted to adopt her as my-my…."

Immediately Carter rushed to her rescue. "Mom can be pretty irresistible, so I understand if you felt pressured to adopt her."

"That she is," Gianna laughed softly. "My mom and dad passed a while back."

Carter felt his gaze grow tender. "That has to be hard. I'm sure you have great memories of them."

Gianna nodded, and he was glad his mother was sensitive enough to reach over and touch Gianna's hand where it rested on the table.

Carter decided to lighten the moment. "If my mother were not such a bad lady, I would loan her to you."

His mother gasped dramatically, and a chuckle burst from Gianna.

Just what he wanted.

He looked at Gianna again, feeling a certain tenderness for her, even though she had a bite to her personality.

"I tell everyone, you're the son with a great heart, so I did not see this coming—you of all people, throwing me under the bus."

Carter chuckled softly.

"Great heart, huh?" Gianna said, looking at him as if seeing him with new eyes.

His eyes on Gianna, Carter rested a hand over his heart. "Now that you've heard from my mother that I have a great heart, will you go jogging with me tomorrow?"

"Go on," Nora encouraged her.

Bad idea. Terrible idea. As if under a spell, Gianna's head bobbed. "Sure."

Carter looked her dead in the eye and flashed a drop-dead gorgeous smile. "That wasn't so hard, was it?"

"No, it-it wasn't."

Even though she sounded breathless, that did not prevent him from taking a victory lap. His eyes pinned her. "Ah, the sweet smell of success."

She flashed him a your-mother-is-in-the-room signal.

The corner of his mouth tipped, and he ignored her signal.

"Are you the first child?" Gianna asked.

Fighting for survival, Carter wanted to laugh aloud. "You think I'm bossy, huh?" He allowed his eyes to go blank.

Gianna's eyes shifted to his mother before looking back at him.

Their eyes locked.

He ignored her your-mother-is-in-the-room signal, again. "Well?" he demanded.

"Don't put words in my mouth," she told him.

His mother smiled, looking from one to the other.

"No. I'm the middle child," Carter informed her. "Paxton is first, and of course, Rylan is the third and last. I have no sister to save the day."

Nora cleared her throat.

"You both should have stopped after I was conceived," Carter insisted.

"You know Rylan will hear about this?" his mother threatened.

"I'll pay up," Carter pleaded, causing much laughter.

CHAPTER 9

Stifling a yawn, Gianna nestled into the pillows against the headboard of the bed in her hotel room. All her thoughts were rushing towards Carter McIntosh. Last night, he had been a perfect gentleman when they'd walked to their rooms. As soon as she had arrived at her door, she'd bade him goodbye. His nearness was rattling her.

What was that about?

She rolled on her side, wondering how to get out of her morning activity with him. She didn't know what she was more afraid of—the way he looked at her with tenderness in every gaze or the way her heart galloped when they were in close proximity.

The ringing of her cell phone disturbed her musing. She reached for it on the nightstand, and a smile popped onto her lips as she answered, "Good morning, Brook!"

"Here I am thinking you were abducted," Brooklyn said, a hint of a smile in her voice. "I only heard from you once since you've been gone. Who has your attention? Is he handsome?"

Gianna laughed out. "I don't know what you're talking about."

Brooklyn did not let up. "I took out my mother-of-the-bride gown, just in case."

"You may want to hold that."

"Oh, dear! I hope you're not there editing and re-editing ReTrac's work. You know what, I'll ask Allison to set up a date with him for you."

"No thanks. He could be a grumpy old man."

It was Brooklyn's turn to laugh. "What's wrong with being old? I'm as they say mature, with sixty knocking on my door."

"And you don't look a day over fifty."

"I'm taking your word on that. What's going on with you? I know that joy in a woman's voice when she has found the love of her life."

"No such thing. I'm about to take an early morning run before the sun decides to beat me into the earth."

"I guess you'll tell me when you're ready."

"Nothing to tell, Brooklyn Morris."

"Oh, that right there—you calling me by my full name—spells guilty."

"You're conjuring up stuff. I'll let you know when it happens."

"And I'll be waiting by my phone. I get the feeling it will be quick. I already created my exercise regimen to fit into my mother-of-the-bride dress."

Gianna sniggered. "No rush. You have time. Is everything good in Seattle? I hope you're not giving Phil a hard time."

"All is well. It's all about work. Remember, we'll be back on Monday."

"Yes, I remember. Oh, boy! I guess I have to wait for more exciting news."

"You sure do. Talk with you soon."

"Bye."

Gianna looked at the screen of her phone. She only had twenty minutes before Carter would be knocking on her door. She rushed to the bathroom to prepare.

Fifteen minutes later, she had donned a baby pink sweat bottom and matching cap-sleeved top and a pair of black sneakers. At the sink in the bathroom, she quickly used a black scrunchy to tie her hair in a ponytail.

She was walking out of the bathroom when someone knocked at her door. She approached the door with a loud, "Who is it?"

"Carter."

Early bird. "One moment, please."

"Sure."

Gianna grabbed her swipe key from the nightstand and placed it in her sweatpants pocket. After that, she made her way to the door and swung it open. She halted, stared at Carter, and started laughing. He was outfitted in brown and beige sweats—the fabric clinging to his well-toned muscles. He looked like he'd stepped off the pages of a fitness magazine.

"Good morning to you, too," he greeted her. "I'm glad I made you happy for a change."

She pulled the door shut and reined herself in. "Good morning. That's my bad."

Appraising eyes studied her. "This I've got to hear."

"It's just that you don't look like you need to go jogging."

He sent her an eyebrow lift. "And why not?"

"You already look fit."

"Thank you," he said, taking her by the hand. "Looking fit is not being fit. Plus, with my job, I need to be in tip-top shape."

She tried to ignore his handholding as they made their way down the hallway. "What do you do for work?"

"I'm an architect by profession. My brother, Ry, and I are in business together. McIntosh Homes." He smiled at her as they reached the second hallway. "As the name suggests, we design homes."

"Is that why you're here?"

"Partly. We started a home site in Tallahassee less than a year ago. The homes are going up fast, but I want to make sure our brand is intact, so I'm doing a drive-by."

A drive-by? A chuckle burst from Gianna, and she used the moment to pull her hand from his. "You're funny. What does Paxton do?"

"Make himself a nuisance. In real life, he's a heart surgeon. He and dad own a medical facility." Carter

60

pressed the call button for the elevator. "Dad's a medical doctor."

"Didn't your parents want you and Rylan to become doctors?"

Gianna stepped into the elevator, and Carter followed and pressed the button to the first floor.

"They sure did. A battle ensued, but I came out victorious." He pumped a fist. "That made it easier for Ry."

"Good for you both."

"It worked out. The job is hectic, but we love it. Would you like to visit the home site with me on Monday morning? I should be heading there around ten o'clock."

"I sup… pose."

The elevator doors opened.

"Don't hide your enthusiasm," he said between his teeth.

She chuckled softly, stepping out of the elevator. "I'm in."

"Great."

"Where are we?" she asked, concerned.

"Don't worry. This is the main gym. We're heading outside.

They walked side by side, passed the gym, and then entered a passageway that led to the outdoors.

"Oh, so *that's* what you do," Gianna asserted. "The rest of us go through a hallway from the main lobby to access the outdoors."

He gave up a big smile. "I'm highly favored. I've stayed at this hotel a few times."

"For business."

"Yes."

"Sounds like you love what you do."

"I do. But so do you. I heard your hearty laughter the first time I saw you."

She smiled. "I do."

He motioned for them to walk the path along one of the gardens. Soon, they stopped at a metal bench.

"Do you need to stretch?" Carter asked.

"Yes."

They both began to stretch.

Less than ten minutes later, they were speed walking, and then their feet hit the pavement in a steady rhythm as they jogged around a circular path.

"How many laps do you do?" Gianna inquired.

"I jog until I'm about to pass…" He paused, laughing because her eyes were bulging.

She stopped, hands akimbo. "Can't you just wait until the Lord is ready for you to come home?"

He cracked up. "I'm kidding. We can jog as long as you can."

"No, you didn't. How about we go as long as *you* can? I'm a natural-born sprinter."

He fist-bumped her shoulder. "Alright, then."

"You better keep up," she said, jogging away.

He caught up with her, and they completed two laps and began walking back. She sprinted away. "Race me to the bench."

"That's unfair."

She made it back to the bench and plopped down, breath laboring. He dropped on the seat beside her, panting too.

"You're a sprinter," he told her.

She nodded in the affirmative as they sat back, both working on breathing slower.

"It's a beautiful day," Gianna mentioned, surveying the scenery.

"Perfect."

"It sure is." A smile curved her lips as she flashed a glance in his direction before turning her eyes back to the landscape. Her eyes widened. *Wait. What? Is he looking at me? Oh, God.*

She dared to look at him again.

He was gazing at her—his light-brown eyes with a hint of desire looked transparent in the early morning light. When his gaze dropped to her lips, she sucked in her breath, knowing he wanted to kiss her.

He leaned towards her, and instinctively, she lifted her head. His intoxicating gaze seducing her, she relished his closeness. And all that mattered was his next move.

And move, he did.

The slight touch of his fingers was affecting her senses as he lightly brushed strands of hair from her forehead.

His fingers stilled... and he pulled back, looking beyond her.

Discombobulated, her heart plummeted as soon as she realized his intention wasn't what she'd assumed. Lips slightly open, she turned her attention back to the scenery, while grappling with several conversations that were competing in her brain. *Am I that desperate for affection?*

"Where do you live?" Carter's quiet voice disturbed her train of thought.

"Orlando," she replied, eyes still on the scenery. "And you?"

"I live in Orlando, too."

She couldn't help the joy that lit her face as she turned to look at him. *Good Lord. My equilibrium is whacked.*

Carter smiled softly.

He looked far too pleased in her estimation.

"Does that mean I get to see more of you?" he asked. And when she wouldn't commit, he moved on. "Is editing your fulltime job?"

"Yes. Night and day." She smiled. "Demanding clients. Luckily, I love reading. I've been at it ever since I left college when I got an internship with BMP. The company took me on after graduation."

"BMP?"

"Brooklyn Morris Publishing House," she filled in, looking at him. "I'm the chief editor."

She watched as his eyebrows jumped to his hairline.

"What?" she asked, puzzled.

He continued to stare at her. "What's your last name?"

"Barrett. Gianna Giva Barrett."

For a second, he looked bewildered before he recovered. She would not let him get away with it. "Do I have horns on my forehead?" she demanded.

He gave a short laugh, then looked at her as if seeing her for the first time. "No, of course not. But you already knew that."

She pursed her lips. "Don't get weird on me."

"I promise I won't, Gia."

Her name rolled off his tongue with a long sound for "G," and she loved it.

"Is it okay to call you Gia?"

"Of course." She looked away, laughing softly. "My parents called me Gigi, and most folks do—Gigi or Gigi B."

"Gigi." Amazement filled his gaze.

She ignored the blush of surprise washing over him and gave his shoulder a gentle shove.

CHAPTER 10

"You look happy," Nora pointed out to Carter.

Carter smiled at her across the table. "I'm always happy, Mom... most times."

He and his mother were having breakfast in her suite.

"Not this kind of happy. Not since Kara."

"Here we go again."

"I know Kara Lawson was special, but you have to admit it's time to let her go."

"I don't know whether to laugh or cry."

"You know I give it to you straight. It's time to start dating again."

"I've dated since."

"Really." His mother's expression was full of skepticism. "When I see Kara's photos stacked away, then I'll be convinced."

Carter frowned. "That is not fair."

His mother exhaled. "I guess I should be glad you don't date as Rylan does."

Carter chuckled softly. "No comment."

"Fine, continue to take his side. Anyway, I can tell you had fun...." Nora paused to wipe her mouth with a napkin.

Carter waited.

She looked him directly in the eye. "Fun on your jogging spree with Gianna."

"Jogging spree?" Carter's forehead furrowed.

"I see you insist on being obtuse this morning."

"Why would you think that?"

"Even so, allow me to break it down for you. Invite Gianna on a date; she would say yes."

Carter eyed his mother. "No matchmaking, remember, Mom."

His mother pretended to zip her lips.

After their jog, Gianna had promised to have breakfast with him and his mother, but following that, she had texted him to say she couldn't make it. He was glad that she got his phone number from his mother to communicate with him. It saved him the trouble of having to convince her to share her number with him.

"Say what you want," his mother addressed him, "but I know you both like each other. Is it because of Kara?"

"Mom, I'm not going to answer that, but I need you to connect a few dots for me. Did you arrange for Gianna to be here? What were you planning to do, threaten her?"

"Oh stop, Carter, I like her."

"I mean before you started liking her."

"Carter, for heaven's sake, I just wanted to get to know her. And, yes, I didn't like the fact that she wanted to stop editing for ReTrac."

"Mom, honest to God, I don't know why you had to do all of that. She had already agreed to be in Tallahassee."

"I just wanted to meet her."

"So why not meet with her in Orlando? You know, have a rational conversation at lunch or dinner. If I was in her position, I would have said no to a trip to Tallahassee."

"I'm sorry, son, I ran ahead of myself."

"Is that why you wanted me to be here? Was I your Plan "B" in case she wouldn't cooperate? Were you expecting me to flirt with her? You know I'm not that type so I don't know what you were thinking."

"Son, you're reading too much into my actions."

"Am I, Mom? You asked me to come here urgently and I'm still waiting to hear why."

His mother remained silent.

Carter exhaled loudly. "I can tell she has trust issues. She will not take kindly to being duped."

"I'm not duping her. As you said, she had already planned to be in Tallahassee."

"You said that you met her on the plane. Did you sit beside her?" He saw the guilt in her eyes. "I don't even want to know how you achieved that."

She looked away. "I didn't do anything illegal."

Carter ignored that. "Is Brooklyn a part of this?"

"No."

He felt relief. *Thank You, Lord.*

"Mom, it's not Gianna's job to fix an author's plot or issues with the setting of a book. She's only responsible for polishing the actual writing. I'm surprised she even agreed to be in Tallahassee. That should tell you something about her dedication to her job." He eyed his mother with some amount of distrust. "What did you promise Brooklyn?"

His mother had the nerve to look shamefaced. "I hinted that ReTrac might be willing to reveal his identity if Gianna kept editing for him."

"This is not good." Carter ran his hands over his face. "Is Allison a part of this secret mission?"

His mother was silent.

Carter released a breath, his mind running in several directions. "For the record, Mom, I am very disappointed."

CHAPTER 11

Gianna dropped her word search book on the bed beside her and rolled onto her back. The joy of unscrambling words was noticeably absent. Her mind was on Carter and their affinity for each other. She was incredibly attracted to him, and she liked having him around. That was scary since she was leaving the hotel next week. *At least we're both in Orlando*, she consoled herself.

She had deliberately not gone to breakfast with him and Nora, because of her growing attachment to them. But she had also committed to having dinner with them. She reached for her cell phone on the nightstand, and group texted them concerning dinner.

Gianna: *Hello! What time are we having dinner? Trying to get my schedule right.*

Carter: *How about 5 PM? Do you mind if we dine at one of the outdoor eating spots?*

Gianna: *5 is good. I would love that.*

Nora: *I already have an important date… with my bed. I'll catch up with both of you tomorrow. [Smiley face emoji]*

Carter: *Gia, thanks for agreeing to dine outdoors. I'll meet you at your door at 5. Mom, rest well.*

Gianna: *Sure, Carter. Nora, enjoy your nap time.*

Nora: *Thanks, loves. [Smiley face emoji]*

Gianna: *You're welcome. [Smiley face emoji]*

Carter: *[Eyes looking skyward emoji]*

Nora: *I can see that, Carter Levi McIntosh, and I can still put you on time out.*

Carter: *[Beating heart emoji] I love you, Mom.*

Nora: *That's more like it. Enjoy dinner, you two.*

Carter: *Thanks, Mom. We will.*

Gianna: *[Smiley face emoji] Thanks, Nora, we will.*
Nora: *[Huge smiley face emoji.]*

Just then, Gianna's phone rang. "Heeeey, Kam!"

"Wait a minute. Who is this person, and what have you done with my Gigi?"

Gianna laughed loudly. "Girl, stop! What's going on?"

"It's more like, *what's* going on with you? Tell me and don't deny it."

Gianna gave a little laugh. "I met someone."

Kamala's loud shrieks almost burst Gianna's eardrums.

"I knew it. What did I tell you? Huh? Huh? Most times, the best cure for heartache lies in the unforeseen."

"Yeah, yeah, you said it."

"I know my best friend. Tell me!"

"His name is Carter McIntosh."

Silence from Kamala.

"Kam, are you there?"

"Yes, I'm waiting for the juicy stuff. Is he handsome? Is he a Christian? What does he do for a living? Where's he from? And last but not least, was the connection electric? Glorious, right?"

Gianna couldn't stop laughing.

"Don't hold back," Kamala implored. "Looks like he's *the one*. I can tell he has clipped your readiness to run."

Loud laughter left Gianna. "You missed your calling; you should be on the big screen. Anyway, I don't know where this goes after we leave here, but at least he lives in Orlando."

"Oooooh, this is goooood. Say more."

"He's handsome in a slightly rugged kind of way. I think he's a Christian, but I will confirm that. I love it when he smiles; it highlights his pearly whites and full lips."

"I like that! Tell me more."

"He looks around mid-thirties. He's an architect. He and his brother are in the business of designing homes, which is partly why he's in Tallahassee. He's the middle child. He has an older brother, Paxton, and a younger brother, Rylan. Rylan is the one he's in business with. I met his mother on the plane when we were both heading to Tallahassee."

"You met his mom? Oooooh, that's great."

"She's nice. She's all but saying, 'Welcome to the family,'" Gianna confided in a hushed tone.

"I'm so glad for that."

"Carter and I are having dinner in a few, and on Monday we're visiting one of his home sites. I mean *a* home site; I don't know if there are others."

"Just wonderful, bestie. Now for the all-important question…"

"What?" Gianna asked, curiously.

"Does he wear Tom Ford Oud Wood cologne?"

An unexpected chuckle left Gianna. "Yes."

"OMG!" Kamala screamed. "Gigi, this is the best surprise ever. Now I know you're onto something special. Important, though: find out if he's a Christian."

"I will." Gianna giggled loudly. "Oh gosh, Kam, when he smiles…."

"He steals your breath."

"Okay, fine, I admit it."

"I can't wait to meet him. Why don't you ask him to be your date at my wedding?"

"Meet him? My date at your wedding? Are you nuts, woman? I just met the man. I don't even know if I'll see him after this."

"I have a good feeling about this. I knew there was a reason you're not on my bridal party."

"I'm not on your bridal party because you already have four sisters who took all the spots."

Kamala laughed a little. "Thanks for jogging my memory. I sense some hesitation from you though," Kamala said quietly.

"I don't want my heart ripped out again."

"Don't let Caleb ruin your opportunity to find love. Take it slowly. You're older and wiser. Above all, pray about it. I'll be praying, too."

Gianna sighed. "I will. So, are you guys having fun in New York?"

"Yes, but not as much as you're having in Tallahassee. This Carter is really looking at you."

"Bestie, you know it. He has a way of looking at me that makes my heart pitter-patter. It's like he's not afraid to let me know he has an interest."

"I love that. A straight shooter."

After more small talk, the two friends said goodbye.

An hour and a half later, Gianna was enjoying Carter's company as they sat at a wooden table under a large umbrella, finishing up their dinner—jerk chicken, steamed rice, and steamed vegetables—Jamaican cuisine, something else they both liked.

"Have you ever felt like doing something you've never done before?" Carter asked her.

Gianna laughed softly. "Nu-uh. I'm not adventurous, but don't let me stop you."

It was his turn to laugh. "I'll be adventurous for both of us. Anyway, isn't that what reading is for? It takes you on many adventures."

"You're right on that. That's why I love it."

He smiled at her. "Have you ever thought of being an author?"

"Oh no, that's too much work," she replied, wiping her mouth with a napkin before placing it on the table. "I'm satisfied with being an editor. That's all the work I'm willing to do. Have you thought about being an author?"

He was momentarily stunned. "Ask me something else?" he said, wiping his mouth with a white napkin from the table.

"Are you a Christian?"

His chin went up. "Yes. I am a Christian."

"I'm a Christian, too," Gianna volunteered.

"I know. I wouldn't feel so connected to you otherwise."

"Awww! That's a beautiful thing to say." She seized the moment. "Are you single? Oh, let me be specific."

"I know what single means," he said, chuckling softly.

"Oh, you'd be surprised, but humor me. When I say single, I mean, not married, not engaged, and not in a relationship."

"Gia," he looked her straight in the eye. "I am single, meaning not married, not engaged, and not in a relationship."

She gave him a skeptical look, which he chose to ignore, and instead asked, "You?"

"Single," she answered without reservation.

He was silent for a moment. "Are you finished eating?"

"Yes."

"Let's take a walk."

CHAPTER 12

When they left the restaurant, Carter extended his hand, and Gianna took it, trying not to look self-conscious as he led her away from the restaurant and onto the path they'd taken when they had gone jogging.

I wonder where he's taking me, she mused.

As if sensing her deliberation, Carter remarked, "We're going for an evening stroll."

"How exciting!" she teased.

He chuckled softly. "I would take you bungee jumping, but I know you would refuse."

"You got that right. An evening stroll is right up my alley."

They continued walking until they came to the metal bench. He released her hand and motioned for her to sit. When she did, he sat and turned to face her. "This is our spot."

"Why do I feel that you're about to carve our names on it?"

He laughed softly. "I like you a lot, Gia."

Momentarily stunned, Gianna gazed at him, taking in his black cargo pants and zip neck Polo shirt, which fit him like a glove. When her eyes eventually met his, he was watching her intently.

"I've rendered you speechless."

"You'd like that, huh?" she said, finally finding her voice.

He stretched out his arm along the back of the bench. "No, I wouldn't. Even though you're a chatterbox with a slight attitude."

"*Well*, tell me how you feel."

Carter lifted a hand. "I'm done for now."

Cheeks flushed, she admitted. "I like you a lot, too, Carter."

"That's a relief. I was about to bury my head in the sand."

"I was a bit slow out of the starting box, but I'm sure you could tell that I like you."

"Perhaps, but confirmation wouldn't hurt."

"That's true," she agreed, staring at his chest. A smile popped out. *Great pecs.*

"My chest fascinates you."

"What? No. I mean, it's a nice chest."

A lazy smile graced his face. "Thanks."

She was blushing like crazy.

"I was engaged once," he said in a serious tone.

She looked at him compassionately, unsure what to say because from his expression and his earlier declaration, it clearly hadn't worked out.

He shifted his gaze to the scenery before them.

"What happened?" she asked.

"She died."

Gianna moved closer and sandwiched his hand with hers. "I'm so sorry. You don't have to talk about it."

She saw him visibly reining in his emotion.

Finally, he looked at her. "I met Kara Lawson in my final year of high school, and we went to the same college after that. The year after we left college, I proposed. We were in the throes of making wedding plans when she started experiencing swelling in her joints, but she was still moving around. In college, she used to have muscular pain now and then, but she took medication whenever it happened," he filled in. "I'd left for Seattle to work on a project for two weeks, and I was comfortable with that. Her parents and my family were on hand to make sure she was good to go. We chatted while I was in Seattle, but I never suspected how sick she was. She made everyone promise not to tell me until I returned. Mom saw the writing on the wall and called me. I flew back the same day that Mom had

74

contacted me. When I arrived at the hospital, I found out that Kara was diagnosed with lupus. Based on her medical history, it was clear that it had gone undiagnosed for years. She died three months later."

He closed his eyes, and Gianna squeezed his hand.

"I'm sorry to hear that, Carter. I know you must have loved her very much."

"I did," he pushed out, then looked her straight in the eye.

"I'm glad you felt comfortable enough to share that with me."

He placed the hand that had been resting on the bench on her shoulder. "I'm at ease with you, Gia."

"That is great to know." She exhaled. "I'm comfortable with you, too. And while we're on the subject, I must confess that I was badly hurt in a relationship, about two years ago. That situation has exacerbated my trust issues, especially concerning men."

Carter gently squeezed her shoulder. "I understand. I'm sorry that happened to you, but not all men are like that."

"I know," she said quietly, "but that was an eye-opener."

They were both silent for a moment.

"This is turning out to be a somber evening," Carter remarked. "That was not my intention."

"No-no. Quite the contrary, it was necessary. And," she bumped him, "we shared our hearts."

"That we did. To be brutally honest, the period after Kara's death was the hardest but the most transparent and transformative phase in my life. It was during that time that I grew the most in my walk with the Lord. I had to realize that the issue I was facing wasn't designed to take me out as I leaned on the God of all comfort."

Gianna nodded with understanding. "I recognize that it was a difficult period in your life, but the results are nothing short of beautiful."

That made Carter smile. "Thank you."

"I have another confession."

His brows jumped. "Will I be able to handle it?"

She thumped his shoulder. "This is a serious confession."

"Sounds like I need my Bible."

"Take that enthusiasm all the way down. This is a mild confession."

"Shoot."

"I came to Tallahassee on business for a client, but the real truth is I'm hiding from my best friend, Kamala, and her bridal party trip to New York this weekend." Gianna crossed her eyes, which sent Carter into stitches.

"Oh-oh, do that again," he said in-between peals of laughter.

Gianna chuckled, playfully rolling her eyes. "I see how much you're enjoying my pain."

"Not really." A loud gurgle popped from him as he watched her expression of unbelief. "Are you her maid of honor?"

"No. Oh, no. We have been friends since our college days, but she has four sisters, so one of them is happily filling that spot. I've been helping Kam with certain things for the wedding, but she's a total bridezilla, so I'm saving myself and loving her from a distance."

His voice dropped an octave. "That's right, save yourself, sister."

She snorted.

"Would you like to see a movie? They have a movie theater on site."

"Sure."

"I hear your joy, and I love it."

He stood and extended his hand to her.
She took it.

CHAPTER 13

"Happy Sunday!" Carter responded to the greeting from a couple who was walking the strip at Lake Ella, a classic in central Tallahassee and the final location Gianna wanted to visit. His eyes drifted to another couple feeding ducks. The weather was a bit nippy but still good for a stroll, dog walking, or eating snacks from surrounding shops on the scenic lake.

Carter opened the buttons on his black coat and sat on the nearby bench. They had already visited another location Gianna had wanted to see—the twenty-four-acre multi-purpose Cascades Park, a nationally registered historic place in the city.

He watched Gianna taking photos with her phone, just like she had when they had visited Cascades Park. Today, she was a bundle of cuteness in her plum dress coat and knee-high boots.

Just then, she turned and smiled at him, and he returned her smile.

"Who are you thinking about, with that soft gaze?" she questioned.

"You."

She grinned at him. "You're good."

"That I am. So, do you think you have enough pics?"

Gianna continued snapping pictures. "I have to make sure I get shots from every angle so I can handle my client's business."

"Right. I forgot you are on a business-and-getaway-from-your-best-friend trip."

"Got that right." Gianna chuckled softly, before turning the camera on him. "Let me get some of you."

He struck several poses, some smiling, and she took them, laughing all the way. When he looked cross-eyed in the last shot, she was gripping her stomach in laughter.

"You thought I would back down, huh?" Carter asked. "Not a chance. Let me get some of you."

"No. I'm good."

"Come on, hand over your phone."

Pouting, Gianna gave him her phone.

"Okay, rock my world."

Ripples of giggles burst from her.

"There you go," Carter said enthusiastically. "You're killing it. Love it."

Gianna was laughing hard. "Enough," she panted. "You're good for my heart."

"Can I get a smile on that?"

"Sure."

She struck a pose and wowed him with her smile.

"Fantastic! You're gorgeous," he exclaimed, taking several shots.

"Awww, thanks."

"Time for a selfie," he said, moving closer to her. He hugged her waist. "Give me that winning smile."

She did, and he took several shots.

"You have a ton of pics," Carter said.

"Yes, I do. Thank you."

"I'm glad I'm helping you to make good memories."

"You are. I miss this place."

"I can tell."

She'd mentioned earlier that she had attended college in Tallahassee.

Gianna smiled at him while adjusting the black beret to cover her ears. "I'm glad I came."

He returned her smile. "Me, too."

79

She sat on the bench, opened her purse, and dropped her phone in. When her purse wouldn't close, she adjusted her word search book and closed it.

"You're indeed a wordsmith," Carter teased, dropping on the seat beside her.

"Yup, a walking dictionary."

He snorted, and she thumped his shoulder.

"It was not that funny."

"It was."

She eyed him with pursed lips. "That's a shameful way to get scraps of joy."

"My bad."

He stifled a smile as they moved towards his Navigator. When she was comfortable in the passenger seat, he walked to the driver's side and hopped in.

"Glad we'll make it on time for lunch with your mom," Gianna mentioned. "She's an on-time person, and I would hate to be late."

"That's Mom for you."

Carter backed the vehicle out, and then they were on their way to the hotel.

"When are you leaving?" Gianna asked.

"Whenever you are leaving."

She chuckled. "Seriously, when?"

He took his eyes off the road for a second to glance at her. "Seriously, whenever you are leaving. When are you flying back?"

"Tuesday afternoon."

"I will leave around that time, too."

"Okay," she said quietly, gazing through the windshield.

"And, on that note, I have to do room service for dinner. I need to review a blueprint to leave with my area manager tomorrow."

"That's fine. I have editorial work to finish up."

"Sounds good. Remember, after breakfast tomorrow, we're going to the home site. Dress comfortably. Perhaps a pair of sneakers would be best."

"Yes, will do."

"Alright, start sending some of those photos to me," Carter said, with some amount of cynicism.

"Fine. What's with the attitude?"

"You are the type that wants to vet every photo before you send them."

"Busted." She snickered softly, retrieving her phone from her purse, which was on her lap. "Since you're a genius, I'm sending all."

"Genius? Will someone hold my head before it swells too big?"

Gianna's melodious laughter filled the air.

Half an hour later, they arrived at the hotel, and Carter hopped out and rounded the front of the vehicle to open Gianna's door.

"Thank you, sir." She climbed out and curtsied.

A gurgle popped from him as he closed the door. "It was my pleasure."

He offered his arm, and she took it.

"Do you need to go back to your room?" he asked as they made their way into the hotel.

"No, I'm good."

Soon, they walked through the foyer and headed towards the dining area. They were just about to approach the reception area when Carter heard someone yell his name. He turned with Gianna's hand still stuck in the crook of his elbow.

He stilled.

Allison Ashworth was sashaying her medium height, curvaceous figured towards them. Her skinny jeans and low-cut blouse fit her like a second skin.

When Allison arrived before them, it was clear that she had been running from somewhere, for her ample bosom was rising and falling with each breath. Her gaze swung from him to Gianna, and he knew he had to put a stop to the madness before it began.

"Alley, hello," he greeted her. With a slight shake of his head, he told her to behave.

A brilliant smile lit Allison's oval-shaped face as she tossed her wavy brown curls behind her. "It's so good to see you, Carter. I knew Nora would be here, but I had no idea you'd be here, too. A pleasant surprise." Allison batted her eyelids and smiled sweetly at him before turning her eyes to Gianna. "Fancy seeing you here, Gigi," Allison said, waving a dismissive hand in Gianna's direction, her hard stare obvious.

"Hi, Allison," Gianna responded.

"See you around, Alley," Carter said.

He was moving Gianna away when Allison spoke. "What's going on here? How did you two meet?"

"Alley, have you lost your mind?" Carter asked.

"Alley, what a surprise!" Nora's voice entered the tense situation.

Carter felt Gianna gripping his arm, and he tugged her closer.

"Nora, hi!" Allison greeted her. "I came to see a client in Tallahassee, but I knew you would be here, so I decided to pop by. But I had no idea Carter would be here."

"Well, now that you're here, perhaps later, we can dine together," Nora suggested to Allison.

"We all can have dinner together," Allison said, sending a playful smile in Carter's direction.

Nut was all he could think.

"No, thanks," Carter responded.

"I'm sure Gigi won't mind if we all eat together," Allison said.

"Maybe she wouldn't, but I would," Carter replied with forced patience.

He nodded at his mother, turned, and moved Gianna towards the dining area.

As soon as they were seated, he knew he had to fix the situation; he felt Gianna mentally slipping away.

"Please give us a moment," he said to the hostess, who nodded and left.

"You don't need to explain," Gianna said, candidly.

"Yes, I do," Carter responded. "We've known Alley and her family all our lives."

"Really?"

"Yes. Same schools and family gatherings."

"I see. I also see that she's quite fascinated by you."

He smiled at her. "Allison's only fascination is with herself."

Gianna looked him straight in the eye. "Did you guys date?"

His smile disappeared. "No. She would be happy with any of the McIntosh men. She tried Pax, then Ry, and now she's looking in my direction. Allison drives a hard bargain, but her bark is worse than her bite."

"I don't know about that. She can be pretty ferocious. She does business with BMP. Brooklyn, my boss, is the only thing standing between me and that dog bite. Allison is a remarkable literary agent, and she has brought Brooklyn some impressive authors."

Carter smiled at her. "I'm sorry about Alley. We will not allow her to ruin our lunch."

"No, we won't."

She returned his smile, and his heart rate climbed.

CHAPTER 14

Gianna took a final look at herself in the full-length mirror on the closet door, taking in her blue jeans, red button-down shirt, and blue sneakers. As she turned from side-to-side, her thoughts rushed to Allison. She could hardly believe that Allison had come to breakfast with the same desperate need—to have Carter all to herself. Oh, she was still wearing her I've-loved-him-for-what-seems-like-forever expression. And, she had all kinds of questions for him. When did he arrive? When did he plan on leaving? Why didn't he mention he was heading to Tallahassee?

Gianna tittered aloud. *Brooklyn is right; desperate is not a good look.* This Brooklyn had told her when she was making moves to get Caleb back. God, she'd been head-over-heels in love with him. She sighed, wondering how she could have been so blind.

Deciding to leave the past where it belonged, she focused on her upcoming outing with Carter. She couldn't wait to see him in action. He'd told her that the home site was being developed in one of the more affluent areas on the north side of Tallahassee. He had divulged, too, that he and Rylan were about to begin talks with the city for another home site, which they were hoping to start developing some time the following year.

A knock at the door told her Carter was ready, as usual, a few minutes earlier than he'd told her. She walked to the bed, picked up her black purse, and made sure the swipe key was in it. After hanging the purse on her shoulder, she made her way to the door.

Carter's wide smile greeted her when she opened the door and she couldn't help but return it.

"You look happy," she said.

"So do you," he remarked, while closing the door behind her.

"Guess it will be a happy day then," she concluded cheekily, taking in his blue short-sleeved Polo shirt. His straight-fit black jeans sat low on his waist and showed off the length of his bowlegs. By the time she reached his gray Felix ankle boots, she was all but singing "Ooh-la-la!" She gathered her thoughts just in time to witness the look of amusement that shone in his eyes.

"Yes, it will be a happy day, for someone who keeps holding on to that twisted hope," he said.

"Oh, gosh! Will you let that go?"

"Why? Because we're in a happy season?"

"That's right. Release yourself, brother."

Smiling, he took hold of her hand—something she was still getting used to—and together, they moved down the passageway. Yet even though she felt his protective instinct, his hold held something else... perhaps, a fear that she would run away.

She looked at him and was greeted by a waft of his Tom Ford Oud Wood cologne. She held back the urge to sniff him. Next, she found herself admiring his fade faux hawk haircut. *Is that a thing with me now?*

"You're not going to be naughty today, are you?" he asked, his eyebrows climbing.

A grin popped from her. "Nope."

"Right," he said dryly. "Nothing but guilt in your eyes."

She pretended to zip her lips.

A few minutes later, they were still chatting as they exited the elevator in the foyer. "Stop talking smack," Carter playfully told her.

She grinned at him. "Like you don't enjoy it."

"Guilty."

He guided her towards the main entrance.

"Hello, you two!"

They both paused as the sound of Nora's voice reached them from nearby.

"Nora!" Gianna beamed as they moved towards her.

"Mom, I thought you had already left for the mall."

Nora held their hands, looking from one to the other, before her gaze settled on Carter. "Not that you both need any help, but I've convinced Allison to return to Orlando with me. I'm waiting for her to accompany me to the mall."

Gianna smiled her thanks but didn't say anything.

"Mom, you didn't have to," Carter told her, even though Gianna could see the relief on his face.

"I needed to," Nora said, releasing their hands.

"Thank you," Gianna mouthed, taking in Nora's long green summer dress. Her sunshades rested on top of her head.

Nora smiled radiantly back at her. "I'm going to take you up on the offer to edit my book."

A soft gasp left Carter, but his mother ignored it.

Gianna glanced briefly at him and then smiled at Nora. "I know that was a hard decision for you, but I'm glad you made it. I would love to edit your book."

Nora smiled self-consciously. "I'm trying to be brave. No one has read it, but I trust you. I'll call you later this week to check on your availability."

"Okay, I will make space on my busy schedule for you," Gianna teased.

Nora grinned at her. "I'm grateful."

"Proud of you, Mom," Carter said, smiling at her.

"Thanks, son. Anyway, I will see you both later. Best to head off before—"

"Carter, there you are!" Allison's beaming voice came from behind Carter and Gianna. They turned to see her rushing towards them.

"Perfect," Nora muttered under her breath.

When Allison arrived at their sides, she let out a low, theatrical sigh, before continuing to address Carter. "I've been calling you."

Gianna could see Carter restraining his immediate negative reaction. "Hey, Alley. What's up?"

Allison knitted her brows. "I thought you said you were working today."

"I am," Carter told her. "And on that note, we're off and running. Bye. Later, Mom." Carter kissed Nora's cheek.

"Bye, son," Nora said, smiling and hugging him briefly.

"See you all later," Gianna managed to say, noting the barely concealed contempt in Allison's eyes.

Carter skillfully moved them towards the entrance door, and before long, they were on the way in his vehicle.

Two hours later, Gianna sat on one of the aqua-blue sofas in the foyer of the office of McIntosh Homes in total admiration of all she'd seen on the tour of the Eagles Wings home site. The picturesque development consisted of two-story and single-family homes and was exquisite down to the last detail.

A terrific investment, Gianna decided. The beautiful landscaping created extraordinary outdoor areas that were both stylish and functional and greatly improved the appearance and aesthetic appeal of the family-friendly environment. The white Greek arbor-style pergolas seemed as if they were divinely inspired to provide relaxing getaways. Gianna marveled at the thick grass that carpeted the entire subdivision, highlighting its elegance and character. And she loved that all the homes surrounded an awe-inspiring waterfall.

"Would you like something to drink?"

Gianna glanced up and into the curious gaze of Megan Bailey, the receptionist to whom she'd been introduced earlier that day. It was clear that she was besotted with her boss and was wondering about his relationship with Gianna. Now, she came for a closer inspection of the competition.

Smiling pleasantly, Gianna responded, "No, but thank you, Megan."

"Okay, please let me know if you need anything," Megan offered with a practiced professional smile.

"I will. Thank you."

Gianna took her phone from her purse, which was resting beside her on the sofa. She was stretching out her arm on the back of the comfy pillow-top armrest when she realized that Megan had not moved.

"Did you need something?" Gianna asked.

Megan looked discombobulated for a moment before she mumbled "No," and quickly moved away.

What on earth? Gianna thought, watching as Megan returned to her seat at a large, cherry L-shaped desk across the room. *Carter had better hurry from that fifteen-minute meeting.*

Once Megan took her seat, Gianna swiped her phone screen and entered the password. She googled McIntosh Homes. Her eyes bulged as she read. *What's in a name?* Oh, McIntosh Homes definitely had a reputation in cyberspace.

She was greatly inspired by what she saw on the company's website—McIntosh Homes, helping you to build your dream home. From the other links that she scurried through, it was evident that the company was one of the nation's most respected homebuilders. They had provided homes that went beyond the standard code requirements of the industry, hence setting their bar higher in standards such as water and energy efficiency, air quality, and sustainability. As she ran through article after article, she concluded that McIntosh Homes was set to have a dynamite year, filled with success.

Gianna glanced up from her research and found Megan eyeballing her before quickly looking away. *Jesus, fix it,* Gianna breathed out, continuing to click a link on her phone. She couldn't help the grin that covered her face as she gazed at a photo of Carter in his navy-blue power suit, physically appealing and beautifully dangerous. She scrolled down the page and stopped at a picture of Rylan McIntosh. He was just as handsome as Carter but was a shade darker, which confirmed to Gianna that there was African American bloodline in the McIntosh family. Still, there was something about Rylan.

Eye candy, for sure.

Watch out, ladies.

Gianna closed the page and put her phone back into her purse. Feeling eyes on her, she glanced up, expecting Megan and her shenanigans. This time, it was Carter, and she welcomed him back with her brightest smile.

CHAPTER 15

Am I falling in love with Carter McIntosh?

That was the question on Gianna's mind as she made herself comfortable in the passenger seat of his Lincoln Navigator. Her breath hitched at the thought.

She watched Carter making his way around the front of the vehicle towards the driver's door. She had noticed that he'd adopted a more professional attitude towards her while they were at the home site. Truth be told, she missed him holding her hand and guiding her around. But she understood the situation.

She was pushing out a happy sigh when she observed that Carter had stopped and was waiting. Megan sashayed towards him while clearly attempting to dazzle him with a brilliant smile. When she stood before him, he nodded courteously as she spoke and then took the package that she handed to him. She strutted back towards the front door of the building as Carter opened the driver's door and hopped in. He closed the door and then placed the package on the back seat.

"Ready?" he asked, throwing her a glance.

She nodded, smiling.

"You look happy," he stated, strapping himself in and then starting the ignition.

"How could I not be? I don't know where to start."

He laughed softly. "I missed something."

"Man, nothing but admiration for the job you're doing at this home site," Gianna gushed. Carter had looked larger than life. *Powerful. Commanding the room without even opening his mouth.*

"Oh, hold the applause," he cautioned as he slowly moved the vehicle forward. "The team is awesome."

"I'm sure they are. The homes are spectacular, Carter. Seriously, they are."

"Thanks. I appreciate that."

He smiled tenderly at her, and she felt her heart rate spiking.

"The team members I met were great. I can tell they have the utmost respect for you and their jobs. They are a bunch of mixed nuts."

Carter laughed out.

"Nuts, in a great way," Gianna clarified as he headed through the main gate.

"You better quit while you're ahead."

Chuckling, Gianna zipped her lips.

"You're forgiven, since you looked cute in your hard hat."

"I did?"

"Yes, you did."

An hour later, Gianna wiped her lips with a paper napkin before putting it on her lunch plate. "Lunch was great. Thank you."

"You're welcome. Glad you enjoyed it."

From their round table in the wooden gazebo, Gianna looked out at the trees. "I lived in Tallahassee for four years and never knew about this barbeque joint."

"It has been here for a while. Not sure how long. It's a popular spot. I'm glad we got a gazebo."

"Right."

Carter observed her from across the table.

"What?" Gianna asked, and when he wouldn't budge, she added, "I saw that look."

A lazy smile stretched across his face like he had all the time in the world. "I was wondering what secret you're harboring. Something in your eyes tells me you're carrying a lot."

"Secret? I could say the same about you."

"Is that so? Want to know one of my secrets?"

Gianna was all ears. "Oh, yes."

"When I was a child, I had a speech problem. I stuttered."

"Really? But it's all gone now."

"Yes. It was not easy to cure, for lack of a better word. Mom and I went through many therapy sessions." He looked away from her. "I hated elementary school. You know how unkind children can be."

"Oh, Carter, sorry about that."

"That's how I developed a love for…"

Gianna saw his eyes widen at his own confession and raced to his rescue. "Writing."

Carter recovered quickly. "Yes, writing and reading."

"It seems like writing has become a family thing. I really don't mind looking at a piece you've written."

"No. You have enough on your plate."

"Even so, here's your chance to write a best seller. This is a golden opportunity to work with the best editor in the world. And it's free!"

"Don't be afraid to toot your own horn."

"Oh, I'm not."

"Love it."

"Quit dodging my suggestion. Does that mean you'll take me up on my offer? You could write under a pseudonym, at first." When he made no further comment, she added, "Think about it."

"Tempting, Miss Chief Editor. What I want to know is what other talents you're hiding?"

"I'm sure you've glimpsed my word search book. It's my fave thing to do."

"Yes, I did."

Gianna found herself thinking about the therapy sessions that Aunt Dorette had accompanied her to in her pre-teens and teens.

"Who do I need to give a beatdown?" Carter asked, playfully beating his chest.

Gianna chortled. "I was just thinking about my therapy sessions."

Carter was ready to listen, but she wasn't inclined to share. "I'll tell you another time."

"That's alright. Ready for dessert? And since I'm letting out secrets, it's my favorite cake. I hope you like it, but if not, you can get something else."

Gianna clutched her hands at her chest in anticipation.

Carter opened the box that was resting at the end of the table to reveal a small black forest cake. Delight danced across his face as he lifted his eyes to hers.

Her bottom jaw hit the ground as if someone had flicked her memory switch on. "Oh, God!" she groaned out.

A look of horror covered his face. "Gia." He sounded as if he didn't know if she was playing or not, but when she started to sob, he immediately moved to her side and pulled her into his arms.

"Shhh. Shhh," he whispered, while rubbing her back.

She continued to sob, clutching the front of his shirt with her head buried in his neck.

"It's going to be okay," he murmured. "Everything will be fine."

After she quieted, she pulled out of his embrace, but one of his hands still rested on her upper back. He handed her a napkin, and she dried her eyes.

He waited patiently.

"I'm sorry," she said quietly, her voice sounding vague and unsure.

"Don't worry. Things have a way of working themselves out. Sorry if I stirred up unhappy memories."

"No. No…" *This would be easier if I didn't have over six feet of muscle watching me.*

He brushed her hair away from her face and pulled her in for a hug. She allowed it. "You don't have to tell me if you don't want to."

She breathed him in, her arms wrapped around his waist.

As he gently stroked her back, she all but purred, feeling the heat of their bodies colliding. *Oh, please don't do that,* she wanted to beg. But she didn't; she loved it. At that thought, her face flamed, and her breath caught in her throat.

As if sensing they were in troubled waters, Carter loosened his hold on her, and she had no choice but to release him. She pulled away, unable to meet his gaze. Eventually, when she looked at him, his eyes had darkened, and his breathing was slightly labored.

Her heart kicked up a beat as anticipation ran through her.

Several wordless moments passed between them as they waited for the storm to dissipate.

"Are you okay?" he finally pushed out.

She nodded, not trusting her voice.

"Okay, let's leave. I don't—"

Gianna cut him short. "I want to talk about it."

Carter gave her a reassuring smile, not taking his eyes off hers.

She couldn't help the tiny smile that popped at the corner of her mouth. She eyed him. "You're not going to treat me like I've gone…?"

"No, noooo," he hastily replied.

She broke eye contact and stared ahead, exhaling quickly.

Carter took hold of her hand, which rested on the seat between them, and gently squeezed it.

His tenderness touched her. It took every ounce of effort not to burst into tears again, but her eyes were welling anyway. "My-my mom…" Her sentence was cut short by a surge of emotions.

He waited.

"My mom used to bake black forest cake for me on my birthday."

"I'm sorry about your parents," he said softly, making movements to close the cake box.

She touched his hand. "I'll have a slice."

"Of course."

"See, you had to put me in the light with this cake."

Carter bumped her shoulder with his. "Not intentionally, my friend."

She watched as he cut a slice, placed it on a plate, and handed it to her. She was ready with her fork. "Thank you! Oh, it looks so good. I haven't had a slice in forever."

"Go ahead," he said, watching as she cut and placed a piece into her mouth.

She closed her eyes, savoring the deliciousness of the rich chocolate sponge cake layered with fresh cherries, cherry liqueur, and cream frosting. "Yum!" she moaned out and dived in again.

CHAPTER 16

Carter watched as Gianna stepped inside her hotel room and turned towards him. They had just returned from lunch. She smiled at him. "Thanks for everything."

"You're welcome, but it's thank *you*. I'm energized for the rest of the day."

They stared at each other, and a part of him wanted to lower his head and kiss her into tomorrow—let his lips chase away all her fears—but that wouldn't be right. He gently pulled her into his arms and brushed his lips against the soft skin of her cheek. Warmth pooled in his lower belly like someone had lit a fire. In a blink, he let her go and almost sprinted to his room.

He eased his own door shut and leaned his forehead against it. But he couldn't be in that position for long; he had business to take care of. He headed to the bathroom and freshened up. When he re-entered his bedroom, he picked up his laptop from the bed bench and headed to the table on the balcony. He had work to do, but his mind was on Gianna. Earlier today, it broke his heart to see her teary-eyed and almost undone. For that and many other reasons, he found himself reluctant to leave her company. No woman had affected him like that since Kara.

As he powered up his laptop, he closed his eyes and whispered a prayer that Gianna would be okay. When he opened his eyes, his lips turned up in a smile. He'd loved the pretty blush that had flooded her cheeks when she had felt the heat between them.

Absentmindedly, he drummed his fingers on the tabletop, wondering if he was ready. *Ready?* His eyebrows furrowed in a frown. He couldn't believe he was thinking it. The idea of falling in love had scared him to death, especially after Kara. One thing was sure—he enjoyed

Gianna Barrett—her intelligence, her honesty, her spunk, and her ability to be herself.

He looked at his laptop and decided work was not happening, at least not right now. He powered it off and went back to the bedroom. After putting the laptop on the nightstand, he kneeled beside the bed and prayed.

"Lord, I thank You for being Lord of my life," he began. "Your word I have hidden in my heart...."

Forty minutes later, Carter knocked on the door of his mother's suite.

"Come in, son," she greeted him, moving back into the suite.

He entered, closed the door, and followed her. He let out a dramatic gasp. "What is this? I can't believe you're ready."

"I was born ready."

Carter hooted. "Put them up." He high fived her, and she laughed.

"You're a mess, but I love you," his mother told him, taking a seat on the large sofa.

"Of course, you do. I love you, too, Mom."

"All that cheekiness."

"Never. You needed to see me? I hope it's not another *urgent* situation," he teased, moving to sit near her.

"Oh, stop that, Carter. I just wanted to chat with you before I go. Allison will be in the vehicle when we head to the airport."

"Okay," Carter said slowly. "You remember, I'm leaving tomorrow, and you can also call me."

"I wanted a face-to-face. What are you doing with Gianna?"

Carter eyed her for a moment. This was just like his mother. Unabashed. Blunt. Straight-forward. He had to admit it would be strange if she didn't behave in this manner.

But he was a grown man.

"I don't understand the question."

"I bet you don't. I noticed a certain spark between both of you." His mother paused and waited, but Carter said nothing.

What was there to say?

His mother continued. "Since you're being daft, let me break it down. I like both of you together. But I must warn you, secrets destroy relationships."

His eyebrows rose of their own accord. "Mom—"

"Oh, you can let your eyebrows climb to the middle of your skull but heed my warning. This will backfire, so you better check your motive."

She waited expectantly.

"Backfire? Mom, you were the one who twisted Brooklyn's arm to send Gia here."

"Twisted? I merely made a suggestion."

"And God knows what you would have done if Gia hadn't come here. You're talking about my motive because yours worked out in your best interest."

"Carter, I know you're grown, so I'm not telling you who to love. I would hate for this to go south, and you lose her."

"I hear you, Mom." He noticed that his mother had deliberately not included herself in the scheme of things.

"Is it because of Kara?" Nora asked quietly.

Carter let out a rugged sigh.

He couldn't blame his mother for thinking that way. After Kara had died, it had taken him more than a few months to climb out of bed, not to mention several months to return to a healthy life.

"I know you love deeply," Nora persisted. "But, honestly, son, I haven't seen you look this alive in a long while. I have prayed for you nightly—that God would send you someone, not to erase the memory of Kara, but someone who will love you as much, and whom you will love." Nora grabbed a tissue from the box on the small table and dabbed her eyes.

"Ah, Mom." Carter moved closer to her and touched her hand.

She sighed and dropped the tissue on the table. "Son, promise you'll take care of it."

"I will, Mom."

She patted his knee. "Good, son, good. Now let's get to the airport. Henry is home, acting as if he has lost the will to live."

"Isn't that just like Dad? You know he can't live without you."

"Carter." His mother paused as if making sure her words were right. But when she looked at him again, a worried expression covered her face. "I know you pray about everything, so I'm trusting you will pray for direction on this matter, too."

Carter knitted his brows in surprise. There was hope yet.

"I don't go to church as often as you do, but when I'm there, I listen to Pastor McCallum's sermons."

Carter flashed her an apologetic glance. "I will, Mom."

His mother smiled contentedly. "By the way, good news. Gianna will start reviewing my book in three weeks."

"Good for you." *And, when did all this go down?*

She read his mind. "She came to say goodbye a few minutes ago. I like her so much. Hint, hint."

Carter had to laugh. What else could he do?

Some forty-five minutes later, Carter hugged his mother goodbye at the airport, then almost had to call airport security to pry Allison off his body. She was pressing on him in places that she had no right visiting. She was clearly kicking things up a notch… several notches. He wrestled her away from his body, and she blew him a dainty kiss that was overflowing with promises of all things naughty. He made sure he looked stoic, but that did not daunt her. She blew another kiss, slipped on her sunglasses, and followed his mother through the revolving door of the airport.

Relief flooded Carter as he hopped into his vehicle, slipped on his seatbelt, and made his way out of the small airport. His phone rang, and he touched the answer button on the dash.

"Hey, Ry. What's up?"

"Hey, bro. Have you dropped off Mom yet? Checking on you. You're noticeably missing. Not even a call."

"You miss your big brother."

"Whatever, man."

Carter smiled. "I just left the airport. Dropped Alley off, too."

"What were Alley and Mom doing in Tallahassee? I spoke with Mom, and she said that she was there to take care of business. I tried to find out exactly what that meant, but she wasn't forthcoming."

Carter pushed out a frustrated sigh. "I can't even begin to tell you what Mom did. I have to talk with you when I get back."

"I'm not sure I want to hear it. How was Alley? Is she still dropping those not-so-subtle hints?"

"I feel so abused right now."

Ry hooted with laughter. "Bro, you know Alley has her sights set on you. The thing is, though, what changed? What brought out her claws?"

"Not funny, man."

"You had your eyes on someone, didn't you?"

"Man, please. Alley needs prayer."

"That we know, but I want to know about this mystery lady as soon as you get back here. I'm meeting you at your place tomorrow."

"Save yourself a trip."

"Will not. Are you near the hotel? I could call you in ten minutes."

"No. Since I'm in the area, I'm about to stop by Greg's company and pick up the package he has for us to review."

"So, you've decided to donate to his charity."

"No. You and I will make that decision. Greg is my friend, but I still want us to look at what his company does and then decide together. Let's pray about it, too. We have to be good stewards."

He and Gregory Talham had been friends since college days, but Greg still had to come through the proper channels. Business was business.

"Okay, sounds good," Rylan said.

"Remember, his company is also working on a marketing presentation for us?"

"Yes, I remember. At last count, Mrs. Blake said that eight other companies had expressed an interest."

"Right. I saw her email. Your assistant is on it, as usual."

"I don't know what I would do without her."

Carter chuckled. "I wonder the same thing. She covers for you, day and night."

"Is that so?"

"We both know it's the truth. That's why she deserves those hefty bonuses."

"Right on that," Rylan admitted.

"When I saw your number pop up, I thought I'd be on a rescue mission. It seems everything is okay with you and Lee-Ann."

"Me and my girlfriend are fine."

"Right, just like you were fine with Sandy. And Karen. And Natalia before her."

Rylan snorted. "I'm a work in progress. But you can rest assured that Lee-Ann and I are fine."

"I'm glad for that. You're setting a record with her."

"We've only just begun, but I think she's the one."

"I hope so, or Mom's party would be in jeopardy."

"Oh, ye of little faith."

"Far from that. Mom likes Lee-Ann. That's a plus."

"Mom doesn't like anyone unless they can do something for her. We should be glad she loves Dad and us."

"Man, stop talking about Mom like that."

"He who feels it knows it. We all know she dotes on you." Rylan sniggered loudly. "Funny how we're all okay with it."

"Whatever you say will not be held against you. I'm parking, so I'll talk with you later."

"Alright, bro. We'll talk soon."

Carter turned off the ignition and took off his seatbelt. He was about to exit his vehicle when the sound of laughter reached him. He looked through his windshield and almost had to lift his bottom jaw off the ground.

Savannah McKenzie was heading towards him. She stopped and hopped into a burgundy Honda CRV two cars away from him. He was of the mindset to race to her vehicle, but something stopped him. He watched discreetly as she drove away.

CHAPTER 17

Gianna watched Carter smiling at her across the breakfast table in their usual spot at the hotel. She'd barely slept last night with her thoughts centered on him. He had taken up residence in her brain. Her cheeks heated every time she thought about how she'd loved when he'd held her tenderly yesterday at lunch.

She had to admit that part of her torment lay in the fact that he hadn't visited, called, or texted her since then. She thought he was sending the I'm-not-in-to-you signal. In the wee hours, she'd called Kamala, and they had prayed about it.

But at breakfast, she quickly learned that Carter McIntosh was a very focused man. Yesterday, he had work to do, so he did just that.

"What time is your flight?" Carter's eyes held hers.

"Four-thirty, so I'll leave here at two o'clock. The hotel bus will get me to the airport."

"Okay. I'm heading to the home site for a meeting, and then I'll be out of here."

"A four-hour drive, huh?"

"Yup." He smiled at her as if she were something precious.

"What?" she asked, her body reacting.

"Nothing," he said, giving up a blank expression.

"So, you're going to look at me in that tone of voice and say it's nothing?"

He was about to say something when one of the waiters approached their table and handed him a small gift bag. Gianna watched curiously as he took the bag and thanked the server.

"Let's roll," Carter said.

Gianna gave him a half-smile and rose as he did.

He held her hand and led her through the breakfast area to the elevators. She prevented her eyes from falling to their connection and instead compelled her brain to focus ahead.

They were both quiet.

She glanced down at their clasped hands, then zipped her eyes to the length of his hairy arms.

"Thanks for making my trip great," Carter said.

"You're welcome."

All this time, her mind was focused on how she was going to let this man go.

She stepped into the elevator ahead of him, and he pressed the number to their floor.

In the silence, she looked at him and found him watching her. Her heart stuttered. To hide her emotions, she let go of his hand and retrieved her swipe key from the pocket of her black jeans.

"Are you okay?" he asked, tenderly.

"Yes," she responded, giving him a tiny smile.

"When I had said, thanks for making my trip great, you know you could have said, 'Likewise, Carter.'"

Bubbles of laughter erupted from her. "That's my very bad. Thanks for making my trip… er… memorable."

"Good job."

"It truly was," she said in all seriousness.

"Well, in that case, I'm glad I was on hand to help."

The elevator stopped, and they stepped out and made their way towards their rooms.

When they arrived at her room door, she stood before it with her back turned to him. Her key was in her hand, but she made no move to open the door. She sensed his body responding to hers, and he hadn't even touched her. Flipping her head back, their eyes locked. He'd bent his head, perhaps to see why she was taking so long, and now their mouths were close. She only had to rise on tiptoes to kiss him.

"Hand me the key," he said.

At the husky sound of his voice, heat washed through her.

He pulled back a bit, swiped the card at the door and pushed the door in.

She entered but did not move deep into the room.

He came in, closed the door, and leaned against it.

Poignant silence felt between them for a few seconds.

"Are you going to be okay?" he asked, his voice sounding like velvet.

"Um…." She honestly wasn't sure.

"I'm going to take that as a yes. We're leaving the hotel, but I assume not each other," Carter stated calmly.

She nodded, and as moisture gathered behind her eyes, she wrapped her arms around her torso.

"Would you allow someone who keeps holding on to a twisted hope to call you?"

She smiled at him, despite the feelings of abandonment that were assailing her. "Of course!"

His eyes gleamed teasingly. "Nice to hear that." He moved into her personal space, and for a moment, she couldn't breathe. "Tell me you're going to miss me," he urged.

She forced herself to look at him, unflinchingly. "I'm going to miss you."

His expression was deadpan. "I don't believe you."

Oh, believe me, Carter. Her yearning magnified, stars exploded behind her eyelids. "I'm going to miss you," she said tenderly.

"I'm going to miss you, too." His voice was low and rumbled slightly.

She took in the contours of his face and then nodded.

"I'll call you later," he reassured her.

He pulled her into a warm embrace, his lips grazing the shell of her ear.

She snuggled against him. It was a temporary fix, but she was taking it.

She felt safe in his arms.

Safe from everything and everyone... but him.

CHAPTER 18

Carter pulled out of the parking lot of the home site, having spent an extra hour at another meeting with a few homebuyers who had insisted on meeting even one of the builders. For the sake of customer service, he'd hung back to meet them.

His mind rolled to Gianna. Goodbye was hard, even though it wasn't really goodbye. He laughed a little, recalling how she'd screamed when she called to thank him for the huge slice of black forest cake, he'd given her.

He was about to enter the ramp that led to the highway when he found himself driving onto a side road and making a U-turn. He ignored the little voice in his head—the one that told him to stop the madness—and made his way back to the hotel.

Half an hour later, he knocked on Gianna's hotel room door. After some movements, she asked, "Who is it?"

"Open the door and find out," he responded.

She yanked the door open and flew into his arms.

He hugged her tightly. "I was expecting confetti, but this is better."

Self-consciously, she pulled out of their embrace and grinned up at him. "Come in. I'm glad to have your company."

He closed the door behind him and followed her. Glancing at his watch, he noticed that it was approaching eleven o'clock. Check out was at eleven, and Gianna was ready in a pair of blue jeans and a stylish pink sweater. Her suitcase and laptop bag were in the middle of the room.

He lifted his eyes to hers and found her watching him.

"I was hoping to convince you to drive back with me," he said.

Arched eyebrows reached him. "Oh…."

His eyes wandered around the room. "Not a problem if you don't want to."

"I would love to."

A smile broke out on his face. "Great."

Twenty minutes later, Gianna had checked out of the hotel and canceled her flight. He loaded her luggage into his vehicle and made sure she was secure in the passenger seat. He all but ran around to the driver's door.

"Let us pray," he said as he hopped in.

"Sure." Gianna relaxed in the seat and closed her eyes.

"Father, we thank You for this great day," Carter prayed. "This is the day that You have made, and we, Your children, rejoice and will be glad in it. Lord, as we leave Tallahassee to head back to Orlando, we pray that You will protect us from all accidents and dangers. Hide us from anything that is not of You. You are our rock and our deliverer, we trust You, Lord. In the name of Jesus Christ, we pray, amen."

"Amen!" Gianna agreed, then proceeded to pierce him with her gaze.

He strapped himself in. "Do you have a question?"

"Yes, but I'll ask it another time."

"Then that's settled." He switched on the ignition. "Please put your address on the GPS."

"I'm right here."

"That I can see, but you look like a sleeper."

"I assure you I don't sleep while I'm in a moving vehicle."

He made a face at her.

"Fine, I'll put it in."

"Thank you, smarty pants."

She sniggered.

He watched as she did, then they were on their way.

"Did you eat?" Gianna asked.

"No, but I'm not hungry. Do I look hungry?"

She laughed a little. "Only you would have come up with something like that. No, you don't, but I have a piece of black forest cake when you get hungry."

"You're so sweet."

"Most times," she told him, and was rewarded with his rich laughter.

"I'm glad you came back for me. I'm looking forward to the scenic ride."

"Scenic ride and great company."

"Oh gosh, yes, Carter."

"I have to drag every compliment out of you. I need therapy."

"Don't be melodramatic. You know I like your company."

"I love the sound of that."

She was silent so he glanced at her and found her looking at him.

She shook her head. "You know you're not right."

Soft laughter left him before he looked at her again. "Did you manage to accomplish everything you needed to do in Tallahassee?"

"I sure did. Business all taken care of. Do you want to know a secret?" she asked.

"Will it cost?"

"Anybody else would have said sure, but you have to be you. Which is refreshing."

"Say that again."

"Whatever. Anyway, the main reason I was in Tallahassee is to make sure my favorite author, ReTrac," she filled in, "gets it right in his manuscript. He's an international bestselling Christian Fiction author."

"He's blessed to have you as an editor."

She smiled. "Not that he needs any help. He's one of the brightest minds in the writing world. An incredible, prolific mind."

He slowed to a crawl as the stop light ahead was showing red. "You sound like you admire him," he remarked, hitting the brakes.

Her smile widened. "I don't know him. He uses a pseudonym. I love his work, though. But, if I can go by the internet, he's every reader's imaginary boyfriend and book boyfriend. Sometimes, I wish he would come out of hiding, but at times, I think it's best that he doesn't. I think, too, that his ministry could be worldwide, but then it is, even with him in hiding."

His heart skittered, and he dared not look in her direction. Still, he had to ask, "Do you want to meet him?"

"Of course."

He got the green light and pulled off, as she continued. "I've been editing his work for five years. But in the grand scheme of things, whether I meet him or not doesn't matter."

That made Carter's heart smile. "You do care about this dude, don't you?"

"Har-har. It's all business. Anyway, I shouldn't be talking about my client. Usually, I don't do that with…"

"Strangers," he filled in quietly.

"Sorry, that didn't come out right, but you know what I mean."

She waited, but he said nothing.

She rolled on. "I mean, we—you and I—aren't really strangers. Ugh! Please say something."

He had to smile. "I know what you mean. Trust me, I do."

"Phew! I thought we'd have to go to therapy to mend this friendship."

"I'm in the friend category? That's a step up."

"Oh, that's a jump. This friendship is sprinting. Usually, I'm more cautious."

He glanced at her and confessed, "Me, too."

They were momentarily silent, then he asked, "Is editing something you've always wanted to do?"

"Yes, I love editing." She smiled. "I get a chance to improve on greatness. Polish that story and make it shine. It stretches my imagination and gives me a chance to learn new things – new words, new empires, new personalities, new situations, new solutions, new equipment. You get my drift."

"I love when you talk like that."

She gave him a toothy grin.

"Lately, I've been feeling as if I want to do something different," she confessed. "A couple of months ago, I had to help in the magazine department when one of the team leads went out on maternity leave. I liked it— several contributors writing their hearts out and bringing their perspectives. I'm strongly thinking of moving to that department. Actually, Brooklyn has informally given me the go-ahead."

"That's great. Congrats!" He flashed her a gaze that was filled with admiration. "You have a great heart for your job."

"You're the same way. Did you always want to do architecture?"

"Yes."

A tiny smile curved his lips as he slowed down because of the flashing yellow traffic signal at the upcoming intersection.

She waited for him to say more.

He carefully moved through the intersection before speaking again.

"As a child, I would not only read and write, but I was always drawing. I buried all of that, though, because

111

somehow, I felt I had to be a medical doctor. It was just a given in our family. After struggling for two semesters in med school, I concluded that it was not for me. So, I followed my passion, and here we are."

"I'm glad you did. You are gifted."

"A compliment? You saw that I almost stopped in the middle of the street?"

"Seriously? Anyway, I'm so proud of you right now, I could...."

"A kiss from you, I will cherish."

She remained silent.

When she spoke again, her face flushed. "Like I would kiss you without being in a relationship."

"You've been thinking about a relationship with me?"

She shifted uncomfortably in her seat. "I don't like where this conversation is going."

He would not let up. "We're grown. We can talk. Do you like me?"

"You're okay, Carter."

He cocked his head briefly. "Just okay! I'm crushed. I'm going to need therapy after this drive."

"Dramatic. Geeesh."

"You crush my heart, then tell me I'm dramatic?" He let out a long sigh.

"I'll have to remember to go easy on you. Tell me one of your favorite childhood memories."

"So many. We are a tightly knitted bunch, which you already figured out. One of my fondest memories is my parents, mostly Mom, reading me bedtime stories. You can understand why I cherish those memories."

"I do. Do you still read before you go to sleep?"

He took his eyes off the road and rewarded her with a smile for her perceptiveness. "Yep. Do you?"

"Yup."

They settled in companionable silence as they hit the highway.

CHAPTER 19

Carter closed the gas tank and climbed into his vehicle. He buckled up, switched on the ignition, and glanced at Gianna, who was sleeping soundly in the passenger seat. They had spent the time chatting and laughing about this and that on their journey to Orlando. During a comfortable lull in the conversation, he had noticed that she'd fallen fast asleep, her head leaning against the window. Smiling, he pulled out of the local gas station and onto the street.

An hour later, following the directions of the GPS, he drove through the entrance gate of the Spring Hill subdivision. He continued straight and then made a left onto Sweetwater Circle. He pulled into the third house on the right and finally cruised to a stop in the driveway of Gianna's impressive one-story single-family home. He took a moment to admire its cream-colored exterior with brown trim. The brick accents and elegant round columns made the dwelling stand out.

Since he was in the business, he was aware of when the builders had started constructing the four-bedroom, three-bathroom, three-car garage residential community, around five years ago. He loved the model home because the master suite was tucked privately on one side of the house while the three additional bedrooms were on the opposite side.

Carter touched Gianna's shoulder, but she didn't respond. He gazed at the soft features of her face before gently shaking her shoulder. "Wake up, sleepy head."

She flashed him several dazed looks before coming to her senses. "What? Where? Did I fall asleep?"

Several gasps left her lips and Carter let out a soft chuckle.

"We're at your home," he told her. "And yes, you don't sleep while you're in a moving vehicle."

She whelped and bolted upright on the seat. "I was just resting my eyes."

"I know." A mischievous smile curled his lips. "There's no cure for sleep except sleep. Not a problem, even though you were supposed to be keeping me alert on the road."

"I did, three-quarters of the journey, so that counts for something."

"No comment."

That did not deter her. "And you were good company. What you lack, you made up for with those soul-stirring gospel songs."

"I could tell you were enjoying the songs. The last I heard of you was when you were rocking out to 'Raise a Hallelujah.' For a moment, I thought you were going to give the singers a run for their money. Head bobbing. Hands in the air. I didn't even know you liked music. Thought you only read."

"Ah-ah. There's a lot you don't know about me, Mr. McIntosh, so don't think you have me all figured out."

"No, ma'am, I wouldn't be so presumptuous."

"Wait a minute! You're a singer. You sounded awesome."

"Was that another compliment?"

"Yes."

"Thank you. I'm putting that in my memory box. And I'm glad you said yes to dinner. Let me get you into your home before you change your mind."

"If you keep being ugly, I might," she murmured.

He laughed softly as he exited the vehicle and walked around to open the passenger door.

Purse and key in hand, Gianna slipped out of the seat and Carter closed the door. He opened the trunk and took out her suitcase and laptop bag, and they made their way along pavers, then up the steps to her porch.

Gianna disarmed the alarm from her phone, then opened the door, and Carter entered and closed it. They walked on beige porcelain tile through an entry way with formal living and dining rooms on either side before entering the huge family room.

Moving forward, his gaze flicked over the loft-styled room—cream-colored walls, shades of blue and yellow accent pillows, exciting artwork, and modern furnishings. A mixture of elegance and comfort. Its tray ceilings provided a spacious feel. Overlooking the family room, the oversized granite kitchen island provided the perfect arrangement to chat while preparing a meal.

Carter placed her luggage near the pastel yellow sofa and looked up to see Gianna opening the blinds. Light flooded the family room and exposed the screened-in lanai, which provided an ideal entertainment spot while escaping the outside elements.

He glanced at Gianna and found her watching him.

"Nice place," he remarked.

"Thank you. I bought it and moved in over four years ago. The layout got me."

He smiled at her. "That's understandable."

"Would you like something to drink or eat?"

"No, but thank you. Your black forest cake filled the gap, and I have an urgent work matter to take care of."

A look of disappointment flashed across her face, but she quickly masked it. "Okay," she said, marching past him and heading to the front door.

He followed.

Hand on the doorknob, she told him, "Thanks for the ride."

"You could at least look at me when you say it."

Sighing deeply, she attempted to open the door, but he'd placed a hand on it to keep it in place. She turned towards him, her lips in a thin line as she prepared to resist what he needed—or perhaps wanted.

He held back a chuckle. She was such a cutie... looking like a fierce cub instead of a roaring lioness.

"I won't become your plaything, Carter," she tossed out, burning him with the fire that blazed in her eyes.

"You will never become my plaything, Gia. I'm not that kind of a person." His words were slow and clear. He needed her to get it.

Her eyes narrowed as she tilted her head, but she didn't say anything else. Instinctively, he pulled her in and hugged her because he knew she needed it. Heck, he needed it, too.

Reluctantly, Gianna hugged him back, burying her head in his chest, and pressing her full weight against him. His blood began to run hot. Her warm breath on his chest was sending chills down his spine.

Heat flared between them, and they both shivered, and then tensed, trying to hold it together. Another wave of heat washed over them, and he heard a groan that was caught in her throat. He all but moaned into her hair. She was driving him mindless with need, and he knew he had to get out of there. He squeezed her tightly and then made movements to release her.

Picking up his signal, she stepped away from him, and all his thoughts merged into one sentence—*I want to love this woman to the moon and back.* Blown away by his thoughts, he jerked his head in a bid to center himself. "I'll call you later," he told her.

She nodded at him, a slight smile adorning her face.

His heart thudding, he dropped a chaste kiss on her cheek and made his escape.

He had to.

She'd stolen his heart without warning.

CHAPTER 20

"Have you heard from Carter?" Kamala asked.

Gianna's heart sank. Now she wished she hadn't taken Kamala's call.

"Nope."

"Keep hope alive."

Gianna could hear the strong call to remain optimistic in her best friend's voice.

"Gigi," Kamala called for her attention, "I know it looks like nothing is happening in the natural, but it's all occurring in the spiritual." Kamala cracked up a little. "Stop rolling your eyes and focus on the road."

"I'll be cross-eyed if you don't stop with that foolishness. I can handle the truth. He's not into me like that."

"You're going to make me cross-eyed if you don't stop talking like that. Where is your faith? Shouldn't you be calling those things which are not as though they were?"

"Don't do that."

"How about this, then? I prayed about my relationship with Reyon before I eventually said yes. You prayed about Carter and you said that you felt the peace of God concerning a relationship with him. So, continue to trust God. Let the Lord lead you and stop doubting...."

Gianna zoned out.

She had to face reality even if her best friend couldn't. And, she certainly didn't need her heart to be on life support again.

Almost two weeks had come and gone since she'd returned to Orlando with Carter, and not a word from him. Her current situation—busy mending her heart before her emotions got out of hand. Maybe the reason their paths had crossed was to remind her of the possibility of love. For what else could it be? Carter and his super-fine-self walked into her life, and all her cynicism flew out the door.

Though she wouldn't admit it aloud, before things came to a grinding halt, she'd been daydreaming about the life they were going to have together.

Soul mates.

Destiny.

Promises of forever.

Happily-ever-after.

Together forever.

How could she not have such thoughts when he was pushing all the right buttons?

Things came to a standstill after day three of no communication from him. She ran out of possible excuses as to why he hadn't called or texted. Secretly, she had hoped he would throw caution to the wind and turn up at her home.

No such luck.

She held back a sigh when she remembered how she'd thrown herself in his arms when he'd returned to the hotel. And when he'd wrapped his arms around her waist, before he'd left her home, she didn't want him to let go. Her body pressed flush against his was pure delight, pulling her rapidly into a vortex of passion. She felt her body letting go, molding into his as wave after wave of heat swamped them.

She had suspected he had feelings for her, but how far did they run? Hers were running deep, and without her permission, sprinting along. Now she was aggravated that she'd allowed her thoughts to run wild.

And what happened to our date?

Carter had looked happy when she'd said yes to his request for a date, but he had mentioned that he needed to check his calendar because he had to be in Seattle that same week.

Oh gosh! I can't believe I'm still thinking that way. Painfully ridiculous.

Insert eye-roll.

Girl, you were a mere tagalong on the trip to Orlando to keep him from boredom.

That thought triggered her fighting instinct, and she sucked air through her teeth.

"You don't have to agree with everything I say," Kamala cautioned.

"Sorry, that was not for you. I'm aggravated at myself."

"Don't be. I'm still not understanding why you refuse to call or text him. Anyway, let's continue to pray and leave the situation in the hands of the Lord."

"I told you—it's a man's job to pursue a woman." Then, in a lackluster tone, "Let's leave it to the Lord."

"I hear you, Gigi, but there's nothing wrong with calling or texting him to say hello or to show that you care. From what you've told me, you've both left a great mark on each other. All I'm asking you to do is reach out to Carter and trust the Father's hand. That's all."

Gianna exhaled loudly. "I'll keep the matter before the Lord."

"I'm happy with that. Now tell me why you're going to your workplace? No one wants you there."

Gianna chuckled. "They all love me. They're hiding it."

Kamala sniggered. "I believe you. I hope you're not spending the entire day, though."

"Nooo. What time is it? A little after eleven. I should leave work no later than one o'clock. I had to get out of the house."

"The rest of us would take a trip, go see a movie, or do something fun, but not you. How many more weeks do you have off?"

"I say two more, but Brooklyn says three."

"Thanks, Brooklyn. You haven't taken a vacation in forever. I'm so happy you decided to go to Nora's. I prayed you would, despite Carter being a no-show."

"I hope he doesn't think I'm doing this just to see him."

"Remember, you made that commitment before all of this."

"Guess so." Gianna pulled into one of the parking spots at BMP and allowed the engine to idle. "I've parked, but I can talk for a few minutes."

"Oh, great! I hope you didn't wear work clothes to let them think you'll be staying all day."

"Gosh, no! I'm in my sleeveless, scoop-neck red jumpsuit and matching heels."

"Whoa! Is that the one with the belted waist?"

"Yep. I was trying to get out of the slump."

"Fresh and flattering. I like that jumpsuit on you. I'm so proud of you right now for rising."

"Awww, thanks."

"Do you want to do something fun, later or over the weekend?" Kamala asked.

"Nah. Your plate is full of wedding planning stuff."

"Not true. Are you shutting yourself away?"

"No, I'm going to get a mani and pedi tomorrow, and I'll start to prepare my clothes that I'll be taking to Nora's home. I'll see you at church on Sunday."

Kamala yawned loudly.

Gianna snorted. "I like to be ready."

"You know what, let's pray."

"Sure."

"Gigi," Kamala's tone begged for her attention.

"What?"

"Please hear me out because I feel a pressing in my spirit to say this."

"Okay."

"You can't get stuck into thinking it's business as usual. Not with Carter. You can't be thinking about him the way you did Caleb. You need to be ready for Carter. There's a reason why you met Carter. There's a reason why he pursued you and will be pursuing you, but it's all about God's plan for both of you. I'm not sure if you realize how the enemy tried to destroy both your lives at a tender age. That's how he operates when he sees greatness. Remember the story of Joseph."

They were both silent for a moment.

Kamala began to pray, "Oh, Lord, You have made the heavens and the earth by Thy great power. We honor You with our lives. It is You who have kept us and have made our way perfect. God, we place this situation regarding Carter and Gianna in Your capable hands. Oh, Lord, You know all things. We declare that Your perfect will be established in this situation. We, Your children, know that You only give good gifts to us. We do not want Your permissive will in this situation; we want Your perfect will. Oh, God, let Thy will be done on earth as it is established in heaven. Do what is right and pleasing in Your eyes, Lord. For Yours is the Kingdom, the power, and the glory, forever and ever. Amen."

"Amen," Gianna agreed. "Thanks, Kam. I promise I'll keep my chin up."

"There's my bestie. Talk with you later."

"Sure will."

Ten minutes later, a black purse in hand, Gianna greeted Maya, who was sitting at her desk.

"You're looking sharp," Maya remarked.

"I aim to please," Gianna said, before moving towards her office.

"Mission accomplished. I'm glad you made it here."

"That's a major change for someone who is always trying to get me out of the office."

"Well, this visit is a short one."

Nearing her office door, Gianna turned to look at Maya.

Maya's face held a huge grin.

Gianna knitted her brows. "What's going on?"

"You tell me."

"I don't have the energy right now, but I'll be back."

"Looking forward to that, Boss Lady," Maya said in a singsong voice.

Gianna shook her head and walked into her office. She stopped mid-stride and almost laughed out; everything was in place. Chuckling, she told Maya, "I'll get you for this. I should have known you were up to no good." Gianna dropped her purse on her desk. "So that's why you kept asking me what time I'll be here. You are something else. I hope I can find—"

She heard movements and looked up... into eyes she couldn't forget.

Carter!

She gasped, just as her heart backflipped.

She was keyed up over him, for sure.

She took a shaky step back.

The coolest fade faux hawk haircut. The navy-blue suit. The highly polished shoes. The flowers. Her gaze zipped back to his face.

Oh God, that smile!

That smile always got her.

Confusion and fear snaking down her spine, her eyes widened, which made his smile grow... his cute dimples teasing his cheeks.

As helplessness welled up inside, she took a second step back, and that was enough to get her feet moving again. *Where am I going?*

A wall was the only thing in sight.

He spoke, but the words didn't register. But when she heard her office door close, that stopped her in her tracks.

She whipped around and leveled her gaze at him.

CHAPTER 21

Carter couldn't help the smile that popped out when he came face-to-face with Gianna. She looked stunning in her red jumpsuit. She was startled at first, but now her eyes held pure contempt. Nevertheless, he wasn't daunted. He locked eyes with her and advanced closer. *Had she always been this gorgeous? Hot? Strong?* He admired her hair—it looked glossy and sleek, falling beyond her shoulders.

This is a time to choose your words carefully, Carter warned himself mentally as he stood before her. His presence had caught her off guard, and she was now acting like it didn't matter that he was in her office.

"Good morning. I'm sorry; I didn't mean to startle you," Carter told her, a smile grazing his lips.

"Good morning, Carter. What do you want?"

I deserve that hostility. He handed her two dozen red roses wrapped in the middle of the stems with a broad red ribbon. "These are for you."

She didn't take them. "Again, what do you want? I have work to do."

"I want you."

Her eyes shot daggers at him. "I'm not available, so you and your flowers can leave."

"You don't mean that."

"Yes, I do. You can't just walk in and out of my life at your leisure and pleasure."

"I'm sorry. At least take the flowers."

"Fine." She took the flowers and placed them on her desk. "Thanks. Have a good day."

"Gia, you don't mean that." He touched her arm, and she shrugged him off.

"I have work to do, Carter, so please leave."

His heart squeezed. "I'm sorry. I just came back from Seattle. I told you I had to be there, but I had to leave earlier than planned."

She straightened her shoulder and quickly constructed a wall between then. "Your phone doesn't work?"

He spoke quickly. "You know it does."

She waited... for the truth.

He tore down her imaginary wall and looked her dead in the eye. "I wanted to make sure the Lord was still holding back the sea."

"Ooookay." Her eyebrows climbed. "I hope for your sake He still is."

"He is. I will tell you about that some other time."

"Say more."

"I was sorting out how I feel about you."

Hands akimbo. "Is that why you were in hiding?"

"Yes."

"I'm listening."

"My bravado was not raring to go," he said in a monotone.

"I take it your *bravado* has returned."

He spotted flickers of mischief in her eyes, and his grin slid sideways. "Yes, it has. I like who I am when I'm with you, and..." he paused, trying to find the right words.

"Ditto. We had already established that we like each other in Tallahassee. I'm not going to do this back and forth thing with you, Carter. If we're friends, we're friends. Let's not run ahead of ourselves. I'm going to back out of this friendship if you pull a stunt like that again."

"I won't. Thank you."

He opened his arms, and she walked into them.

"I missed you," he said, his lips grazing her ear.

"I missed you, too." He felt her shiver as she hugged his waist as if she was afraid he would disappear.

126

A heartbeat later, they pulled apart, both aware of their non-relationship status.

The heat in Carter's belly kicked up, but he had to focus and reassure her he was here to stay. "I promise I won't disappear again."

She looked at him cautiously. "So, you say."

"I won't," he said firmly.

She nodded.

"You look great," he told her.

"Thank you. So do you."

He flashed her a teasing smile. "Another compliment? I don't know if I can handle it."

A tiny smile peeked out. "I'm sure you'll find a way."

"What are you doing at work? Let's go."

"Wait a minute. You can't pop back into my life and start throwing out orders."

"Far from that. You're supposed to be on vacation."

"I came to hang around then collect a few things... which I see are packed."

Gianna turned her gaze to a small white bag on her desk. She eyed Carter suspiciously. "Do you know Maya? Did she help you pull off this stunt?"

"My lips are sealed, but this I will say—I have connections."

"I will get her for this."

"Ready?"

"What's the rush? You should have called ahead, but no, you think I can just drop everything in my life and—"

"Gia, it's just lunch. A special lunch with your favorite dessert."

A tiny smile popped out. "You know I don't like you, right?"

"I know. But on my way here, I was talking to the Lord, and declaring those things which are not as though they were."

Gianna eyed him, sighing softly. "Let me check this bag."

From the contents, she took up a small notebook and her cell phone stand, dropped them into her purse, and zipped it.

Carter smiled as she secured the straps of her purse on her shoulder.

She glanced up in time to catch his smile... and she returned it.

"What's the plan?" she asked.

"We will leave your vehicle at your home, and then we'll take mine to the picnic spot."

"You're not dressed for a picnic."

"I had two meetings this morning. Planning to lose the jacket and tie. Will that do?"

She laughed briefly. "Yes, that will do."

She took up the flowers and brought them to her nose. "Nice. Thank you."

He moved closer to her. "You're welcome."

Instinctively, she slipped her hand into his, and he couldn't help that his fingers tightened around hers.

Soon, they were out of her office and facing a smiling Maya, who was still sitting at her desk.

"That was your shortest workday ever," Maya teased Gianna mercilessly. "I hope we can arrange for many more of those."

Carter laughed as Gianna eyeballed her. "We will definitely be talking. Have a good day."

"Thanks, Boss Lady. You know I will."

Chuckling, Carter moved Gianna forward.

CHAPTER 22

Bedcovers pulled up to her neck, Gianna lay frozen on her back, staring at the ceiling in her bedroom. For a moment, her eyes wandered to the balcony door where the sunlight was hitting it at an angle. Her thoughts were all over the place, yet they were all focused on Carter McIntosh. He'd made her heart his home. Air burst from her lips, followed by soft laughter as she recalled Carter's words—*my bravado was not raring to go.* Carter's innate goodness and the way he had said those words did not allow her to question his sincerity. *At least he's honest.*

Their picnic date was the bomb. They had quickly weathered the initial awkwardness and settled into effortless conversation and shenanigans. The meal—garlic butter baked salmon, baked potatoes, and green beans— was good too, and the black forest cake was yummy. Carter had picked up the food he had ordered from Panoramic Seafood Restaurant, which was near their picnic spot at Lake Apopka. While they ate, she tried to press him to reveal what he'd meant by "I wanted to make sure that the Lord was still holding back the sea." He didn't explain his statement but told her he would when the time was right.

As if the picnic wasn't enough, on Saturday evening, he had taken her to see a musical at the Dr. Phillips Center for the Performing Arts. Her stomach filled with butterflies as she recalled their two dates. Though he'd exhibited care, she noticed that he had entered her home and made sure everything was okay then gave her a quick goodbye hug. Still, their attraction to each other was relentless. She relished being in his arms; the gentleness in his strong fingers circling her waist always made her chest tighten.

Gianna reached for her phone on the nightstand and touched the email icon on the screen. Her eyes widened with excitement when she saw the first email. ReTrac had sent his revised manuscript, at two o'clock that morning. *Admirable.* She couldn't wait to see if he'd accepted her suggested changes, and she was particularly interested to know if he had made changes to the Tallahassee settings he'd mentioned in the book. She expanded her arms in a long stretch, and a lazy yawn slipped out. *Definitely looking forward to checking this out after breakfast.*

Her cell phone vibrated. It was Nora.

"Hello, lovely lady!" Gianna greeted her.

"You're good for me, Gianna. Good morning, my dear."

"And to what do I owe this pleasure?"

Nora gave a short laugh. "Please don't say no. I need some girly advice."

Gianna knitted her brows because she was sure Nora had friends and many others vying for her friendship. "How can I help?"

"I want to reassure you that this is not a bid to encourage you to join the family. Carter told me that you live almost an hour from my home. You had said that you would be visiting next Wednesday and leaving on Friday, but I was wondering if you could spend the weekend and attend my party on Saturday. Please say yes."

"Well…" Gianna's thoughts were all over the place for a second time that morning.

"I promise I won't get in your way," Nora pleaded. "I need some female company in the house, and your take on a few things."

Gianna smiled inwardly at Nora's apprehension. *She's good company and I like her.* "Okay, I will," Gianna said.

"Ooh, thanks, Gianna."

"You're welcome. I'll be glad to help in whatever way I can."

"Okay, great. If you need anything special while you're staying with us, please text or call me. If not, see you next week," Nora said joyfully.

"I sure will. Bye."

"Bye."

Without another thought about the matter, Gianna swung her legs out of bed and headed to the bathroom.

An hour later, she had eaten breakfast and washed the dishes she'd used. She paused at the island to admire the red roses Carter had given her.

Next, she sat at the nook table and began to read from her laptop. Soon, she was beaming. ReTrac was on point. He had accepted all her suggested changes. Plus, the Cascades Park and Lake Ella settings were brought to life in his manuscript and provided the backdrops for the emotional impact of his story. *Depth and dimension. A brilliantly conceived storyline.* She was sure this new series would be made into a movie just like his other books.

Suddenly, her heart rate spiked. *He visited Tallahassee. Was he there when I was there? Guess I wouldn't know.*

Her eyebrows furrowed, for it dawned on her that ReTrac had rewritten or revised most of the scenes that had anything to do with physical or emotional connections. These cozy scenes were far from wildly intimate, but the way he wrote the eye-to-eye, hand-to-hand, arm-to-waist, and mouth-to-mouth contacts between the protagonist and his female interest were pretty telling. Her eyebrows climbed. What had changed since the previous draft he'd written? He seemed much more emotionally invested in the manuscript now than he'd been before. Could he be in love? *Ahhh, maybe I'm reading too much into this.*

Her thoughts rolled to Brooklyn. She glanced at the clock on her laptop, and it registered 10:30. She hadn't spoken to Brooklyn in a few days, which was unusual.

131

Gianna retrieved her phone from the island and headed to the large pastel yellow sofa. Stretched out on the couch, she swiped her phone screen and called Brooklyn.

"Well, well," Brooklyn greeted her. "I was beginning to think I'd lost the only daughter I will ever have."

"Never," Gianna assured her, laughing.

"Word on the street is that you've found a new man *and* a new mama."

"Word on the street? You mean Maya was telling stories. I will have to call her again. She's already on time-out for pulling a stunt on me. Anyway, you cannot be replaced. We have been together through thick and thin. I dare not lose you. That thought already has me stirred all the way up." Gianna gurgled loudly, finding herself funny.

"If you say so," Brooklyn said dryly.

"You know I love you, right?"

"Yes, I do. And I love you, even though you're giving up on our mother-daughter relationship."

"I can't win," Gianna lamented playfully.

"So, to what do I owe this call? I was about to go into a meeting, but when I saw that it was you, I told Julia to ask Phil to manage the meeting."

"You know Phil can handle it."

"That is so. Good help is so hard to find. I'm glad to have Phil."

"I'm sure Phil wants to *have* you, but he dare not ask."

"Don't start that mess again."

"There's nothing wrong with having someone in your life."

"Who is this? Please put Gigi back on the line."

Gianna cracked up.

"This has wrong written all over it," Brooklyn continued. "I can't date my employee. We have company policies against such things."

"I wonder who wrote those policies?"

Brooklyn chuckled. "I can't rewrite what makes sense."

"It's a pity. Phil adores you. He looks at you like you are an earth angel."

Brooklyn snorted. "Stop reading those love stories; they're making you twisted."

Gianna was unrelenting. "Here's an idea for you. If he retires, would you date him?"

Brooklyn paused but long enough for Gianna to know her interest was piqued.

"I don't know, Gigi," Brooklyn finally pushed out. "I don't have the time to think such thoughts. I'm about to lose the chief editor for my Christian Fiction and Non-Fiction genre, so I'm busy thinking about that."

"You do realize she's talking with you now. Anyway, you would be happy to know that she has decided to wait until you find a replacement. In fact, she will help to find, and train said replacement. And there's more good news. She will continue to edit for ReTrac when she moves to the magazine department, if that's okay with the management of BMP."

A huge sigh of relief came from Brooklyn. "Thanks, Gigi! Thanks so much."

"My pleasure. Seriously, it is. I've had a good run in my current position, and I won't say I will never return, but I need something new right now."

"That I understand, and I appreciate your thoughtfulness."

"You're welcome, Big Mama."

Brooklyn laughed loudly. "Girl, you're all kinds of wrong today."

"You will keep laughing if you date Phil. He has been your right hand for what seems like forever. I think he's here just to be near you. You know it's not for the money. He has money of his own."

"Thanks for letting me know your thoughts. So how is the young man you're seeing?"

It was Gianna's turn to pause.

"Don't go quiet on me," Brooklyn insisted. "Word is all over these streets. Kidding. So, what's up with him?"

"Er, I don't know what to say. Well, we're not dating, we're just friends. I met him at the hotel in Tallahassee."

"You've gotten close in the few days, but I supposed when the connection is right, it's just right."

"It's nothing like that."

"You're too old to be fooling yourself. Seems like he hasn't made a move, but you must know he's scouting out the lay of the land before he moves in."

"I don't know about that."

"Hand holding. Hugging. Kissing your cheek. Laughing at your bad jokes. Staring at you, intensely. And, I bet you're telling him things you've never told anyone, excepting those close to you. What do you think is going on here? No, you didn't have to mention any of those things to me. I've been around the block a few times."

Gianna remained silent.

"Just take your time," Brooklyn warned. "Go slowly. Let me say that again: go slowly."

"Okay."

"Is he a Christian?"

"Yes, he is," Gianna said quickly.

"That's good to know. Since you're not ready to talk about him, I will be praying."

"His name is Carter... Carter McIntosh. No need to Google," Gianna said. "He's co-owner of McIntosh Homes.

He took me to his home development site in Tallahassee, and it was amazing," Gianna gushed. "He's amazing. His mom stayed at the hotel that I was at and sometimes we had breakfast and dinner together. In fact, Nora, his mom, invited me to her sixtieth birthday party. I'm going to stay at her home next Wednesday all the way through the weekend. The party is on Saturday. Isn't that something?"

No response came from Brooklyn.

"Are you there?" Gianna asked.

"You should tread cautiously down that road," Brooklyn pushed out.

"Do you know Carter and Nora?"

"You barely know this woman. If the party is Saturday, why would you be going to her home from Wednesday?"

"I did say you cannot be replaced, right?" Gianna teased, attempting to lighten the moment.

"You think that's what this is about? I understand the role that I play in your life."

"Then, it's settled," Gianna said. "For the record, I'm going to review a book Nora is working on. Don't worry; it's not a paid job. I know company policy."

There was a momentary silence, and then Brooklyn spoke. "Gigi, I don't know much about Nora's children, but all my encounters with Nora McIntosh have not gone well. People like her will chew you up and destroy you if you are not willing to go along with whatever they say."

Gianna exploded with an exasperated sigh. "Weren't you the one telling me to quit the emotional shielding and self-sabotaging behaviors? *Apparently*, I misunderstood."

"I have your best interest at heart. I want you to be happy, but I don't believe this is a good situation. Please put the matter before the Lord."

"I'm already doing that."

Bristling silence.

"Everything will work itself out," Brooklyn said. "Talk with you later. Julia is here."

"Okay."

Gianna gazed at the phone screen, still mystified by Brooklyn's reaction. She slid from the sofa to her knees.

"Father, it is in the name of Jesus that I come," she prayed. "Thank You for being Lord and Savior of my life. Lord, help me to fix my gaze on You concerning my relationship with Carter. Open the eyes of my heart, so that I can hear and understand what the Holy Spirit is saying…."

CHAPTER 23

On the balcony outside his father's home office, Carter stared straight ahead at the lush vegetation.

Seated near to him on a matching light-brown sofa, his father watched him eagerly. Waiting for an answer.

Not that Carter couldn't respond. He didn't know the best way to do so without going overboard. Gushing all over the place was not cool. It was not even in his makeup.

For all that he felt in his heart about Gianna, it was still hard to express it, when even he had not acknowledged the truth.

"It still feels surreal," Carter began, finally looking at his father. "I just met her, Dad."

Henry smiled at him, adjusting his lean, coffee-colored frame in the corner of the sofa. "Sometimes, that's how it happens."

"Tell me about it. Completely unexpected." Carter couldn't quite understand his affinity for Gianna. "It's not hard to say why I'd stopped to look at her," Carter continued. "I heard her laughter, and that pulled me in. She was not in sight when I heard her laughing, but eventually, when I found her, not only was her laughter beautiful, but she was gorgeous." He was babbling, but he didn't care. "There was something about her; the air around her was positive, even though she appeared a bit shy. But, when she opened her mouth, she was authentic. The more I got to know her, the more I realized that she looked and sounded like my...."

"Uh-oh! Don't leave me hanging." His father chuckled loudly, then ran a hand over his low-cut salt-and-pepper hair.

Carter shook his head. "She looked and sounded like my queen, my wife."

Silence descended as that revelation hit.

His father spoke quietly. "That's wonderful, son. Gianna has struck the major chord in your heart. I often wondered if you would love again because I know Kara's death hit you hard. But, son, I'm glad to see that aspect of your life on the rise. You buried your head in work all these years, and that did your business well, but there's nothing like having a family, people to share all that success with."

"I don't know about that yet, Dad, but Gianna sure hit a nerve in my heart."

"That's a great start. And, I'm glad she knows the Lord."

"Me too."

"What's your next move? It sounds like Gianna is interested in you, too."

"Next move? I don't know. It's not that I'm afraid. I like Gia, but while my heart is tripping over itself, my head is busy pressing the brake—left, right, top, bottom, and in every direction."

"It's not easy to step out again." His father looked thoughtful. "You had said that you would never visit—"

"No, Dad." *I don't know why you would bring that up.* "I don't want to. In any case, I don't know how that would help."

"You would be surprised, son. You would be surprised. Think about it."

"I don't even want to make that promise, because that's not in my sphere of thoughts."

"I have something for you. This is the moment to give it to you."

Carter eyed his father. "That sounds... interesting."

His father chuckled. "I don't want to say anything else, but I love this new thing that is happening to you."

Carter smiled. "I was wondering if I was getting carried away, but I've prayed about it, and I feel at peace concerning a relationship with Gia."

"Son, God developed you in the dark after Kara's death. You had gone through a rough season after her death. But God incubated you in the dark during that period, and now, it's time to step into the light, and make new memories." Henry paused to make sure that Carter was attentive. "I will be praying for you."

"Thanks, Dad. I'd like that."

"It's all good."

Carter nodded, then cleared his throat. "I haven't told Mom yet, but you'll never believe who I saw in Tallahassee: Savannah McKenzie."

"Savannah? But she disappeared."

"I know, and took Ry's heart with her."

"Did you talk with her?"

"No. For some strange reason, even though she was right there, I didn't."

His father chuckled. "To think she was just up north."

"I couldn't believe it. She was coming out of the building that houses Greg's company. I had planned to ask Greg if he knew her, but he had an emergency at work the day I stopped by."

"Did you mention seeing her to Ry?"

"No. Noooo."

His father laughed loudly. "You didn't want to risk him heading to Tallahassee with a shotgun, huh?"

"You know it. Savannah had him—"

"Savannah?" Nora said, coming towards them from the doorway.

"Hey, Mom! Heard you were in the shower." Carter rose and hugged her, not missing the expression of shock running across her face.

"Hey, love!" Nora soaked up Carter's affection.

139

Carter released her and returned to his seat, watching as his mother pecked his father on the cheek before sitting beside him.

"Oh, my two loves in one place," Nora said, sighing contentedly.

"Mom, what if Pax and Ry walk in and hear you?" Carter asked. "Do you want me to be left in a pit by my brothers, and then sold? Geez! Pax and Ry can take so much and no more. They're only humans."

His mother laughed loudly. "Okay, Joseph, you just wrote a whole story. But tell you what, if you all don't say it to them, I won't."

"I won't," Carter said, playfully. "I'm sure Dad won't."

"I won't," Henry said, "even though Pax is dropping by."

"Awesome!" Nora perked up, looking from one to the other, then her brows furrowed. "Pax is dropping by. Again. I hope he's not planning to marry that—"

"My eldest son can't swing by?" Henry asked, with crinkled brows.

"Of course, honey," Nora said, smiling to appease her husband.

Carter raced to the rescue. "Mom, you know Pax is always hanging out with Dad."

"It's not enough that they work together," they all said in unison.

Everyone laughed.

"Did you both plan to dress alike today?" Nora questioned.

Carter glanced at his father, who was dressed in a pair of black jeans and a royal-blue Polo shirt. "So observant, Mom," he harassed her.

She rolled her eyes. "Isn't it enough that you all look like each other? Your father is the most handsome, though."

"Don't forget—and the tallest," Carter said cheekily. He and Paxton were almost as tall as their father—six feet three inches, while Rylan was two inches shorter.

"I can still put you over my knees, Carter Levi McIntosh," his mother threatened.

Laughter burst from Carter. "Trying to help, Mom. Just trying to help."

"Right? What were you saying about Savannah?" Nora inquired.

"I glimpsed her in Tallahassee," Carter said, omitting where exactly he had seen her.

His father looked at him puzzled, but from his expression, he understood. Everyone in the family knew that there was no love lost between Nora and Savannah.

"I see," Nora said, then chuckled to herself. "She gave meaning to the word 'disappear.'"

"Come on, Nora," Henry chided.

"You know the trouble that, that… er, girl… caused Rylan. You all need to keep her in the past and away from him. My poor baby."

"You made things hard for her, Mom," Carter insisted. "If I were her, I would have disappeared, too."

"Forget about that girl," Nora said with a shrug, then smiled brightly. "How is Gianna?"

"She's great. We're hanging out tomorrow evening."

Nora clapped her hands in glee. "I love that. I love her."

"I can't wait to meet this Gianna," Henry stated.

"And you will, dear," Nora piped up. "Next Wednesday is on the way." She looked at Carter. "And I'll have her all to myself because someone is traveling."

"Well, rub that in, Mom."

"I won't because I know you will be calling her day and night."

Both men chuckled knowingly.

"I hope you've had that conversation with her, Carter. If you didn't, I would encourage you to do so speedily. She is the type of woman who's hyper-intelligent but doing some amount of emotional shielding." Nora laughed a little. "Truthfully, we're all dysfunctional, some more than others."

"You speak for yourself, dear," Henry stated. "The good Lord has cleaned me up… nicely, I might add."

Carter remained silent. Only his immediate family and Allison knew about his pseudonym. *Coming clean?* Truth be told, he wasn't quite there yet. Just maybe he was a bit insecure, competing with the superman ReTrac.

"Tell her sooner, rather than later, son," his father encouraged. "Your mother and I had *that* conversation about how you all ended up in Tallahassee."

"Oh, honey, I told you I was just trying to help," Nora said sweetly, flashing a brilliant smile in the direction of her husband.

"I'm sure you were." Her husband mimicked her tone, causing bubbles of self-conscious laughter to rush from her.

Carter had to laugh, too. His father wore the pants in this house. After almost forty years of marriage, his parents had each other down pat.

"I'm going to my study," Nora said, rising and making her way to the door. "No love is coming from you two." She stopped, turned, and opened her mouth, but Carter and Henry were on it.

"Like father, like son," they said in unison.

Dramatically, Nora lifted her hands and eyes towards the ceiling before dropping them and moving through the door.

"Love you, honey!" Henry yelled after her, holding back laughter.

"Love...." Carter was chuckling so hard; he couldn't get the words out.

"She'll be alright," his father said, rising. "As you know, it's your mother's way or the highway. I have to be on the church's prayer line in a few, and I know you've got some thinking and praying to do."

"Right on that, Dad."

"Let's go into my office so I can give you what I was hoping to part with way before now."

"Can't wait," Carter said, not sure what to make of the situation. He followed his father into the office and watched as he opened the safe and retrieved a baby pink envelope.

"I was told to hold this until the appropriate time. I think now is the time." He handed a puzzled Carter the envelope. "This might be what you need for the next leg of your journey."

Carter took the envelope and looked at the writing on the front. When he looked up at his father, his face paled. Before he realized it, he was wiping his eyes with the back of his hands.

CHAPTER 24

The doorbell chimed, announcing Carter's arrival, and Gianna rushed to the door and swung it open. The sight of Carter anchored her and sent sparks of joy to her heart.

"Hello," Gianna greeted him with a wide smile, then shifted out of the way so he could enter.

"Hello to you, too." He smiled at her, stepped through the door, and closed it behind him.

In one sweeping glance, she took in his navy-blue jeans and short-sleeved green Polo shirt. "This way, please," she said, moving through the entryway that led to the living room. "What did you bring for dessert?"

Silence.

"Carter." She turned to locate him and had to retrace her steps. He was standing at the front door. "What's going on?" she questioned, eyes wide.

"I'm here waiting for my hug, if it will ever come."

A gurgle popped from her as she took in his child-like expression. "Oh gosh, you're so spoiled." She walked over, threw both arms around his waist, and embraced him. He hugged her tightly with one arm.

She patted his back. "Are you happy now?"

"A little more, please."

She hugged him a little longer, and then on tiptoes, she gently kissed his cheek. Somehow, she felt he needed it.

Big mistake.

He showed no sign of letting up.

And, just like that, she was breathless. His cologne was kicking up a storm in her.

She made movements to release herself, and when his arm finally dropped from her waist, they both pushed out quiet sighs.

Laughter spluttered.

"Come on, dinner is already on the table," she told him, moving towards the living room for a second time.

He followed her. "Great. Hungry Howie's is here."

She chuckled loudly.

"It wasn't that funny," he remarked.

"Man, you're in a mood this evening. What's up? Did someone steal your cookies at school?"

He chortled, moving through the living room to drop the cake box he was carrying on the island. He eyeballed her, where she stood at the opposite end of the island. "What is this? I hope it's not beat-up-Carter evening?"

"Not at all," she reassured him.

"Can I take your word for it?"

"You can. Thanks for the dessert. Black forest cake?"

He smiled at her. "Got that right."

"Yeah." She returned his smile.

"Do you like to play Chinese Checkers?" he asked.

"Yes." She looked at him, puzzled. *That came out of nowhere.*

He jerked his head towards the box marked "Chinese Checkers," which was, in large part, hidden by magazines on the island.

"Very observant," she told him. "Dinner is on the nook table. I hope you don't mind?"

"No. It's more intimate."

Did he say intimate? She shut down her thoughts. "Right... on that," she pushed out vaguely.

"Which part? Intimate?" Forced innocence laced his voice.

She felt the heat rising on her face. "You *are* in a mood."

"No, I'm not."

145

"I'll take your word for it," she said, moving to the nook table.

He followed her.

"You can sit where you are," she told him.

"Thanks."

After they were both seated, he blessed their meal.

"Well done," Carter said, his eye sweeping the table.

She had taken the time to prepare bourbon pecan chicken, curried steamed rice, potato salad, green beans, vegetable salad, and fruit punch.

"But you haven't tasted it yet."

He smiled at her. "I didn't tell you about my gift—I can see the future."

"That's a wonderful gift. I don't have any superpower."

"Don't worry. It will come."

She smiled at him and his foolishness. She liked Carter McIntosh... a lot.

He placed food on his plate, and so did she.

"Would you like to attend church with me on Sunday? I don't mean to take you away from attending your church."

"No problem. I would love to."

They had discussed the churches they attended on the drive from Tallahassee.

"I will pick you up at nine o'clock," Carter said. "And I will attend church with you whenever you like."

"That's nice."

"You're making me sound like a cream puff."

Gianna had to laugh.

They ate in silence for a while before Carter wiped his mouth with a napkin from the table. "The food tastes great. Who taught you to cook?"

"My aunt Dorette. She's my mother's sister; she is my only aunt. I lived with her and Reginald, her husband, in Chicago after my parents died. Uncle Reginald passed over seven years ago in a car accident."

"I'm sorry, Gia," he said quietly, his gaze growing tender.

"Me, too." She nodded with understanding, and then smiled at him. "Well, the good news is—the dark clouds over you are lifting."

Carter let out a soft chuckle. "Would you like to have dinner with me on Sunday, after church?"

"Sure." It was out before she could think about it. She mentally rolled her eyes.

Carter cracked up. "I saw that. Any suggestions on where we can eat?"

"Yes… somewhere with food."

He snorted. "You're good."

Gianna couldn't help the happiness that lit her face. "Oh, I just changed your life with that. I'm good at those sorts of things."

An hour later, they sat on the colorful rug with the large sofa at their backs and the Chinese Checkers board between them as they competed for the position of champion.

"Are you going to make a move or what?" Gianna asked.

"I'm on it."

"No, you're not. You're very distracted. No, make that extremely distracted. Don't think I haven't noticed."

He sighed, moving one of his marbles on the board. "There."

"Do you want to talk about it?"

"No. I'm okay."

She noticed that he didn't make eye contact. "Okay," she said, preparing to make a move.

"You may not want to make that move," Carter goaded her.

"I'm making it," she said, jumping over several marbles. "Great move, huh?"

Carter groaned.

She patted his shoulder. "At least you saw that coming."

In quietness, Carter made his move.

Gianna whelped. "Oh, no. I didn't see that coming."

No matter which way she moved, he was bound to win.

"I tried to help you, but you keep holding on to that twisted hope."

"Aha! I don't want to play anymore. We were supposed to be watching a movie, anyway."

"Make your move, woman."

"No. Stop being ugly."

He eyed her. "You could at least lose gracefully."

"Fine. You win."

"Look at that attitude. I don't know if I can accept my gift."

Her head swished to look at him. "What gift?"

"A gift is involved." He dazzled her with a smile. "A gift for the winner."

"A kiss is not a gift. And I've heard all your rebuttals already."

He chuckled while turning his body towards hers.

She mirrored his movements.

His mouth quirked in a slight smile. "You know that man was a fool to leave you?"

She looked at him, trying to read his thoughts, but couldn't.

He held her gaze, resting his head in the cup of his hand, his elbow on the sofa.

"Thanks," she said quietly, looking away from him.

In a smooth move, he cupped her cheek, turning her head towards him.

Senses spinning, she puffed out, "Ca-Carter."

"Don't worry. I'm not going to kiss you."

Disappointing. She met his hooded gaze, wondering what he was looking for. She dared not ask, for she was already battling the sensations that were roaming her body. She focused on his hairy hand, and screeching brakes echoed in her mind. She wanted to run her hand along his arm. "Carter, please—"

"I like looking at you, Gia," he murmured, releasing his hold.

What...? She worked to slow her breathing.

"And I suspect you like looking at me, too. Am I right?" he asked.

She couldn't make eye contact.

"Don't get shy on me now," he teased. "I'm blessed with many talents, but reading minds is not one of them. I want to take that off my list of the great unknowns."

When she still wouldn't respond, he leaned in, filling her senses with his nearness. Unable to help herself, Gianna gazed tenderly at him.

"Yes," seemed to squeeze out of her before she drifted into the swirling kaleidoscope of bright light he'd created.

CHAPTER 25

On Saturday morning, Carter punched in the code and entered his home office, which was upstairs, opposite his master suite. He'd gone for an early morning run instead of burning time at his home gym. He needed to clear his head, too many thoughts running to and fro. After his run, he'd showered then made breakfast, even though his appetite was shot. After playing with the food on his plate, he had left it on the island.

He slid into the brown leather chair behind the executive desk just as his cell phone buzzed. He reached for it in his pocket and noticed that it was Rylan calling.

"I didn't know if I should answer," Carter greeted him. "Isn't this a bit early for you?"

"Man, don't you see I'm trying to get my life together? Thanks for the encouragement."

"That's a good thing."

"It's none of your business, but I got up early to commune with the Lord, then I went for a run. Just had breakfast and now trying to make sure you're living right."

Carter stared at his phone. *Never say never.*

"Are you there?" Rylan questioned.

"Yes, bro. Proud that you're trying to take it higher."

"Trying? No, bro. I'm succeeding, even though old habits are weighing me down."

"Tell me about it," Carter muttered.

"Did you read it?"

"I told you I couldn't. Soon though."

"Have some fortitude man, some courage. Do I need to come over?"

"No need. I've got this."

"I'm giving you two hours, and if I don't hear from you, I'm coming over."

"That's not what that key is for."

"This is an emergency. See you soon. Bye."

"Okay, bro."

Soon, Carter powered on his computer, hoping to catch up on his writing. *That will keep my mind occupied.* However, he found himself retyping the same paragraph. He pushed back in his chair, letting out a frustrated moan as images of Gianna's smiling face filled his thoughts.

He loved being in her presence.

He loved looking at her.

He loved touching her.

But more than that, he was falling in love with her. He constantly felt the need to protect her, to keep her secure.

A tortured expression filled his eyes. *Am I betraying my love for Kara?* Even on her death bed, he wanted to marry her, but she would have none of it. She didn't want that for him. In her words, she loved him too much to do that to him.

His eyes welled, and he ran his hands over his face, thinking about the letter she'd left him. He had felt the envelope a few times and surmised that it was a letter. He hadn't read it. Afraid he couldn't handle it.

He stared at the photo of himself and Kara that was in a gold frame on his desk. They were smiling happily at Rylan as he snapped them leaning against each other at a family brunch in his parents' backyard.

Good times!

A single tear rolled down his cheek. He opened the middle drawer on his desk and took out the letter. He wiped his eyes with the back of his hand and stared at the envelope. A tiny smile lifted a corner of his mouth. Pink was Kara's favorite color—all shades of pink. For Kara, pink represented compassion and love—love of oneself, and love for others. Above all, it symbolized a right relationship with God.

His courage grew, and Carter opened the letter, trying to get out of his own way. He pushed out a long sigh, recognizing Kara's handwriting, and then started to read.

My dear Carter,

I love you with all my heart. And I know that you love me with all your heart. The Lord has given us many years, and for that, I'm grateful. Dry your tears, for we both know I'm in a better place... and so are you. That means you've done away with that break-the-glass situation. Don't be surprised that I'm aware of this. My love, I know you.

Carter gaped, and then a smile crept up his face. She was right on the money. Back in the day, he'd lost the will to live, so he had created his will and made Paxton the executor of his estate, just in case. Thankfully, he was still alive and kicking. Grateful too, for parents who would not let him go.

Carter mopped his eyes with the back of his hand before he continued reading.

That break-the-glass situation is over. Thank God! I know because this letter would not be in your hands otherwise. I'm happy that you've found the one—someone whom you can't stop thinking about, someone whose presence brings you joy, someone whom you want to protect, and someone whom your soul loves. And, yes, as crazy as it seems, someone whom you've fallen in love with.

I know you will treasure and honor my memory, and because she loves you, she will too. This goodbye is what you need for the next leg of the journey. Take it. I love you, and so, with all my love, I give you my blessing. Be happy. You deserve it.

God bless both of you. Go on, Carter, love her with all your heart. Goodbye, Dearest Carter.

With all my love,
Kara

Tears rolled down Carter's cheeks, but no sound came from him. He was not sure how long he stayed in that position, but when he came to himself, he was praying.

CHAPTER 26

"I ought to bury my shame in my backyard," Gianna lamented, throwing her back against the sofa in her living room. "He's wavering, Kam; he's wavering. I'm quitting before it's too late."

"Gigi, stop it," Kam called out, her voice filled with reprimand. She pulled to the edge of the smaller sofa across from Gianna. "You cannot throw yourself on the grenade right now. For God's sake, have faith."

"You don't understand; I'm all the way in, and now I need to pull back. Leave with my dignity."

"Leave! You haven't even started a relationship with Carter, and you're already giving up."

"Go ahead. Speak from your heart, why don't you?"

"Okay, I may have come down on you a bit heavy, but don't distance yourself from him. Be patient."

Gianna let out a short laugh. "Distancing myself. Oh, I invented that. I don't want to be played with. I feel like I'm competing for his affection, competing with a ghost, at that. I'm telling you, Kam; something wasn't right with him. I think he's having separation issues, separation from a ghost, and I have no intention of—"

"Relationships take time to form and build. He was going to marry this woman."

"Her name is Kara," Gianna told her. "And for your information, I've been in a relationship."

"Really?" Kamala's eyebrows shot up as she spoke. "Your longest relationship is with the last book you read."

"What's that supposed to mean?" Gianna straightened her back as her brows furrowed.

"You heard me, and we've had this conversation. Caleb was not my favorite, and I told you that a thousand times. But, he didn't stand a chance, and he knew it. You had that poor man running behind you for six months

154

before you went on a date with him. Then, you obliged him by entering a relationship with him. Then, you suffocated him in the relationship. By the time you realized what you had in your hands, he was gone."

Silence descended, and Gianna eyeballed Kamala.

"I see," Gianna pushed out, her voice flat.

"See, that's what you do, hide your emotions. Gigi, I haven't seen you this alive in forever. I'm not trying to hurt your feelings, but I would hate to see a good man pass you by. Worse yet, I'd hate to see *you* pass *him* by."

Thinking, Gianna swiped her mouth to the side, for she knew Kamala was right. She had trust issues, and because of that she had needed to know Caleb's every move. Tiring for her, and him. Gianna pushed out a sigh. "How do you know Carter is a good man?"

"I feel so in my spirit. He invited you to church, for starters. Yes, I know he's working to resolve some issues, but who isn't?" Kamala looked Gianna in the eye. "The least you can do is continue to trust the Lord in this matter and let Him lead you. And, continue to pray for Carter."

"I don't know if I want to," Gianna confessed.

"You know fear is not of God, right? You must let someone in, Gigi, at some time or the other. No one is going to marry you without knowing you."

Gianna's eyes bulged, and Kamala laughed aloud.

"Not knowing you, like that," Kamala hastily added.

"That's a relief," Gianna responded, clutching her chest. "I know you have my back, but I cannot afford to have my heart ripped out."

"I don't see myself as a matchmaker, but from what you've told me about Carter and from what we've read, he seems like one of the good guys. Now, if you had fallen for his brother, Rylan, then I would have told you to sprint away."

155

Gianna chortled. "Yep, social media has not been kind to him. It seemed weird, though, considering his two brothers seem to lead normal lives."

"You always have that one black sheep in the family. At least he's equally handsome. What a handsome brood! Daddy McIntosh looks pretty dapper, too."

"Yes, they're a good-looking family. Ry is the shortest of the men."

"He's not that short," Kamala retorted. "According to the internet, they're six three while he's six-one."

"Can't be good for a huge ego, if the little Carter mentioned about him is true. Anyway, we can't believe all we read on the internet. At one time, the internet was sure ReTrac was a woman, but we know, thanks to Brooklyn, that he's a man."

"Right on that." Kamala eyed her. "I'm glad for that. And I'm glad, too, to see you letting go of your imaginary boyfriend and embracing the real deal."

Gianna pouted. "I wish I had your confidence."

"You know where you can find your confidence," Kamala replied, moving to sit next to her.

"In the Lord," Gianna said quietly. "Thanks for the reminder."

"You're welcome, bestie."

They were quiet for a moment.

Kamala smiled at her. "Ready?"

"Yes, let me get my purse."

"It's going to rain, so grab an umbrella."

"Will do."

An hour later, Gianna and Kamala exited Kamala's black Honda CRV in the parking lot at Restwell Cemetery. Gianna tucked Kamala's hand in the crook of her elbow as they took the walk on a paved pathway.

For a Saturday afternoon, the temperature was pretty cool, and Gianna could hear the wind rustling the

156

branches of nearby trees. The sun cast shadows on the predominantly white tombstones, filtering through green tree leaves, and the strategically planted colorful blooming flowers on the thick grass.

As far as Gianna's eyes could see, most of the graves had beautiful bouquets, but some had weather-beaten flowers or other gifts. Visitors and mourners were scattered all over the cemetery. Ahead, the concrete walkway glistened like a mirror, reminding visitors that they were alive… even though loved ones were dead.

Gianna felt Kamala shiver. "Are you going to be okay?" Gianna asked.

Kamala put on a brave smile. "Yes."

Ever since they'd become friends in college, they had visited Kamala's parents' graves on the anniversary of their deaths.

"That's good to know, but don't break my arm," Gianna said, looking at Kamala's hand in a death grip on her arm.

"Oh gosh, sorry," Kamala pushed out, relaxing her hold.

"No worries. I've got you. Let's pick up the pace. We don't want the rain to catch us."

"Right," Kamala responded, eyeing the long umbrella sticking out from under Gianna's arm. "I'm glad you're prepared, though."

Gianna smiled at her. "Always."

They continued to walk in silence, then soon veered left and followed another path.

"Thanks again for getting the flowers," Kamala said, eyeing the bunch of red roses in her hand before glancing at another bunch in Gianna's hand.

"You're very welcome. Even though I don't know if the bunch you're carrying will make it."

A gurgle popped from Kamala. "It will make it."

"Good," Gianna said, smiling at her.

The pair halted before two graves, the white tombstones announcing Gregory Tayson and Dawn Tayson in black ink. Kamala's parents had died in an airplane crash when she was fifteen years old.

Gianna wrapped an arm around her friend and allowed her to cry. Around ten minutes later, Kamala released herself from Gianna's arms and laid the flowers on her parents' graves. She then kneeled between the graves mumbling words of gratitude and love.

Half an hour later, a few raindrops splattered, and Gianna opened the umbrella over their heads. Gianna sensed that Kamala didn't want to leave, but they had to before it started pouring. In silence, they walked back to the vehicle. Suddenly, Gianna halted and gripped Kamala's arm.

"He's here," Gianna whispered, pulling on the umbrella in Kamala's hand to shield herself, and then moving them along.

"Who?" Kamala asked in a hushed tone.

Panicked, Gianna mumbled, "Carter."

"Umm, *who*?"

Gianna pulled on her hand to keep them moving, and Kamala obliged.

"Did you say Carter?" Kamala asked.

"Yes."

"Are you sure?"

"Yes, they are on the right. He's with someone."

Kamala cast a furtive glance in that direction. "How do you know it's him? Their backs are to us."

"It's him. I know it. I'm not sure who the other man is."

"Gianna, really?"

"Yes, hurry. I don't want him to know I saw him."

As soon as they were back in Kamala's vehicle, a long sigh left Gianna. She turned to face her friend, who was watching her curiously.

"I know it was him," Giana blurted. "And no, visiting your parents' graveside was not too much for me."

"Gigi, you—"

"Kam, it was him. I told you I am competing with a ghost." Gianna sulked, strapping herself in and then staring out the window.

Kamala did not say anything.

"Can we go?" Gianna begged, anxiety evident in her voice.

"Of course."

Kamala switched on the ignition and pulled away. The ride to Gianna's home was mostly quiet. Any conversation Kamala struck up with her was pushed away. By the time Kamala pulled onto the driveway, the vehicle was heavy with ominous silence.

"Thank you," Gianna said, not looking at her.

"You're welcome. I'm coming in."

Gianna paused, her hand on the door, tears brimming. "I need to be alone."

"No. The last thing you need is to be alone."

Gianna swung her head in Kamala's direction, ready to lash out, but Kamala beat her to it.

"I'm not the enemy. Stop feeling sorry for yourself. Stop beating yourself up. And stop trying to put the pieces of the puzzle together because you don't have all the parts. Plus, aren't you seeing Carter tomorrow?"

An endless stream of tears rolled down Gianna's cheeks. "I don't want to be hurt again," she said between sobs. "It's like I'm allergic to happiness."

"No, you're not. Stop declaring that."

"Didn't you see him at her graveside?" Sadness choked her voice.

"That's what you get when you start spying on people. That's no way to get the full story. You know what I think? Carter is in preparation mode to enter his new relationship. He's smart. Goodbye to Kara is what he'll need to take the next step... with you."

Hope flared in Gianna's heart.

CHAPTER 27

"You look stunning," Carter gave Gianna a broad smile when he entered her home.

"Thanks!" Gianna walked ahead of him to the living room. "You're early," she remarked when they stood near the small sofas.

"Always. I didn't want to keep you waiting. But the question is, why do you look like someone stole your thunder?"

She eyed him guardedly. "I'm fine. Just have a lot on my mind."

"Anything I can do?" he asked with genuine concern.

He was moving closer, and Gianna had to resist the urge to back away. "No, I'll be fine," she said, turning to pick up her purse and Bible from the coffee table.

After her little pity party yesterday, she'd been determined to enter her home and have an even bigger pity party, but Kamala would have none of it. She had insisted on coming in, even though Gianna knew she would be late for her bridal party meeting. Gianna allowed her in, and Kamala went into Mama mode. She would not leave until Gianna agreed to submit the matter in prayer to the Lord. In the end, she'd prayed and also apologized to Kamala for ruining their sacred ritual.

It was hard to miss Carter's silence, so Gianna fixed her expression before facing him. "I'm fine," she said, looking him in the eye. His expression of unbelief caused a tiny smile to curl her lips.

Opening his arms wide, he sang, "I see sunshine on a cloudy day."

She had to laugh at his foolishness.

"There she is," he teased.

She relaxed a bit. "Did you have breakfast?"

161

"Yes. Did you?"

"Yes. You look great," she told him, her eyes sweeping his navy-blue slim fit suit, complemented by a white shirt and a red and white tie.

"Thanks. Shall we?" he asked with a sweep of his hand towards the front door.

"Sure."

Forty-five minutes later, Gianna walked with Carter on beautiful green grounds to enter the huge red brick building that housed Fellowship of Living Word Church. Rays of sunlight bounced off the upstairs floor-to-ceiling glass windows creating a kaleidoscope effect and playing with her senses.

They entered the beautifully decorated foyer, and Carter escorted her into the high-ceiling theater-style sanctuary. As they walked along the burgundy carpeted floor, Gianna observed that flowers were everywhere, their fragrances providing a sweet, soft scent.

When they moved up the middle aisle, Carter greeted members of the congregation, and to some, he introduced her as his friend. Gianna smiled politely and returned their greetings. There were a few raised eyebrows, but everyone remained respectful. Soon, Carter motioned for her to enter the third row of plush velvet burgundy chairs in the middle aisle, and they took their seats.

"Carter," someone called out from nearby.

Both Carter and Gianna looked in the direction of the voice.

"Hi, Mrs. Vella," Carter responded. "Good morning!"

The slender African American woman moved closer. "Good morning to you both!" she said, flashing a charming smile.

"Good morning," Gianna replied under the woman's watchful gaze.

162

"Carter," Mrs. Vella said, her gaze shifting to him, "Pastor McCallum needs to speak with you."

"Sure," Carter told her, before turning to Gianna. "I'll be back."

She smiled at him. "Okay."

Gianna watched as Carter made his way from the pew, then her gaze shifted to the screen of her phone. Noting the time, she calculated that the worship service would begin in twenty minutes. After dropping her phone into her purse, her eyes swept the inviting sanctuary—ivory-colored walls, gold chandeliers, paintings, and brass fixtures.

From her barely-there conversation with Carter, while they were on the way in, she knew that the sanctuary could hold approximately two thousand people. The seats were filling up fast, and the congregation was, for the most part, quiet. It was much larger than the church she attended, but she felt equally comfortable. An overwhelming feeling of inner harmony settled in her heart as instrumental music filled the air. She closed her eyes and prayed.

Slight bustling sounds caused her to conclude her prayer. She opened her eyes to witness the musicians taking their places. The altar was now illuminated with dramatic red and gold lighting that highlighted the cross on the wall. Gianna watched intently until movements to her right caught her eyes. Carter was entering the pew.

"Everything okay?" she asked quietly as soon as he took his seat beside her.

"Yes," he said, turning towards her. "Pastor McCallum is asking me to lead praise and worship. The praise and worship leader for today is not feeling well."

Gianna's eyes widened. "Is that something you do?"

"Yes, we're on a roster."

"That's wonderful," Gianna said, her enthusiasm on display. "Do you have the songs all lined up?"

163

"You bet. I stay ready," Carter quipped.

"I love that."

"I need to meet with the praise team in the back, so I'll see you after church. Mom and Dad will sit with you."

"Okay, thanks. I'll be praying for you."

"Thanks." Carter flashed her a grateful smile then moved away.

A few minutes after Carter left, a smiling Nora greeted Gianna. Delighted, Gianna rose and hugged her. As soon as they withdrew from their embrace, Nora introduced her to Henry, her husband.

Gianna smiled at him, taking in his pleasant disposition. His low-cut salt-and-pepper hair stood out against his still youthful coffee-colored skin. He was handsome, with well-defined cheekbones, chin and nose. His dark-brown eyes were framed by thick brows. He was a little taller than Carter, and she saw who was responsible for the long dimples in Carter's lean cheek.

"Nice to meet you, Dr. McIntosh," Gianna said, extending a hand to him.

"The pleasure is mine." His voice was deep but pleasant, and his handshake firm. "Dr. McIntosh? Oh no. When people call me that, they usually want medical advice or a favor," he teased. "Please call me Henry."

A sense of humor. Gianna's smile widened. "Henry, it is."

"I'm glad to finally meet you," Henry said. "You're all Nora talks about these days."

"I hope only good things," Gianna remarked, her eyes rushing to Nora's.

"Only good things, I assure you," Nora told her, smiling.

"Great then," Gianna said, returning her smile.

"Good things," Henry agreed as they all took their seats.

A few minutes later, a man walked to the podium. "Good morning, church! Let us worship God," he said zealously.

The congregation rose in high praise, and Gianna stood, too.

Henry and Nora followed suit.

"For those of you who don't know me, I'm Deacon Paul Nader," the man continued. "It's a pleasure to have you in the house of the Lord this morning."

The congregation responded with shouts of praise.

"Let us pray," Deacon Nader said.

He waited a few moments for the congregation to settle down before praying. "Lord, we exalt You. Glory be to Your name. Father, in the name of Jesus Christ, we pull down strongholds and cast down vain imaginations and every high thing that seeks to exalt itself against the knowledge of God. We declare that You are our God, our God, who has girded us with strength and has made our way perfect. Father, we pray that miracles and wonders will take place in this worship service. Lift, oh God, feelings of heaviness and depression. Lord, we commit this service to You. May we leave changed in our hearts and minds. May we leave strengthened and uplifted. In the name of Jesus Christ, we pray, amen."

Loud amens rang out in response to the prayer.

As Deacon Nader rested the microphone on the podium and moved away, a loud, "Praise the Lord, church!" rang out.

The congregation responded likewise.

"Praise the Lord!" the somewhat familiar voice continued. "Come on, clap your hands and shout onto God with a voice of triumph."

Gianna's head jerked up, and a smile broke out across her face when she saw that it was Carter—confirmed when he moved to the spot recently occupied by Deacon Nader.

"Come on, give God the praise and glory that's due to Him," Carter encouraged, preparing the congregation for a powerful worship experience.

Gianna joined the congregation as they clapped and shouted praises to the Lord. Even so, she had to slam her mouth shut. She was mesmerized by this newfound side of Carter.

"Let everything that has breath praise the Lord," Carter announced.

"Praise the Lord!" the congregation roared back.

Celestial sounds of music and worship filled the air.

"Praise Him in the Sanctuary," Carter declared, "Praise Him in the firmament of His power. Praise Him on the high-sounding cymbals. Let everything that has breath praise the Lord."

The band struck heavenly chords, and Gianna couldn't help but worship.

"Come on, people of God, take up your positions in the Lord!" Carter cried out. "You are children of God. You *are* the apple of His eye." Carter raised a hand in the air. "Hallelujah! Let us sing praises to our God, for with God, all things are possible."

As the instrumental introduction to "This Is a Move" by gospel artistes, Brandon Lake and Tasha Cobbs Leonard, began, the atmosphere became euphoric. Applause filled the air as Carter, arms wide open, effortlessly belted out the song with emotion and ease.

The momentum was heavenly.

Backed by the engaging praise team, Carter's tenor voice was incredibly worshipful, beautifully raspy, and altogether wonderful. The rise and fall, and ebb and flow of their powerful voices empowered the congregation to worship, and the people of God were full of joy alongside them.

Gianna tried to remember to worship, for she could hardly believe it was Carter... yet she could. She wished he would never stop singing. His beautiful heart was on display before the Lord, and she found herself staring at him with fresh admiration.

After praise and worship was finished, Carter sat with the praise team to the left of the podium. Next, they listened to Pastor Raymond McCallum as he spoke under the theme, "Reach for Your Destiny," to bring home the full spectrum of their spiritual experience.

The sanctuary was quiet as the man of God boldly delivered his message. "The enemy knows your potential, and that's why he tried to snuff you out," Pastor McCallum told the congregation. "Don't let your brokenness take you off the course of your destiny. Let it go and be healed. God kept you here because there's oil in you. Yes, there's still oil in you."

CHAPTER 28

Taking his eyes off the road for a split second, Carter glanced at Gianna, who was busy throwing compliments his way. Fascinating how her mouth, which always bordered on the verge of a smile, was displaying a wide grin.

"What's up with that look?" she asked, a glimmer of mischief in her eyes.

"Are you going to stop?"

"Nope. Praise and worship was on fiiiiire. From now on, you're Psalmist McIntosh."

Carter chuckled. "I didn't realize you're a troublemaker."

"We're both making discoveries today."

"If you want to put it like that. The good thing is—you're back."

Her forehead furrowed. "Back?"

"You were more than a little reserved this morning when I picked you up."

"I had a lot on my mind, but I left it all at church. Plus, I wasn't prepared to be wowed, starting with praise and worship."

"I'm glad you were blessed. To worship like that is God's doing. When suffering slaps you in the face, you see exactly what you're made of," he admitted quietly.

"Oh, Carter."

He glanced her way and smiled. "The great thing is that the Lord gave me enough for the journey, and He made sure I had more than enough to sustain me wherever He needs me to be. It's my pleasure to be able to minister the nature of our Father."

"That's beautiful. Your worship inspired me to lean in, into a closer relationship with the Lord. I want to allow

God to use the challenging situations of my past to create ministry like that."

"That's great. If you ever need my help or for me to pray about a situation, let me know."

"Thanks. I will. I know your ministry was birthed out of your challenging circumstances, and it wasn't easy for you. You cannot minister like that unless you know God on an intimate level. I appreciate that you allowed the Lord to use you. You have been a blessing to me. Thank you."

"Just hearing you say that made my struggles worth it. You're welcome, always. I had said that I would take you out to dinner, but we're going to eat at my home instead. I hope you don't mind."

"Not a problem, unless you cooked."

He laughed. "Woman, I can cook."

"I like that passion, but I'll be the judge of that."

"Now, I'm thinking I should have taken you out to eat."

"No," she said quickly. "I'll eat whatever you provide. I'm sure it will be good."

"Alrighty."

Carter returned her smile, loving the appreciation displayed in her eyes.

Soon, he pulled onto a private road and traveled a one mile stretch through beautiful flowering trees, before driving through the entrance gate of his custom-built gated estate home. Walking a fine line between modern-day and timeless, the two-story home sat in the middle of three acres of fenced lush greenery and flowers.

Brick accent walls, majestic columns, and arch-topped windows provided the right touch to the dignified front of his gray and white dwelling. His home boasted a three-car garage to the right of the circular driveway. He opened the double doors, parked, and turned off the ignition.

He looked at Gianna. "You're quiet," he stated matter-of-factly while closing the garage door.

She perked up. "Your home is stunning. Did you design it?"

"Thanks. Yes, I did."

"Great job! I can't wait to see inside."

"Let's go then."

They alighted from the vehicle, and after disarming the alarm, Carter opened the door to a long, wide hallway. He reached in and flipped on the light switch.

"Go ahead," he encouraged, and Gianna stepped in.

He followed suit and closed the door behind them.

They were moving down the hallway when a beaming Gianna exclaimed, "Wow! These are gorgeous!" She paused to admire one of the lovely large paintings that lined the cream-colored walls.

"Thanks," he said, moving her along.

"Do you…?" Her voice trailed off as she halted to look at a picture of a beautiful waterfall. "This looks familiar," she said, staring at the portrait before her head whipped right to look at him.

He stilled. He'd forgotten to take the piece down when he was removing all evidence from the general areas of his home. "That's Dunn's River Falls in Jamaica. It's one of the country's natural attractions."

She gazed at the picture. "You've been there?"

"Yes."

Gianna looked at him, and he tried not to hold his breath.

"I haven't been to Jamaica, but ReTrac had mentioned Dunn's River Falls in one of his books. Wow! He described it exactly right."

She moved forward, and he all but breathed out a sigh of relief.

"It's a beautiful scene for sure," Carter added, just as they entered the living room. "Make yourself comfortable."

"I sure will," she responded, walking deeper into the room and placing her purse on the marble top coffee table.

"A bathroom is in the passageway on your right if you need one."

Gianna turned towards him. "Thanks! I need a tour of...." she paused when she heard gentle barking, followed by the clicking of running paws on the immaculate cream-colored porcelain tiles. She turned and saw a tan-colored Pomeranian dog bounding towards her.

"Help!" she shrieked, racing towards Carter.

"She won't...." His voice trailed off as she threw herself against him, clutching the front of his jacket.

He caught her and held her against his chest. "She won't hurt you. She's affectionate."

"I-I...." she panted, trying to catch her breath.

"Look at Nya. She's giving you a wounded gaze. She was just trying to be friendly."

Gianna had his jacket in a death grip. "Are you sure?"

He was still holding her against him, and he loved that, although she was shaking a bit, her head now buried in his chest.

As if realizing what was happening, Gianna swung her head to look at Nya, but she was now bathing his neck with small puffs of air.

Nya was standing nearby, looking up at them.

"See, she won't hurt you," Carter told her encouragingly.

Gianna looked at the small dog, who was now wagging her tail and watching them with hopeful eyes.

"Nya, lie in your bed," Carter commanded.

The small dog scampered around a bit before running away to climb into her bed near the large brown and beige wood trim sofa.

A sigh of relief left Gianna, and she relaxed her hold on his jacket. "Sorry about that," she said self-consciously, not meeting his eyes.

"Not a problem. Now I know, you're afraid of dogs."

"She took me by surprise."

Gianna made movements to remove herself from his arms, but he tightened his hands around her waist.

"Ca-Carter," she puffed out.

"My eyes are up here," he teased. His two fingers pressed under her chin, forcing her head up.

Her startled eyes finally found their intended destination.

His eyes fixed on hers, he leaned in and heard her suck in a breath. He wanted to kiss her full, tender lips. Unable to help himself, he gently kissed her cheek and then released her.

"I'm glad you're here," he told her. "Even though you're abusing my friend's dog. Good thing he's coming for her tomorrow."

Face flushed, Gianna looked mortified. "Nya came out of nowhere. Oh, she belongs to your friend."

Carter touched her shoulder. "Don't worry about it. I can tell you're not a dog person. And don't think I didn't hear the relief in your voice that it's not my dog."

She smiled at him. "I happen to like dogs. She's cute, too. She surprised me, that's all."

"I might as well take your word for it."

"You can take my word for it. Okay, let's tour this fabulous place."

"Before we eat?

"Yes. I'm not sure I'll be able to move after I eat."

"Let's do it then," he said, leading her across the living room.

A little whimper behind them told him Nya wanted to join in the fun, but she was too well-trained to move from her bed.

Carter eyed Gianna. "Thanks to you, Nya is in solitary confinement."

"Oh, no!"

"She will need therapy after you're gone."

"Then you better release her from jail."

"On it."

Carter took a few colorful plastic balls from a box near Nya's bed and placed them on the burgundy rug under the coffee table. At his command, Nya jumped from her bed, ran towards the balls, and circled them several times. As if putting on a show for them, the dog rolled back and forth, making happy woofing sounds before playing with the balls as if she'd discovered hidden treasures.

"Will she be okay alone?" Gianna whispered when Carter joined her.

"Yes, she'll be alright."

"Good job."

He patted his chest. "Dog-whisperer-in-chief."

Gianna covered her mouth with her hand to prevent her spontaneous outburst from distracting Nya.

Shortly after that, Carter gave Gianna a tour of his home, which was decorated mainly in shades of ivory, with touches of burgundy and yellow accents. The exquisite floor plan boasted large windows, French doors, and wood painted tray ceilings in the living spaces.

On the ground floor were the formal living, dining, and family rooms, kitchen, nook, gym, washroom, bathrooms, and a few other habitable spaces. The second floor held another living room, home offices, four bedrooms with bathrooms, and a massive master suite.

Winded after the tour, they were ready for dinner. Together, they warmed the food in the oven and microwave and lay the dishes out on the table in the formal dining room.

Gianna cleared her throat and Carter looked at her. "The food was delicious. Thank you," she said. "I can't believe you can cook, and you woke early to cook."

He had prepared grilled chicken, peppered steak, steamed brown rice, baked macaroni and cheese, tossed salad, blueberry muffins, and orange juice.

Carter smiled at her. "You're welcome. I enjoy cooking."

"That's nice to know. Who taught you to cook?"

"Marian. She worked with my parents when we were growing up. She could whip up a tasty dish in no time."

"A man of many talents. What other talents do you have, I wonder?"

They eyed each other for a moment, and nervous laughter left her.

"Don't answer that," she quipped, backing away at break-neck speed.

He pushed out a soft sigh. "What other talents do you have?"

"No other talent... none that you don't already know."

He knitted his brows. "That response was way too quick. I know there's more in you."

"Perhaps," she conceded.

He could tell she was holding back. "I knew it."

174

She gave a short laugh. "I dabble in a bit of home decorating."

She wasn't telling all, but he was willing to wait.

"That would explain your beautiful home."

"Thanks. Did you decorate here?"

"Noooo. I'm a builder. Mom helped, and I had an interior designer. Now, I have you."

"I said, dabble."

"You more than dabble."

She didn't take him on. "I wish all my clothes and shoes could live together, like yours."

He laughed. "My walk-in closet was by special design."

"I noticed the matching closet next to it is empty. You have more like a walk-in closet suite. Is it my imagination that it's a bit larger than the one you occupy?"

"Not your imagination. I built it for my wife."

Her mouth opened in a perfect O, then she snapped it shut.

"You know women have more clothes and stuff than men," he added.

"That's thoughtful of you," she added bashfully.

He smiled at her, and she looked away.

"Would you like us to move to the family room?" he asked.

"The dishes, first."

"You don't..." he paused, chuckling at her expression. "Okay, dishes first."

"I refuse to let you cook and then wash the dishes." She twiddled her eyebrows. "I want to participate. And let's do it the old-fashioned way." At his puzzled expression, she added, "No dishwasher."

"Alright. Let's do it."

They moved the plates and leftovers to the kitchen.

While he placed the leftovers in containers, she washed. When he was through, he dried and stacked the dishes. Next, they put the leftovers in the refrigerator and wiped the countertops. Mission accomplished, they stood next to the sink, smiling at each other as they dried their hands with sheets of paper towel.

"Why are you smiling?" she asked, as a gurgle popped from her lips.

He took the damp paper towel from her hand and walked to drop it along with his in the aluminum trash can at the end of the cupboard. When he came back to her, she was still waiting for a reply.

"I'm smiling at you because you're smiling at me," he told her. "And it's nice to have company—good company—here."

"Do you bring a lot of... people here?"

"You mean a lot of women?"

"No. That's none of my business," she said hastily.

He gazed at her for a moment. "I think you know I live a quiet life. My family and friends visit, but no special lady has graced my home. Don't get me wrong, I've gone on a few dates, but no, I'm not in the habit of bringing women here."

"I see," she said quietly, clearly uncomfortable with the turn of the conversation.

"I know you're not in the habit of inviting men home."

"Got that right," she said.

He moved closer and held her hand.

She looked at him curiously. "What?"

"I want to show you something—my favorite spot."

She smiled at him. "That's nice."

That smile caused his heart to stutter.

CHAPTER 29

Carter and Gianna moved from the kitchen and accessed a passageway on the right.

"For a moment, I thought you were going to show me your home office," Gianna told him.

"Is that so? It's a mess. Blueprints everywhere."

"It must be an important room. Keypad access."

"Very observant of you, but it's pretty boring. Actually, it's two offices, one would be for my wife."

Gianna tried not to squirm. "Again, that's thoughtful of you."

"It was the right thing to do. I'm using it now, but when she arrives, I will clear out."

Carter opened the door leading to the back patio and Gianna stepped out.

"That's a nice...." The view muted her train of thought. "Wow," she breathed out.

The back patio covered the length of the home and led to the pool and flourishing vegetation in the backyard.

"This is quite a view," Gianna remarked, moving towards the patio steps leading to the backyard. She halted, gazing around.

Carter stood beside her. "Since you're excited, I'll definitely show you my favorite spot."

"Show me!" She clutched his fingers.

He responded likewise, and they moved forward.

Almost an hour later, Carter and Gianna strode up the back patio. They'd taken the electric cart to a beautiful lake at the edge of the property.

"How do you find the discipline to leave home in the mornings?" Gianna harassed him. "This backyard would keep me outside, and that view of the lake is a writer's dream."

A spontaneous chuckle left Carter. "It's hard, but my clients need me. Church needs me. Do I need to go on? But feel free to use it anytime."

She eyed him as they neared the back door. "I wouldn't want to intrude. Even though the gazebo overlooking the lake is tempting."

"Only the gazebo?"

She opened her mouth to speak, but the heated expression in his eyes halted her breath. He was sending shivers all the way to her toes. She felt her body leaning in and had to catch herself. "You... you need to stop doing that," she mumbled, shifting her weight from one leg to the other.

"Doing what?" he asked innocently.

"You know, Carter," she pushed out, looking away.

"Tell no one," he said quietly, causing her to look at him.

"What?"

"I enjoy looking at you," he said softly.

She gaped at him, her thoughts running wild.

He pushed out a ragged breath and opened the door. "I'm not sure why, but when it comes to you, my heart is an open door."

Stunned by his confession, she could not find appropriate words. But images of him standing at his deceased fiancée's grave hit her, so she moved swiftly through the doorway.

Carter followed, closing the door behind him. As they moved up the passageway, Gianna searched for something to return them to the happy-go-lucky mood of a few minutes earlier. Then she remembered—she'd glimpsed a keyboard in one of the rooms when they rushed by during the tour earlier. The keyboard came to the rescue when she spotted it again through the crack of the door.

She stopped abruptly. "Is that a keyboard?" she asked, pointing towards the door.

"Yes, it's the music room. Would you like to see it?"

"Sure."

He pushed back the door to expose a large room equipped with several musical instruments, a soundboard, microphones, royal-blue padded chairs, and a wooden L-shaped desk and hutch.

"Nice," she said, entering the room. "You have the whole she-bang."

He chuckled softly. "The entire family plays and sings. It's kind of our way of staying in touch."

"Are you serious?"

"Yes. Dad and Mom play the keyboard, so we all learned when we were kids. I play mostly the keyboard and electro-acoustic guitar. Ry loves the keyboard, acoustic guitar, and drums. Pax is into the saxophone and drums. The story from Mom is that Dad taught her to play the keyboard when he realized she could sing and dance." Carter chuckled softly. "We have yet to hear the rest of that story, but it must have been back in the day because we only know Mom as working alongside Dad as director of business operations."

"Sweet." Gianna's eyes wandered around the room, and she walked towards the keyboard. "A musical family, huh?"

Carter moved to stand next to her. "You could say that."

Gianna stared longingly at the top-of-the-line Yamaha Genos digital workstation. Just what all keyboard buffs needed to expand their musical knowledge. "When do you practice?"

"Twice monthly or as the need arises, followed by dinner. First Saturday of the month, practice is at Mom and

Dad's home, and then for the next rehearsal me, Pax, and Ry rotate to have it at our homes. As you know, I'm on the roster for praise and worship, so this is where I get my extra practice. Pax and Ry are backups for the band at church. Sometimes, we sing as a family."

"Nice," she said absentmindedly, her eyes were still on the keyboard.

"Can you play?"

"I-I... yes."

"Whoa! You are full of surprises. Do you want to play?"

"No," she said quickly. "I haven't played in forever."

"Would you like me to play?"

"Er-er...."

"I take it that's a yes. We are practicing for Mom's party. Dad put in a special request."

Gianna felt her eyes widen. "That is soooo nice. Are you singing?"

"Yes. I'm singing 'Nobody Loves Me Like You Do.' Do you know it? Whitney Houston and Jermaine Jackson sang it back in the day."

She nodded eagerly. "One of my faves."

"According to Dad, he and Mom have a history with that song." Carter's eyebrows climbed. "History, which we can never know about. I told him that was too much information."

Gianna grinned at him. "Awww. I love that. That's a duet. Who are you singing with?"

"Ry's current girlfriend."

"Current?"

"Yes," Carter said, taking a seat at the keyboard. "For several years now, he has been banging his head against the same wall, in terms of his choice of women, hoping that things will change. Well, at least Lee-Ann has been around for a little over three months, so that's good."

"Oh, gosh."

"Pray for my brother," Carter said, twiddling the buttons on the keyboard. "What do you want to hear me play?"

"Hmmm!" She stalled, still reflecting on his comments about Rylan.

He smiled at her, and her heart flipped. Too many times. Her teeth displayed right back.

"How about 'Nobody Loves Me… *Like You Do*'? I can sing both parts." His eyes darkened, overflowing with more than a hint of desire.

She swallowed hard. "Yes, that-that will do."

In effortless movements, his fingers stroked the keys, and she felt a scorching wave of pleasure racing through her core. *Lord, have mercy*, she cried out mentally, shifting her gaze from his to clear her mind. But when his soulful voice hit her eardrums, her head whipped to look at him. She was mesmerized.

His voice was like a sweet caress. Singers Peabo Bryson and Brian McKnight wrapped in one package. Each time he sang the line, "Nobody loves me like you do," she all but shuddered with desire and moved into a kind of limitless space.

He was watching her with intense interest, fervently devouring her with his eyes. And when his gaze grew even more tender, she heard herself whelp, for the promise in his eyes floated to her—he couldn't wait to bathe her in the fervor of his love and clothe her with everlasting protection.

By the time he was finished singing, the yearning in her eyes had matched his, and she was basking in happiness on overdrive. Of their own volition, her feet moved from side to side, for delight and hope were blooming in her

181

heart. Undeniable chemistry flaring, they stared at each other, riding the wave of intense emotions that were running back and forth between them.

Oh, God! The heat was deliciously subversive in her core. In the next breath, she was berating herself, for she wouldn't be his playground. Attempting to escape her contradictory feelings, she quickly backed out of the room.

"Gia!" Carter called out.

But she didn't stop.

She had to get away from him.

She was running scared.

From the sounds behind her, she knew Carter was making his way to locate her, but she did not stop moving until she heard a vibrating growl. Gianna halted; her breath coming in small puffs as her eyes landed on Nya. She'd disturbed Nya's play area.

Nya moved towards her and stopped abruptly. Head raised with pricked ears, tail held erect and rigid, Nya gazed at her as if she'd accepted a challenge of a sort.

"Help," Gia squeezed out, looking around wildly for Carter.

"I've got you," he told her, circling her in his arms.

She pressed herself against him, trying to avoid the ferocious beast before her.

"Nya, lie in your bed," Carter commanded.

A small growl left Nya, followed by a moment of silence, and Gianna assumed she'd wandered off to rest.

"Are you okay?" Carter asked tenderly, rubbing the small of her back.

"I-I'm fine," Gianna responded, untangling herself from his arms. "Thanks. I'm sorry about that. I didn't mean to startle her."

"Would not startling her have made this situation any less awkward?"

When she didn't answer, he watched her a little while before quietly asking, "Why did you leave?"

The care in his tone undid all the longings in her heart, and she buried her head in his chest and wept.

CHAPTER 30

Carter prayed for Gianna until her crying subsided. "It's going to be alright," he told her, holding her close. His eyes brimmed, and he blinked rapidly to clear them. He wondered what could have broken her heart.

Gianna made movements to separate from him, and he let her go but still held her hand. She was not looking at him, but when he motioned for them to move to the large sofa, she obeyed.

"I'm sorry," she mumbled, her gaze bouncing all over the room.

"Don't worry about it," he said. "Let me get you some napkins."

He walked to the kitchen and retrieved the napkins. When he returned to the living room, Gianna was still perched at the edge of the sofa where he'd left her. He handed her the napkins, and she took them. She lifted off the top one and dabbed her eyes.

"Gia, if there's anything—"

"You cannot help me," she told him bluntly.

He sat slightly away from her, feeling that she needed space. "I'm sorry you feel that way."

"You can't, because you cannot erase my past."

"We all have a past with something in it that we would like to forget," he said tenderly.

"There's no escaping mine. It seems to follow me everywhere, making sure I never forget." A little laugh left her. "It's determined to destroy me."

"Careful now," Carter cautioned.

"You just don't know," she eyed him, "being born is my problem." She held up a hand to stop him.

Not that he was about to say anything. As much as it pained his heart to hear her morbid declarations, he was content to let her get it out.

"Twisted as this may sound," she let out, "if I hadn't been born, my parents would be alive."

Misplaced guilt. "Gia, no," Carter pulled closer to her. "Don't say that. I, for one, am glad that you're alive."

"Careful about that. I lose everyone I love, and I know you've had enough of that, too."

His silence made her look at him. "I'm sorry, Carter. I shouldn't have said that." She rambled on. "I know that was a painful period in your life."

"You have no idea," he pushed out. "But let's talk about what's ailing you."

"Back in the day, I played the keyboard and sang and danced. My parents taught me, just as yours did. Then, they thought I had potential, so they got me into classes to hone my skills."

"That's nice," he encouraged.

"I stopped after my parents died," she said quietly. "I caused their deaths."

"You can't believe that."

"They were rushing from work to see me play and sing at the national finals of a singing competition." Her voice grew melancholy. "They knew I loved to have them in the front row at all my performances. They were running late, and they called and told me to go ahead even if they didn't make it. Usually, after school, I stayed at Aunt Dorette and Uncle Reginald's home. So that day, Aunt Dorette had taken me to the event. Even when my name was announced as the winner that night, they still hadn't shown up. When I accepted my trophy and went backstage, Aunt Dorette and two police officers were waiting for me. I will never forget these words— 'There has been an accident.'"

She clutched her hands to her stomach, and he knew she was recalling that day. He wanted to hold her so badly.

"It took three seconds for me to realize my life would never be the same." Gianna looked at him, fighting back tears. "I was twelve years old when it happened. You may not have heard the news. We were living in Chicago during that time. After that, I lived with my aunt and uncle, and then I moved away to attend college in Tallahassee, and eventually, I settled in Orlando."

Carter waited, knowing there was more.

"My aunt and uncle were fervent Christians, so while living with them, I developed a personal relationship with the Lord. Back then, I used to have panic attacks. My aunt accompanied me to therapy and thank God I learned how to control the feeling when it's coming on. That's why I started exercising regularly. It reduces anxiety naturally. Then, one day, not sure when, the panic attacks stopped. I give thanks to God for that. I used to be so afraid when I had them because I felt like I was dying. The keyboard just reminded me of my past." She smirked. "Well, there you have it, my life story."

"I'm sorry, Gia," Carter said quietly. "You have been through a lot. It must have been hard to lose your parents at such a tender age. I'm thankful to God that you survived."

"Sometimes, I wonder if I did," she confessed. "I have been through grief counseling, but the memories will not let me go."

"I feel you," Carter acknowledged. "I have learned to deliberately choose the happy memories that I have of Kara. Knowing her, she would not want me to live my life in an unhappy state, but for me, everything was a process. I'm encouraging you to think about the happy times with your parents."

"Thanks. I miss them so much."

A broken sob left her, and again he wanted to take her in his arms, if only she would allow him. He tried for comforting words. "I understand, and that's normal."

He waited.

"What else did you do?" she asked.

"The short version is, I only survived the loss because daily I gave it all to the Lord. I had to. I was killing myself and everyone around me. I would find Scriptures that would encourage my soul. I started with one Scripture a day, and that kept me for the entire day. Now I do devotions in the morning and at nights, and I pray as often as I can."

"What's your Scripture for today?"

"Saint John fourteen verse twenty-seven. 'Peace I leave with you, my peace I give unto you: not as the world giveth, give I unto you. Let not your heart be troubled, neither let it be afraid.'"

"That just hit me. It's beautiful. I'm taking it."

He smiled at her. "You sure can. And you must forgive yourself. You were a child back then. Your parents were only trying to give you the best that life has to offer. This is too much for you to carry. And you shouldn't carry it. That's why the Scripture encourages us to cast our care upon Jesus."

She sighed loudly as if she'd heard it all before.

"Gia," he called for her attention.

She watched him cautiously.

"I understand what you're feeling. Sometimes, healing takes time. I know what it's like to feel a hurt that cannot be expressed...," he paused, "you feel so hurt that you can't find the right words to express it. No words to articulate how badly you feel."

Understanding lit her large, luminous eyes as they locked with his.

"When Kara died, I wanted to die, too. I couldn't confess that to anyone except my pastor because somehow, I thought that confession made God look bad. We don't like talking about things like that in the church. But that was a period in my life when I was right at the edge."

He shook his head. "I, me, Carter Levi McIntosh, wanted to die. I was Holy Ghost-filled, and I wanted to die. I was so pressured by my situation that I didn't want to be around. As a Christian, it was the hardest thing for me to admit. After all, people always called on me; I was their hope. How could I tell them that I'm fighting suicide and dealing with depression?"

Carter paused, taking in her eager expression.

How did you overcome? She wanted to know.

"While I was going through," he filled in, "I had to come to terms with my situation. It was beyond my capacity. I knew that, but I also knew that if I didn't resolve my heart issues, I would start feeling the effects in my body."

He sighed loudly.

"We are as sick as the dark things and dark thoughts that we allow to circulate, percolate, and then take over our lives. So, I made myself go through a series of counseling sessions with Pastor McCallum. During the sessions, we talked through the issue but at the end of each, Pastor would share a Scripture and pray. Though he'd shared several Scriptures during the sessions, Second Corinthians one verse eight kept running through my mind, and that Scripture kept me. Do you want to know what that Scripture states?"

"Of course." She was all ears.

He gave her a wry smile. "'For we would not, brethren, have you ignorant of our trouble which came to us in Asia, that we were pressed out of measure, above strength, insomuch that we despaired even of life.'" He eyed her. "That one Scripture told me that I was not out of my mind, that it was okay to have feelings. For if Paul, an Apostle of God, could write that he despaired of life, I was in good company, so I didn't feel so bad."

Carter shook his head. "Let me tell you how bad it got. I didn't know how I would make it from day to day so I created a will and made Paxton the executor." He smiled at her. "But, look at me now. It took a while, but I can safely say, God has kept me. He has been my refuge and my strength. *My* God, in Him will I trust."

Their gazes collided, and they smiled at each other.

"One night as I prayed, I heard the Spirit of the Lord saying, *Give me you, and I will make you dream again.* So, I gave my life to the Lord—all of me, withholding nothing. After surrendering my life to the Lord, my days became much better. It was like the fog was gone, and I was able to dream again… to live again. It was crazy; my creativity began to flourish. Everything around me started to flourish. But do you know how I know that I'm healed?" he asked.

"Tell me." Her voice was filled with admiration.

"You burst your way into my heart, and my heart was ready… I allowed it."

And in that beautiful moment, she reached for him, and he took her in his arms. She wrapped her arms around his waist and melted into him.

He held her and told her, "You were a child; you did *not* kill your parents. You are carrying a burden that has nothing to do with you. Release yourself from that situation. God has always been with you. He was with you in that challenging situation. He's here with you now. Through it all—every second. Every minute. All day. Every day. God is with you. There's no mistake, no—" he gulped, overcome with emotions, "—no situation that you can't recover from because He is with you. Give Him all of you, Gia. He will fix the situation and make you whole again.'"

A wail left her.

Carter knew she'd needed to hear those words.

Tears streaming down his face, he prayed for her. "Oh, God, I'm confident that You are Lord through the power of the cross. I declare that the plans of the enemy against Gia will *not* stand. No weapon that is formed against her will prosper. I rebuke the spirit of condemnation in the name of Jesus Christ. I declare that she now looks from a position of faith, and not fear. Father, I thank You that her breakthrough has come, her joy has come, and that she will move forward in Jesus' name. I declare, Lord, that all her days are hidden in Christ and that You, Lord, will fight all her battles. I declare that You will do exceedingly abundantly above all she will ever ask...."

CHAPTER 31

Peace I leave with you, my peace I give unto you: not as the world giveth, give I unto you. Let not your heart be troubled, neither let it be afraid. "Ooooooh!" Gia squealed joyfully, rolling back and forth on her bed.

That had been her mood for the last two days—her heart was thrashing about because of the joy that was returning to her life since she'd released herself from her past. Truth be told, her heart was tumbling around, too, because of the heartthrob with light-brown eyes. The prayer warrior who had prayed her through, and her newfound crush—a beautiful spirit called Carter Levi McIntosh.

She reminisced about the time they'd shared after church last Sunday. Carter had been nothing but kind and sensitive to her challenges. He'd even made her promise to sing again. Her quiet response, *I will.*

She did not hold back her disappointment when he'd told her he would be heading to Seattle for work the following day. Just as well, because their newfound understanding of each other was creating a closeness that she didn't think they were prepared for. Still, she was excited each time he'd called or texted. She couldn't wait to see him on Saturday at Nora's party. *Three days to go. I can do this.*

Gianna hopped out of bed and straightened the blue gold-trimmed comforter. She twirled and began singing "This is a Move", which was on her heart. Hands in the air, she worshipped, before shimmying to the bathroom. She was smiling all the way.

An hour later, she had eaten, washed the dishes she'd used, and was making her way back to the bedroom when her cell phone rang. A wide smile covered her face when she saw Carter's name.

"Hey there, a happy Wednesday to you," she greeted him as she entered her room.

"Good morning. I don't have to ask how's my girl doing. She's doing great."

"Oh, I'm your girl now?" She threw herself on her bed and rolled onto her side.

"Yes, you are. You should know that."

"Well, good to know."

"You like that, huh?"

"Best leave that alone. I thought you were at work."

"I am, but I'm in between meetings and wanted to check on you. Are you all packed?"

"Yes, I am. I told Nora I'd be there late in the afternoon. I need to finish up work."

"I thought you were on vacation."

"I am. But ReTrac is our special client."

"I'm beginning to feel the green-eyed monster entering the boardroom."

Gianna laughed softly. "There's no need for you to feel jealous."

He sighed dramatically. "Makes a guy wonder…"

"You're the real deal, Carter."

"That sounds good. Say more, how about, I'm…."

I could say many things. I bet your kisses would be delightful.

"Kisses?" Carter asked. His voice held pure mischief.

Eyes about to pop from their sockets, Gianna attempted to close her gaping mouth.

"Kisses?" Carter repeated with interest.

"Er-er…."

"I'm going to keep it one hundred percent with you." Carter lowered his voice. "I feel like I was challenged. I accept."

Gianna laughed. "Stop the foolishness."

192

"I'm going to let it go, but I'm sure it will come up again."

She cracked up. "Whatever."

"I would like to take you out on Friday if that's okay with you. Around seven o'clock," he said quietly.

"Friday?"

"We can do it next weekend if you're not available."

"No-no. Friday is good. I was just surprised. You had said that you'd be back on Saturday."

"I miss you, so I want to be back by tomorrow night or Friday morning."

Miss you, echoed in her ears unendingly, and she burst into delightful laughter.

"Is this a new side of you that I need to discover?" he demanded playfully.

"No," she managed to say. "I'm just happy. Overjoyed. I miss you, too."

"Nice. Dress up. I'm taking you somewhere special, and I need to talk with you about something."

"That sounds mysterious. Anyway, I'll be ready in my regal attire. Hurry and get back here."

"My queen, I will leave no stone unturned to return to the castle."

"I like that."

Gianna heard laughter in the background and figured that his staff had entered the room.

"Got to go," Carter said, "eavesdroppers have invaded the land."

A gurgle popped from Gianna. "Have fun. Bye."

"Bye."

Gianna disconnected the call, and her chuckles rang out in the room. *Oh, to see the look on the eavesdroppers' faces.* "Tee-hee!" escaped her.

She was still chuckling when she slipped off the bed, straightened the comforter, and headed for her home office. She had the last six chapters of ReTrac's book to edit. Soon, she pushed back the French doors to her command post and sat around the classic-style cherry wood executive desk. She kept her desk clutter-free, stacking all her documents and paraphernalia in an acrylic desk organizer set for easy access.

She placed her cell phone on its stand and powered on her laptop. Mentally, she shook her head because she was still smiling. But nothing could wipe that smile from her lips. She glanced at the twenty-three-inch all-in-one computer that stood to the right of her desk, beside a framed picture of her parents. *Should I turn it on?*

As she deliberated, Gianna's gaze traveled her beautifully styled office—before her desk sat two light gray fabric accent chairs with diamond tufted backrests that contoured to the body for added comfort. A few framed pictures hung on the walls, but her all-time favorite was the cover of ReTrac's first bestselling novel. Behind her desk stood the matching three-piece cherry wood built-in bookcase, which provided ample storage space for books and collectibles.

Deciding that she didn't need her computer, Gianna pulled her laptop towards her, entered her password and then opened the Word document to ReTrac's manuscript.

She prayed and then got to work.

Two hours later, she was still sitting in the same spot, but this time she was grinning at the ingenuity of her favorite author. "Good job! No, great job!" She beamed as her mind replayed a part of the final scene when the hero proposed with a ring and a gift—an eighteen-karat gold bracelet with a Madeira Citrine gemstone.

"Great storytelling, dude," Gianna announced. It was as if she'd watched it all unfold. She had to write a comment at the scene—*You scored! Love this!*

Madeira Citrine was her favorite gemstone because of its warm deep red-orange color, but mainly because of the Madeira Citrine stud earrings that her parents had given her on her tenth birthday.

Gianna reached into the glass jar on her desk to grab a Jolly Rancher. She opened the wrapper and took the candy into her mouth. After dropping the wrapper in the small black trash can, she wrote a quick note to her assistant and copied Brooklyn on it.

I'm finished editing another masterpiece from ReTrac. Please return it to him. Thank you!

She knitted her brows as she powered off her laptop. It was the first time she hadn't personally returned ReTrac's manuscript to him. *I must be growing up.*

Gianna relaxed on the chair, thoughts of Carter swirling in her mind. She held back laughter when she remembered how she'd unintentionally mentioned his kisses aloud. *Oh gosh! Definitely burying that in the backyard.*

She couldn't help but love this period in her life. Indescribable—this joy she was feeling. The kindness and sincerity with which Carter treated her had opened a different window in her heart for him.

She swiped a yellow Post-it, wrote CARTER in all caps, and began generating words from his name. Finding all the small words hidden inside a long one used to be one of her favorite pastimes as a child.

Car.

Cart.

Care.

Tar.

Race.

Racer.

Crate.

Rrrrrring!

Before answering her cell phone, Gianna quickly pulled out a word search book from her desk drawer and dropped the Post-it into it.

"Brooklyn, gooood morning!"

"Morning. Oh, lower the volume."

"What volume?"

"On those joy bells."

Gianna gave a short laugh. "I don't know what you're talking about."

"Moving on then. I just saw your note to Maya. It struck me that it was the first time you've had her return a manuscript to ReTrac."

Silence.

"You're right." Gianna finally chipped in. She was wondering where Brooklyn was going with this conversation. When Brooklyn didn't say anything, she added, "That's what I do for all my other clients."

"I know, but I don't want you to lose your relationship with him. You know how this business works."

"Understood. I'll drop him a note."

Brooklyn breathed out a sigh of relief. "Thanks. What time are you leaving?"

"Within another two hours or so."

"I received an invitation to Nora's party," Brooklyn said dryly.

"That's great! Wait a minute. Do you know her like that?"

"No, and I thought of not attending, but since you're going, I will. I told you I keep my interaction with that woman sparse. I'm sure she'll have a lot of influential people at her party. High society. This is not just a party;

it's a way for Nora and her family to maintain their edge in these parts."

"The strange thing is that Nora reminds me of you, in some ways."

"I'm tough, but I'm not unkind. Be careful, okay?"

Annoyance rose from deep within Gianna. "I'm not sure why you keep mentioning Nora. And, do you know something terrible about Carter? You haven't exactly been forthcoming concerning him, but I sense you know something about him and don't want to say it. Or, are you using your relationship with Nora to judge Carter?"

"I'm going to leave that alone."

Really. "You've never been one to cool things down. What exactly is going on?"

"Don't you think it's odd that Carter says everything to you except 'I love you'?"

Gianna's heart sank. Now she was sorry she'd mentioned to Brooklyn what had occurred between her and Carter last Sunday.

"You don't know Carter," she defended him, her displeasure evident. "For the sake of our relationship, I won't mention Carter or Nora again."

"Don't say that. You know I wish you well."

Gianna's countenance saddened.

Brooklyn had always been honest with her, even when she didn't want to hear the truth. But the trepidation in Brooklyn's voice every time she mentioned Nora or Carter told her Brooklyn was not being upfront with her.

"I don't want to hide behind a glass cage anymore, Brook. Carter is not perfect, but I've never had a connection like the one I have with him. I feel the Lord leading me in that direction, so I want to explore this. The least you can do is pray for me, for us."

Brooklyn relented. "I will. Have a safe drive to Nora's home, and let me know when you get there. I have to run."

"I will. Bye."

"Bye."

Gianna stared at her phone as the screen faded to black. *What on earth?* She had always trusted Brooklyn's judgment, but in that moment, she decided she wouldn't listen to anyone who wanted to kill her newfound joy.

CHAPTER 32

"I know you. If you thought anything was wrong, you would be out of there in a jiffy," Kamala said, then hastened to add, "I prayed for you this morning. Not just this morning, always."

"Thanks, Kam," Gianna said. "I appreciate that. I wish you were coming to Nora's party."

"So I can be a third wheel? I love you, but no. You'll be fine. I've seen pictures of that man—Christian and ridiculously fine. I approve." Kamala sniggered loudly.

Gianna snorted. "This is wild stuff. I can't handle you so early in the morning. I'm not even at home where I can reach into my arsenal."

"You know what, I bet your home misses you," Kamala said dryly.

"Agreed," Gianna shot back, refusing to acknowledge the shade she was throwing.

"I know what really misses you—those word search books."

"Not at all. I was on it here last night."

"To keep your mind off Carter?"

"Yes, and Brooklyn."

"I told you to forget what Brooklyn said. I'm glad you've found someone who loves you and whom you love."

"Speaking of love… I didn't want to tell you, but Brooklyn is more than hinting that Carter never said that he loves me. She sounds like she thinks Carter is hiding something."

"Why would she even say that? I love her, but good Lord."

"That got me thinking, too. I don't want to be hurt again," Gianna admitted quietly.

"Now stop that," Kamala admonished. "Didn't you say you prayed, and you felt the peace of the Lord concerning a relationship with Carter?"

"Yes, I did."

"Well, let God work out the details."

"But what if it's just me, and my desire for him?"

"That's fear talking, and you need to get that under the control of the Holy Spirit. You're being tossed to and fro by your emotions. The Word of God says, 'I will instruct you and teach you in the way that you should go. I will guide you with my eye.' I suggest that you cling to God's Word. And I hope you're praying for Carter."

"That I'm doing."

"That's great. You have a date with him, right? And he did say he wanted to talk with you about something. Sounds serious, and he said to dress up."

"Right. I kind of feel weird with him picking me up from here for the date. I haven't even mentioned it to Nora."

"So tell Nora you have an event, and you're going home Friday evening and will return Saturday morning. Then, you can tell Carter to pick you up at home."

"Good thought, but that's almost an hour drive," Gianna lamented.

"You'll be more comfortable if you do that."

"True."

"I'll visit you tomorrow to make sure you get the dress-up part right."

Gianna laughed softly. "Okay, my third mama."

"Roger that," Kamala laughed joyfully.

"Kam, I forgot to mention that when I had dinner at Carter's home, some of the walls had spaces like pictures had been hanging there, and he took them down. I think they were photos of Kara, and he took them down since I was coming over."

"That's a good thing, right?"

"I suppose so."

"Yes, it is. That was thoughtful of him. I wouldn't overthink it."

"I kind of felt bad."

"No, no, wrong emotion. I don't mean to be callous, but she's dead, and if he's trying to move on, then having those photos on the wall would be a turn-off for any woman. So, yes, he did the right thing."

"I see what you're saying."

"Now stop making up excuses to sabotage your love life. Prayer and the Word of God are your weapons."

"Roger that."

"Got to go. Me and my baby are about to go and finalize plans with our wedding planner. I thought of recommending Lisa to you for your wedding planning, but I'm sure Nora knows many high society wedding planners."

"Are you ever going to stop the madness?"

"Madness? I'm trying to keep you straight. See you tomorrow."

"Thanks. You're the best."

"I got you, bestie. Bye."

"Bye-bye."

A smile crept up her face as Gianna rolled onto her side in the luxurious upholstered king-size sleigh bed that was a part of a set with nightstands, dresser, and chest of drawers. Her eyes swept the gorgeously decorated bedroom that struck a happy balance between tranquil and chic. A green theme ran through the entire room, from cooler tinges of jade green to a warmer kind of yellow-green. These colors definitely gave the occupant a good night's sleep… albeit sleep had eluded her last night.

Glancing at her cell phone screen, Gianna saw that it was eight twenty-eight. Prior to this, she'd eaten breakfast with Henry and Nora and had come back to her room to freshen up. She would be meeting Nora at nine o'clock to talk more about writing. Last night after dinner, they had sat in the family room and discussed her aspirations for her memoir before she'd emailed it to Gianna. The game plan was for Gianna to browse it and give her writing tips. She would make the recommended changes and email it to Gianna the following week. Eventually, when Gianna returned the manuscript, Nora would do the rewrite and go through the proper channels to hopefully have BMP become her publisher.

Cell phone in hand, Gianna climbed out of bed and straightened the lime-green embroidered bedcovers and cushions. Deciding that it was too early to make her way back downstairs, she slipped on the black indoor flats that were on the cedar-green shag rug. She walked on the warm hardwood floor towards a set of army-green sofas. However, she did not linger there but made her way to the balcony door.

Just then, her phone buzzed, and a text popped up on the screen. A huge smile lit her face.

Carter: *Babes, I'll definitely be making it home tonight. Late though, around 10. I will be in meetings all day. Be in touch when I can. [Heart emoji]*

Gianna: *[Smiley face emoji] That's good news. Travel safely. See you soon. I'm praying for you. [Heart emoji]*

Carter: *Go for a walk later. You'll like it.*

Gianna: *[Woman running emoji] Great thought!*

Carter: *[Two beating heart emojis]*

Gianna's heart skipped a few beats, and her smile grew as she slid the large glass double door open. Tilting her head, she soaked up the burst of sunlight. It was just the right temperature—warm on her face. Soon, she stepped out onto the balcony and walked to the wooden rails to take in the picturesque scenery—a breathtaking view of the beautiful natural vegetation.

Henry and Nora's world-class Mediterranean-style private estate was nothing short of a modern masterpiece that sat on five acres among the most prestigious home sites in Orlando.

Yesterday, after clearing security, she'd driven the winding driveway highlighted by trees, shrubs, and flowers. As she approached the superb dwelling, she remembered thinking that it was reminiscent of a timeless architectural period.

A member of the house staff had welcomed her, and soon, she was standing face-to-face with Henry and Nora, who were thrilled to see her. After she'd settled in, Nora had given her a mini-tour of the ten-bedroom, twelve full baths, and three half-baths home. The grandeur of each room captured the charm and appeal of yesteryear with its heirloom furnishings and prominent decorative carvings, paintings, and family portraits. Painted mainly in beige— the go-to neutral for many interior designers—the home signaled that it was the setting for countless memories and peaceful moments.

Maybe I will *go for a walk later*, Gianna mused as she stepped back into her suite, and closed the door. She refreshed herself in the bathroom and changed into a long hot-pink cotton halter dress and matching sandals. She moved quickly to retrieve her laptop from the coffee table and exited her room. She couldn't wait to reach the grand curved double staircase with gold banisters. Soon, she hurried along the circular landing and stood at the top of the staircase to survey the scene before her.

From her vantage point, she could see the exquisitely decorated circular entryway.

Simply beautiful, was her only thought.

CHAPTER 33

"You look beautiful."

Gianna's gaze flitted all over and finally located Nora at the entrance of one of the double staircases. "Nora. Hi! Thank you. I didn't realize you were standing there." With that, Gianna began to descend the marble steps, which were designed for a royal entrance.

"I was waiting for you," Nora said, smiling. "Truth be told, I got a bit anxious. I can't wait to hear your thoughts."

"You have nothing to fear," Gianna told her.

"Really?"

Gianna attempted to go down each step swiftly. "I'm sure you'll be okay."

Nora was quiet for a moment, then she spoke, "You're trying to make me feel good, aren't you?"

"No. I never joke about my editing gigs."

When Gianna arrived before Nora, she noticed that Nora had clasped her hands to her chest like a child who was happy to receive a good grade. Gianna couldn't help but smile encouragingly at her. She knew many authors, even the bestselling, world-renowned ones, who went through emotional anxiety about their work.

"Together, we're going to make sure your manuscript shines," Gianna encouraged.

"I like that. I appreciate that you're doing this for me," Nora confessed.

"It's my pleasure. Where do you want us to work?"

"In my home office. I've already set it up so we can both use the desk."

"Sounds great."

Nora motioned with her hand, and together, they moved forward to the right of the entryway. They kept moving to the extreme right then rounded a corner to enter a passageway to access Nora's office. Nothing prepared Gianna for the magnificent semi-circular office with huge glass windows.

Elegant and sleek.

Surprisingly, the walls were painted the same beige as the rest of the house, which Gianna thought went against Nora's vibrant personality. Nevertheless, as she took in the setting, she determined that it was distinctively designed to accommodate a busy, well-lived life.

Before the huge classic-style, cherry oak executive desk sat two red upholstered fabric accent chairs with button tufted details on the seat. As expected, the three-piece built-in bookcase was some distance behind the desk. The lounge area with red sofas and side tables masterfully blended in the home office. Near the lounge area was a cherry oak six-seater oval conference room table.

"Your office is beautiful," Gianna remarked.

"Thanks, dear."

At the desk, Gianna started her laptop while Nora powered on her twenty-seven-inch all-in-one computer.

"Look at your boys," Gianna said, peering at a photo of Nora's three sons in high school garb.

"Yes, my heartbeats. Not teenagers anymore." Nora gave a short laugh. "For sure. Now they're trying to manage me."

Gianna laughed, too.

"And speaking of my boys, I see how attached you and Carter have become."

Gianna shifted uncomfortably.

"You don't have to say anything," Nora told her, smiling. "I approve. So does his father."

"We have a growing friendship," Gianna managed to squeeze out quietly.

"That's a good thing."

"Thanks," Gianna said, not knowing what else to say. "I have an event on Friday evening, so I'm going to leave on Friday afternoon and return early Saturday morning. It won't affect our plans."

"No problem. Are you sure you can manage to return on Saturday morning? Maybe you should return in the afternoon to get ready for the party."

"No, I'll be fine."

Nora pushed out a sigh of relief. "I appreciate that." Her gaze bounced around the room before settling on Gianna. "Thank you."

Gianna reached over and hugged her, knowing this woman was not accustomed to needing anyone.

Nora hugged her tightly.

"I understand that you invited my second mom to your party," Gianna said, after they released each other.

"Yes. I've known Brooklyn for some time, though we're not particularly close." At Gianna's puzzled expression, she explained. "I invited her because of you and because of her influence in society."

"That's kind of you. She…."

"I know. She thinks I'm a monster. Our interactions have been a little on the unpleasant side."

"How did you know she's connected to me?"

"I've been around these parts for a while, so I consider it my duty to keep informed."

"I see. No doubt you did a background check on me."

"No, I didn't. But I'm aware that Alley has clients with BMP, so I asked her about you."

Gianna lifted her eyes skyward. "Allison and I only have a business relationship. A decent working relationship, I thought, but since we recently met in Tallahassee, and she realized that I know Carter, she has become hostile, for lack of a better word."

Nora shook her head. "You must forgive Alley. She has known my sons since they were children. She has managed to convince herself that she's destined to marry one of them. I don't think it matters which one."

"Oh, I see," Gianna said quietly.

"She'll be here after lunch for a brief meeting with me. I'll keep her out of your way. I need a literary agent, and I have to admit, she's good at what she does."

"Thanks for that. Yes, she's good at her job."

"Most authors want to be published by BMP. Not to mention work with one of the finest editors in the business. I'm grateful for the opportunity."

Gianna smiled gently at her. "To God be all the glory. Thanks for the opportunity."

Nora returned her smile, admiration in her gaze.

"Do you mind if we pray before we begin?" Gianna asked.

"Not at all," Nora beamed with satisfaction.

They bowed their heads and Gianna prayed.

Some two hours later, they decided to break for lunch.

"Why don't you just write my memoir for me?" Nora asked, her expression looking like someone had burst her bubble.

Gianna touched her shoulder. "You're a great writer. I'm only polishing your work."

"If you say so."

"Yes, I say so. You have good writing skills, and while there's a place for ghostwriters, you're perfectly equipped to write your story."

"Thank you." Nora smiled happily.

"You're very welcome. I'll work on this in my room for the rest of the afternoon."

"Sounds like a plan. Let me see what Henry is up to. Lunch will be ready in less than half an hour. We're eating on the balcony outside the kitchen."

"I'll meet you there. I have notes I need to jot down while I remember them."

"Okay. See you then." Nora left the desk and made her way towards the door.

"Nora," Gianna called out.

"Yes." Nora stopped and turned to look at her.

"Would you like to go walking with me later today?"

Nora smiled widely. "Sure. I'd love that."

Gianna smiled. "Me, too."

Nora's smile widened further before she left the office.

Ten minutes later, Gianna jerked upright at the sound of a loud knock at the door. Allison Ashworth was staring her down. Gianna refused to flinch under her hard stare as she moved closer.

"Allison, hello. I heard you were popping by after lunch." *What on earth? Why did I even say that?*

"Popping by," Allison scoffed with a wave of her hand. "This is like my second home."

Gianna remained silent, her expression asking if there was something that she needed.

"You do not understand the state of play here," Allison said, as if they were continuing a previous conversation.

Gianna pushed out a soft sigh. "Allison, I don't know what you're talking about, and I don't want to know. As you can see, I'm busy."

"You think you can just waltz in here and take Carter from me."

"Excuse me?"

"'Excuse me,'" Allison mimicked. "I guarantee you that he's just distracted by you right now, so get all you can while you can."

Silly woman. Gianna eyed her pointedly. "If you're finished, I'd like to get back to work."

"Finished? Far from it. You better up your game."

Mystified, Gianna eyeballed her. "Is this a cry for help?"

Clap! Clap! Clap filled the air. "Such grown-up talk," Allison said sarcastically. "My mind is reeling."

Lord, have mercy. "Allison," Gianna called for her attention as if speaking to a child, "I'm not doing this with you, so please move on." *Just go away. Please.*

"Not a wilting wallflower, I see," Allison sneered. "I hope you realize Carter is just playing with you, *and* you're letting him."

That brought Gianna to her feet.

Allison took a step back, a hand flying to her chest.

Gianna gave her a steely glare. "Do not speak to me unless it's about the business of BMP." With that, Gianna popped down on the chair and pulled her laptop forward.

Without another word, Allison left the room.

CHAPTER 34

"I'm glad you made it home safely," Carter said. "I'm looking forward to our date."

Fervor and expectancy. Gianna loved the way he said that. She moved her cell phone from one ear to the next, then mimicked his zeal. "Can't wait, either!"

"I love that."

"Right, but don't think I've forgotten your little misadventure. You owe me, big time."

"You'll never let me live that down, will you?"

Gianna laughed out, then spread out on her sofa. "Oh, take me out of that little equation. That was all you. Who falls asleep on someone he's trying to impress? That hero act fell through a hole."

"You know I had a hard day, then jet lag. For the record, I wasn't trying to impress you, woman."

"Jet lag, yes. That's why I tried to get you to hit the sack, but no." Gianna mimicked his voice. "'I'm okay, Gia.'" She laughed some more. "All I heard a minute after that was loud snoring. I don't know how I'm supposed to feel."

"You'll be alright."

"Wait, are you giving me attitude? What if your brothers find out about your little secret?"

"No, you wouldn't. I can't believe you would take advantage of my sleep deprived state."

"Try me."

"How can I make it up to you?"

"Luckily for you, I need a favor. Will you accompany me to Kam's wedding in five weeks? I'll give you the details."

"Sure. Anything else?"

She snorted. "Don't sound so eager."

"Your happiness is my priority. Remember, I'm picking you up at seven, sharp."

"*Sharp?* Did you do that male thing? I'm a timely person."

Carter laughed aloud. "This is going to be fun."

"Your mom told me you bullied her into letting me leave earlier than I had planned."

"Bullied?" Carter laughed aloud for a second time. "Bullied and my mother in the same sentence? What's wrong with that picture? Unnatural."

"That's wrong on so many levels."

"I merely made a suggestion," Carter confessed. "You and Mom are two strong-willed women. You all do what you want, whenever you want to. I'm constantly thinking of ways to bring my 'A' game when I'm around both of you."

"You're such a smart man."

"Okay, smarty pants, go get dolled up. See you later."

"See you later, hon, I mean Carter. Bye." Gianna bolted upright, clutching her chest. *No, I didn't.*

She dropped the phone beside her and rolled her eyes, then cracked up when she remembered Carter snoring loudly as she was telling him that his parents had walked the grounds of their home with her.

Not an exciting subject. I get that now.

She had an hour and a half to go but did not want to start dressing so early. She picked up her word search book and pencil from the coffee table. When she opened the book, a yellow Post-it fell to the floor. She picked it up and saw that she had been using it to generate words from Carter's name. She went to work again.

Rear.

Act.

React.

Tear.

Art.

Tracer.

Acer.

Crater.

Carte.

Trace.

Gianna was about to add another word when her phone rang. She pushed the Post-it back into the book and grabbed her phone.

"Hi, Kam," she answered happily.

"The sound of joy. I like that. I'm in your driveway."

"You are?"

"Girl, open the door before I use my key. I'm getting out of my vehicle."

"Yes, ma'am."

Gianna hung up, and before long, she was swinging the front door open. "Come in."

Knitted brows greeted her as Kamala stepped inside and rushed by her.

"Let's go!" Kamala said.

Mouth gaping, Gianna stared after her, then closed the door. She caught up with Kamala, who had moved through the living room and was already heading towards the passageway to access the master suite.

"Hey, slow down."

"There's much to do," Kamala threw over her shoulder before disappearing into Gianna's bedroom.

Gianna hurried after her and found her standing in the middle of the room. Her paraphernalia were already dumped on the bed bench.

"What's going on?" Gianna asked, concern lacing her voice.

Kamala's eyebrows climbed. "I have more work to do than I anticipated. I need to get moving. What's up with your hair?"

Gianna's brows crinkled. "What do you mean?"

"I can tell you haven't been wearing a sleep cap; your curls are almost gone."

"You're too much."

"You're playing with the big guns now. You know it's a catfight at that level."

Right. Gianna moved to sit on the bed, remembering how Allison had shamelessly confronted her.

"I'm not beating up on you. I know Carter is a Christian, and he'll do right by you, but I need to beef you up a bit for your date. Remember, he said to dress up. I won't do anything that will make you uncomfortable."

"Okay, let's do it."

"That's my bestie. You could have dropped a few rollers in your hair, though."

"And I'm sure you'll fix that."

But Kamala had moved on; she was inspecting the royal-blue dress that was laid out on Gianna's bed.

"You like?" Gianna asked, amused by her ecstatic expression.

Kamala enclosed her in a tight hug and then released her. "You did well," she twirled happily. "I loooove it. You're holding out on me."

"I went shopping with Nora this morning."

"Oh, sweet! It's worth the small fortune you no doubt spent on it."

"Everything was discounted. Nora is a preferred customer, so I received the same discount. Anyway, she wouldn't have it any other way. She insisted on buying my gown for her party. I told her I already had a gown, but apparently the color wasn't right."

"What do you mean, the color wasn't right?"

"She wanted the family to wear red." Gianna grinned at her. "Apparently, I'm family."

"That's a good thing."

"Sometimes, I wonder. I offered to help her with her book. Now we're scheduled to do everything together since I've been there. She has her staff taking care of my needs. Good Lord! I'm like the daughter she never had."

Kamala eyed her. "Tell her I'm your sister from another mister. She can pamper me at any time. All those blessings are coming to you and you're second-guessing God's goodness."

"Actually, I like it. I haven't been fussed over in forever."

"That's because you won't let anyone in. Just make sure you put in a good word for me with your mother-in-law."

Gianna gave her a side-eye. "I don't want to be Debbie Downer here, but I cannot put the cart before the horse."

Kamala shook her head. "What am I going to do with you? My job is to highlight your best features, but you'll have to reach for what you want. Put yourself in a position to win, to be happy."

Gianna watched her, not knowing what to say.

Kamala touched her arm. "Let's get you dolled up. That dress is gor-ge-ous!"

"I'm glad you approve. I was beginning to feel hopeless."

"Hopeless?" Kamala waved her away. "Never."

CHAPTER 35

Gianna was taking a final glance at herself in the dresser mirror when the doorbell sounded. She felt great in the chic attention-grabbing A-Line dress with its one-shoulder neckline and flowing bell-shaped right sleeve. The ultimate allure was the long, breezy, royal-blue chiffon skirt beneath the waist-defining sash. A dainty gold choker hugged her neck and matched her stick linear drop earrings.

After making her way to the living room, Gianna left her purse on the coffee table before moving to the front door. Carter was ten minutes early, but so was she. She looked through the peephole, and her breath halted. *Wow!*

She swung the door open and greeted him with a warm smile. "Hello."

"Hello to you, too. Wow!"

Mission accomplished. Gianna held back girlish giggles and stepped aside for him to enter.

He didn't move and was evidently unaware that he was gaping as his eyes took another sprint over her body. She could see the moment reality dawned for him. He let out a low chuckle then let go of an alluring smile.

Her heart leaped.

"Are you coming in?" she asked, wondering why her voice was dripping with honey.

"Yes." Carter stepped in and closed the door behind him.

When they reached the living room, he handed her a bouquet of red roses. "These are for you."

Gianna took the flowers from his hand. "Thank you. They're gorgeous." She wanted to kiss his cheek but held back.

"Do you have a vase?" Carter asked.

"Yes. In the kitchen."

The folds of the fabric teased her slender legs as she moved away. She felt his eyes burning into her back and decided to check. *Heck!* He was in the same spot, watching her like she was his favorite new toy. She pretended not to notice. "Come and help me."

"Sure."

In the kitchen, she reached into the cupboard for a transparent glass vase and filled it with water so he could put the flowers in it. She spent a few seconds looking at the roses before smelling them. Smiling, she turned to look at Carter; he was smiling at her, causing her smile to widen. "Thank you."

"My pleasure." His gaze rolled over her once more. "You look beautiful. You took my breath away when you opened the door."

She gazed at him coyly. "That's a good thing, right?"

"Uh-huh. I love your hair."

"Thanks."

She loved it, too—a curly, messy updo with long, soft tendrils draping her cheeks. She owed Kamala big-time.

"You cleaned up well," she told him. "Handsome."

He guffawed softly as her gaze swept him from head to toe, admiring his trendy black slim fit suit. He completed his fabulous look with the matching vest, white shirt, and red polyester tie. His attire was kicked up a notch with a deep red pocket square, and black matte dress shoes provided the finishing touch. As always, his fade faux hawk was on fleek.

"Wait. I just realized why you look so different," Gianna gushed.

"Different? Is that a good thing?"

"Yes, and I love it," she hastened to say. "Your sideburns are gone."

He'd shaven off his tapered sideburns, highlighting his pronounced jawlines. Now he was sporting a pencil mustache with a square connected goatee. A slight smile curved her lips, and she reached out and briefly touched his cheek. She wanted to kiss him, but a touch would have to do.

He watched her for a few seconds as if he wanted to say something but suddenly changed his mind. "Ready?" he asked, his voice taking on a husky tone.

"Yes. Can you please put the vase on the dining room table?"

"Of course," he said, reaching for the vase and moving away.

Gianna stared after him. *Lord, help us.* She followed him, seizing the moment to fill her eyes with the magnitude of the man.

An hour and a half later, they were still in The Z Cuisine Restaurant, tantalizing their taste buds. Offering classic cuisine and a show, the restaurant's posh dining featured an open kitchen counter, which permitted them to feel the warmth of the fire while watching as the chef prepared their meals. They were finishing up dinner—she was enjoying grilled Scottish king salmon while he was devouring barbeque chicken with pineapple salsa.

Mouth-watering food.

Stimulating conversation.

On top of that, she and Carter were constantly smiling at each other as if they each knew something the other didn't. Carter was great company, and Gianna hoped he was enjoying her company, too. Still, she couldn't help but notice that he was wearing his protector-in-chief badge, making sure everything was to her heart's desire.

"Are you sure you don't want to try my chicken?" Carter asked. "It's almost finished."

"Okay, just a tiny piece."

She prepared her plate to receive the chunk he was cutting. When she looked up again, he was holding his fork with a piece of chicken on it.

"Uh-oh." Flushed, she opened her mouth, took in the meat, and chewed it. It tasted like heaven.

"Good, huh?" Carter said. "The pineapple gives it a slightly sweet taste."

"Yes. I will have it the next time."

"Here's another piece for you."

Again, she took the meat in her mouth, noticing he enjoyed feeding her. *Oh boy!* "Thank you," she mumbled, then busied herself with the rest of the food on her plate.

"I love your hair, but I told you that already."

"Yes, you did. What do you like about it?"

"The curls. I want to pull on them, and they emphasize your heart-shaped face."

"Thanks," she pushed out self-consciously.

"Dessert?" Carter asked.

"I don't think I can have dessert."

"Me either. Do you want to take something home?"

"Yes. What do you recommend?"

He picked up the menu nearby. "Let me see."

She waited, knowing she would be happy with anything he selected.

"The wafer brownie," he said, handing her the menu and pointing to the brownie.

"Looks good," she said, then read the notes, *house-made brownie with nuts, berry sauce, and your choice of ice cream.* "Hold the ice cream, please."

Carter nodded in agreement.

He motioned for the server, placed the order, and indicated that he needed the check.

Why isn't he saying, I love you? Gianna deliberated. *I can tell he does.*

"What's with that face?" Carter asked. "I thought you were having a great time."

Carter's teasing tone roused Gianna from her pondering, and she dropped the thought as quickly as she'd acquired it.

"Yes. I'm having a great time."

His eyebrows raised in a faux surprise. "I must be seeing things."

She tittered. "I am. I promise."

"I'm working extra hard because I don't want my secret shame to get out on the street."

"Keep doing what you're doing." She leaned in and confidentially told him. "No one will know about your snoring."

"Your eyes tell me I can trust you."

"I think you're on to something."

Gianna felt a smile spread across her face, and she mentally admitted she was defenseless against Carter McIntosh.

Carter returned her smile, and her heartbeat ramped up to full throttle.

Saved by the server.

Carter paid the check, and then they were on their way with dessert on the back seat of his dark gray metallic BMW 750i.

Forty minutes later, Carter asked, "You're not dozing, are you?"

"Oh, no. In this friendship, only one person can hold the trophy for dozing off in a jiffy."

A gurgle popped from Carter. "Are you ever going to let that go?"

"Oh no. I'm milking it to death, but since you've been great, I'm going to give you a break."

"You mean, you loved our date, and I've been amazing."

"Oh, I was just getting started."

"I love that."

She laughed a little. "I had a great time."

"Me too."

Carter pulled into her driveway. "We should see more of each other."

"I'd like that," was out before Gianna realized it. *Oh boy.*

"Great to know."

It could be her imagination, but it seemed as if his voice had dropped an octave, and it was endearing. She watched as he cut the engine, and the dim roof light came on.

They stared at each other, and then both started to laugh.

They were stalling.

She didn't want him to go.

And he didn't want to go either.

"I like your car. Is it new?" *You have no interest in his car.* She almost rolled her eyes.

"Thanks. I got it late last year. I haven't driven it in a while, but I thought this was a good occasion to use it."

"Nice."

"I need to reach into the glove compartment," he said.

"Okay."

He leaned towards her, and she held her breath as his head neared hers. *Oh, God, you're too close.* His Tom Ford Oud Wood cologne filled the air, but it was the tide of warmth in her body that was causing her alarm. Their eyes met, and she bathed his face with a puff of air as her lips parted to receive his kiss. He lifted his head and pecked the tip of her nose before reaching into the glove compartment.

Disappointed, she slammed her mouth shut and reprimanded herself.

She didn't even realize Carter was looking at her until he spoke. "This is for you." He handed her a small green gift bag.

She took it. "Thanks. Are you coming in? I could make us cocoa or tea." She almost mentally berated herself. *So lame.*

"I'll come in for a minute," he said quietly.

Her lips twitched into a small grin.

CHAPTER 36

Carter slipped out of the car, and Gianna watched as he rounded the front of the vehicle to get to her. He opened her door, and she stepped out and watched as he closed it. When he moved to take the bag with her dessert from the back seat, she busied herself, using her cell phone to disarm the alarm to her home. He locked the vehicle, and together, they moved towards her front door.

Gianna felt Carter's hand burning right through to her waist as she retrieved the house key from her purse. She quickly located the keyhole, opened the door, and stepped in. Carter followed her and then closed the door.

She flipped on the light switch near the door and hurried towards the living room, her legs seemingly eating up the distance.

"What's with the rush?" he asked.

"No rush."

She paused near the coffee table, placed her purse on it, and attempted to lighten the moment. "I'm about to open my gift."

"Okay." He walked towards her.

She opened the gift bag and pulled out two small bags of Jolly Ranchers. "I love these. Thanks. This is your favorite candy, too."

"Right. I was getting some and thought I'd get some for you."

"Thanks. You're so…." She paused as he made movements to hug her. To avoid his arms, she turned and rushed towards the kitchen.

"Did I miss something? What's with the rush?" he asked for a second time.

"No rush. Just getting the kettle." *Getting the kettle. Eye-roll!*

When he said nothing, she looked over her shoulder and saw that he was relieving himself of his jacket. Near the nook table, she switched on the kitchen light. After placing her bags of Jolly Ranchers and the gift bag on the island, she took the kettle from the countertop near to the sink. Her movements felt jerky and stiff as she filled it with water and plugged it into the white wall socket.

"Everything good out there?" she asked, pressing the button to turn on the kettle.

No answer.

She turned and collided with his hard body, his cologne filling her nostrils. "Ouch!" she whelped for no good reason.

"Got you." Carter snaked his arms around her waist, locking her to his rock-hard frame.

Hmmm, came from her lips as she took in the magnitude of his pecs. *Ripped.* His jacket and vest were gone, and he'd rolled up the cuffs of his button-down dress shirt and loosened his tie.

His heart was beating at an unhealthy speed.

Or was it hers?

"Up here."

His teasing voice reached her, and she forced her gaze up.

"Would you like to see it?" he asked.

"Er…." *Whoa! What?* "See-see what?" she stammered.

"You seem to have developed a serious addiction to my chest."

Her bottom jaw hit the ground, and a slow sigh escaped her lips as she processed.

Carter touched her shoulder. "I'm messing with you. Lighten up."

"Oh-okay. I'm fine," she insisted as if he'd asked her. She made movements to escape, but he didn't let go.

Her eyebrows pinched. "You know you're in my personal space, right?"

"I am, but I think you like it."

"Ca-Carter…" She could hardly string a sentence together. He was sexy-eyeing her, generating some serious heat between them.

"I like being in your personal space, Gia."

For the love of God, you cannot say my name like that. She kept looking at him even though her brain was begging her to look away.

"I like to hold you in my arms," he confessed.

She was sure she shuddered. *Oh, this will not end well. God, save the queen. Like, send help out of Zion. Seriously.*

Carter released her and took a step back. Barely.

Oh gosh, I'm staring at his chest.

As if sensing she needed space, he stepped away.

She stared at him as he walked and stood near the island, his back to her. He turned and looked at her. "Come, I need to talk with you."

Fear gripped her because she was afraid he was going to break her heart. She turned towards the kettle, tears brimming. "I'm making us tea," she said, hating the tremor in her voice.

"You and I know that tea is the last thing on our minds."

The seriousness in his tone caused her to look at him, but her feet refused to move. He came to her and held out his hand. She took it.

Carter reached around her to unplug the kettle, and then they moved forward. He led her to the living room and indicated that she should sit on the sofa. He sat next to her.

She raised anxious eyes to his, but before she could speak, he reached for her hand and spoke. "It is clear to me that I have not done a good job communicating how I feel about you. So, I want to assure you that I love you." His eyes shone with affection. "I love you."

Her mouth popped open.

Time appeared to have suspended itself as she stared mindlessly into his bright, light-brown eyes. It was a moment to shine, but she was speechless. She felt him gently tugging her hand to bring her back, but her brain refused to defog itself. Her heart pounded. How she'd longed to hear those words from his lips! *I love you, too.* The words wanted to rise from her mouth, but she had no breath to speak. Her eyebrows went up and she flew into his arms.

Carter pulled her snugly against him, his fingers rubbing small circles on her back and mumbling sweet nothings as tears streamed down her face and drenched his shirt.

Soon her tears subsided, and her breath fanned his chin. "I love you, too," she finally got out between breaths.

"I'm glad you do," he teased.

She eased herself from his chest and watched him through watery eyes.

"Let me get you a napkin," he said, gently putting her back against the sofa. He walked to the kitchen, returned with a few napkins, and gave them to her. He sat next to her, his arm on the back of the sofa. He waited, watching as she mopped her eyes.

When she was finished drying her tears, she put on a brave, tiny smile and looked at him. The love, care, and concern in his darkened gaze gripped her heart and her jitters evaporated. She touched his hand and hastily told him, "I'm fine."

He held on to her hand. "That's reassuring."

His dramatic tone caused a giggle to pop out. "I was just stunned."

He caressed her hand with his thumb. "Sorry about that, babes. I fell in love with you the first time I saw you. You lured me with your laughter, and I've never been able to get you out of my head or my heart. I thought you knew it was game over after that."

She gave a short laugh at his expression. "I don't want to be hurt again."

"Gia, I love you. I have no intention of hurting you."

"Thanks." She touched his cheeks with both hands and couldn't stop touching them.

In the next breath, his hand found its way from the back of the sofa to her neck. She sucked in a quick breath, as he slowly dragged his fingers through the hair at the back of her head. "I've been wanting to touch your hair all evening."

Oh-oh God. It was a simple move, but it was spiking her heart rate. She looked beyond him as she felt her eyes glossing over with pleasure.

"I want to help you to grow into all that God wants you to be," Carter told her, "and I was hoping you would do the same for me."

"I will," she pledged. Then she spoke up. "You are giving me all that you are, and I love you for that. I know it hasn't been easy since Kara, and I don't expect you to dishonor her memory. The blank spaces on your wall at home looked unnatural, so I figured that you had taken down portraits of her because I was coming over."

He nodded. "I didn't want it to be weird."

"Thank you for thinking about me. I'm a work in progress with God. Since I have met you, you've opened my eyes in many ways because you're...." She paused to gather herself. "You're caring, thoughtful, and giving. You have a way of settling me that I absolutely love."

His eyes displayed many emotions—admiration, joy, peace—but love dominated.

"I love what God has done with your life," Gianna said. "You're a testimony that God can put it back together again when you think you've lost it all."

"Thanks. God is good." He smiled at her. "There is so much potential in you, Gia. When I look at you, I think of dynamite. You look unbelievably gentle, but I know there is something powerful in you. I want to see you flourish in the Lord."

She returned his smile. "Thank you."

Suddenly, he stood.

Instinctively, she rose, too.

Expectancy filled the air.

"Stay there," he commanded, moving to take up his jacket.

She watched as he reached into one of the pockets before dropping it back on the sofa and making his way to her.

"I thought a lot about us when I was in Seattle. I'd planned to do everything after the party, but here we are. I suppose we can break the news after the party."

"News? What news?" Gianna felt her heart doing a pitter-patter dance.

"This news."

Carter went down on one knee, and Gianna gaped. She was sure she was dreaming.

"Gia, you're powerful. You're special. You're amazing. The Bible says that 'there is no fear in love; but perfect love casts out fear, because fear involves torment. But he who fears has not been made perfect in love.' And with you I feel no fear. I love you. Will you marry me?"

Her eyes floated over his face then widened and widened some more as she tried to take it all in.

He waited.

"Carter, oh my God! Yes, I will."

He released her hand and opened the black velvet ring box to display a timeless gold trellis engagement ring with a brilliant oval cut center diamond and a cluster of three stones forming a triangle on each side.

In her excitement, Gianna gripped his shoulders to hasten the process. He took the ring from the box and placed it on her ring finger. She was sure she had floated several inches off the ground. She gazed at the ring and then smiled at him. "Honey, it's gorgeous. I love it."

Carter placed the ring box on the coffee table, and as he rose, she threw herself into his arms.

He hugged her tightly.

She lifted her head and told him. "I love you."

"I love you, too."

His strong arms tightened on her waist, just as her arms circled his neck. That was all the encouragement he needed. He leaned towards her, and she was on tiptoes, ready for their first kiss—the first of many to come. When he took her mouth, she parted her quivering lips and kissed him back. His lips caressed hers tenderly at first, but in a second the intensity grew—heated and full of need. Wild tremors racked her body, and she clung to him as the floor tilted. He was evoking sensations in her body that were foreign to her. Just when she couldn't take any more, he broke their kiss.

Breathless, they gazed at each other.

He lowered his head again, and she moaned in anticipation. He kissed the corners of her mouth and then her forehead, and she whimpered with pleasure. But when he pecked her lips ever so softly, she was giddy with delight.

"I've wanted to kiss you since forever," he whispered. "But no more kissing. We'll be in trouble."

His husky tone drawing butterflies in her heart, she groaned and buried her head in his chest.

As if sensing her need, he wrapped his arms around the small of her back, and she melted into him, pressing in to get more of him. Even so, she wanted him closer.

CHAPTER 37

Beep, beep, beep...

The alarm woke Gianna, and for a split second, she wondered where she was. She was back at Nora and Henry's home and had decided to take a nap on the large sofa in the lounge area of her room. Her eyes widened and her body jackknifed into a sitting position. She lifted her left hand and grinned at the ring on her finger before her spontaneous shrieks of joy filled the air.

Seconds later, she picked up her cell phone from the coffee table and turned off the alarm. She returned to her cozy spot on the sofa and found herself smiling... delightful images flitting across her mind. She was on cloud nine.

She was bright-eyed and bushy tail after her engagement and following that, spending time on the phone with Carter until the wee hours. She rolled her eyes dreamily, still feeling the flutters of his touch. Quiet laughter escaped when she recalled she'd fallen asleep while talking with him. *We're equal now.* He made sure she knew that this morning when he'd called. She had denied it, but they both knew she'd lost her edge over him.

Thank you, Lord, for my fiancé.

They'd prayed together before she left home this morning, and she made sure to let him know she'd arrived safely. Thanks to Carter, Nora's chauffeur had picked her up at her house. He had insisted that he wanted them to travel back together on Sunday. No, she didn't object. She'd given in to him and his swoon-worthy voice.

Her phone chimed with a text message, and she reached for it and fell back onto the sofa. Her face broke out in a huge smile.

Carter: *Thinking of you, my fiancée. I love you.*
          [Beating heart emoji] See you soon.
Gianna: *Thinking of you, too, my fiancé. I love you.*
          [Beating heart emoji] Looking forward to
          seeing you.

She re-read the text, loving the way it made her feel. She raised her left hand and gazed at her engagement ring. *Blessed.* That's how she felt—marrying the man of her dreams and a man whose faith was strong in the Lord.

Knock! Knock!

Celia is here.

When Celia Gaither, the head of the household staff, had met her on arrival, she had indicated that she would visit to run over the schedule for the day.

Gianna rose, placed her phone on the end table, and made her way towards the door. Running a hand over her hair, she opened the door and came face-to-face with a beaming Nora.

Gianna smiled at her. "Hi, Nora."

"I couldn't wait to see you," Nora said, moving through the door and closing it. She embraced and released Gianna. "Celia is waiting. I told her I needed a moment with you."

"Is everything okay?"

"Yes. Carter told me he popped the question."

Gianna grinned at her. "He did. But he told me he would wait until after your party to inform the family."

"I'm glad he didn't wait. Welcome to the family. Now let me see the rock."

Smiling, Gianna lifted her left hand and watched as Nora admired the ring.

"It's gorgeous," Nora beamed. "I hope you're planning to wear it later."

"Now that the cat is out of the bag, I will."

"Thank you, Lord. I see the light at the end of the tunnel," Nora said dramatically.

Gianna laughed softly, knowing she was at last seeing grandchildren in her future.

After Nora left, Celia entered and ran down the list of activities to be performed before the party, which was scheduled to begin at six o'clock.

"Do you need anything else?" Celia asked from the sofa in the lounge area.

Gianna couldn't help but smile at the Caucasian woman, but what was the fuss about? She looked like she was bursting with excitement. Like the rest of the house staff, Celia was dressed in black slacks and a long-sleeve button-down white shirt.

"Thanks, Celia. Nothing else."

"I don't mean to be forward, Gianna, but I wanted to say congratulations on your engagement to Carter. He's a good man, and he loves the Lord."

"Thanks. You're right on both accounts." Gianna held out her left hand for Celia to see her engagement ring.

"It's beautiful," Celia gushed.

"Thank you."

"I've assigned Lissan Rivers to help you. If you need a snack or something to drink, she will be able to get that for you. You can also call the kitchen, and they'll bring up whatever you want."

"There's no need for that. I'll get it myself."

Celia smiled warmly at Gianna. "Perhaps, but you're going to need help for this occasion."

Gianna nodded. "Thank you."

"Dr. and Mrs. McIntosh told us, the staff, that you're to be treated as a biological daughter, with all the rights and privileges that come with that."

Gianna's eyes widened. "Really?"

"Yes. They pray with us at six o'clock every morning."

"That's wonderful. I'll join tomorrow morning."

"We all get to sleep in, so prayer will be at ten tomorrow."

"Okay, I'll be there."

"That would be great. Then, you can meet the rest of the staff." Celia handed Gianna a cream-colored card with the list of activities. "I'm leaving you now, but please call if you need anything. Be mindful of the time you have with the hairdresser and makeup artist, because they need to go to Mrs. McIntosh when they are finished with you."

Gianna took the card. "I sure will. Thanks, Celia."

After Celia left, Gianna retook her last position on the sofa. She inspected the card, which had GIANNA written in all caps at the top.

11:00 AM – Mani and Pedi

12:30 PM – Lunch in the Sunroom with Dr. & Mrs. Henry McIntosh

02:15 PM – Hairdresser Appointment

03:40 PM – Makeup Appointment

04:00 PM – Getting Ready

05:00 PM – Final Touches

05:15 PM – Escorted by Carter to the Ballroom

05:30 PM – Cocktails

05:45 PM – Mrs. Nora McIntosh enters Grand Ballroom

06:00 PM – Party Time

Gianna placed the card beside her on the sofa, and her mind turned to the difference between Brooklyn's and Kamala's reactions when she had announced that she was engaged.

Brooklyn's cool "Congratulations" was in sharp contrast to Kamala's shouts of joy. She wished Brooklyn would relax and be happy for her.

Knock! Knock! Knock!

The urgency of the knocks caused Gianna to hurry to the door.

"Who is it?"

"Carter."

She flung open the door, and he rushed in, closing the door behind him.

They wrapped each other in a warm embrace.

"I'm so glad to see you," she told him when they parted.

"Glad to see you, too. I hear you have a strict schedule." With a mischievous expression, he asked, "Is Mom trying to steal you away?"

Gianna smiled at him. "Not at all. We're sharing a hairdresser and makeup artist."

"Only that?"

"Pretty much."

"Mom and Dad are elated about our engagement. I called to let them know this morning. It was really to tell them that I changed my plans."

"Good for you. Declare your independence."

His chest seemingly puffed out. "I told Brooklyn, too, but she said you had called her."

Gianna's eyebrows climbed. "You spoke with Brooklyn?"

"Yes. I'd spoken to her before all of this to get her approval to marry you. She's your second mom, right? You mentioned that on our trip from Tallahassee."

"How did—?"

"I told you I have contacts, little lady." He rested his back against the wall near the door.

"Brooklyn never said a word about it to me."

"Forgive her. She was sworn to secrecy."

"Well, she could have at least said something this morning when I told her I was engaged."

"I don't know what to say about that. When I heard that you're having lunch with Mom and Dad, I invited myself. I'm in my old room on the other side of this floor."

Gianna patted his chest. "Oh, brave one, I'm glad you were fearless enough to tread through uncharted waters to get to your queen. You shall be greatly rewarded."

"I like that." He wrapped an arm around her waist and pulled her closer. "No one will snatch our happiness."

"Agreed," she said, gazing up at him.

"I have something for you," he said, reaching into the back pocket of his black jeans and handing her a small box wrapped with shiny red paper.

"Another gift. Thank you. You're spoiling me." She took it from his hand and lifted the cover.

"Not at all."

"You're so…" She paused as she laid eyes on a gold bracelet with three Madeira Citrine gemstones surrounded by diamonds. *Stunning.* She lifted it from the box and placed the box on the marble console table near the door.

"How…?" She was at a loss for words.

"Do you like it?"

"I do, very much. Thank you."

He took it from her and clasped it on her hand.

They both admired it as it glimmered, reflecting the ceiling light.

He held her hand and brought it to his lips, and as their eyes collided, fear gripped her. *Wait. How did he…? How could he have known?* Thoughts in turmoil, she yanked her hand away.

Carter gaped.

"How did you know I like Madeira Citrine gemstones?" she asked in an accusing tone.

"I didn't," he spoke quietly. "I went to get Mom a birthday gift at the jewelry store and decided to get a gift for you. Something I was hoping you would wear to the party."

Suddenly, Gianna felt foolish. "Hope you didn't spend the family fortune," she said, attempting to lighten the mood.

"I did."

That caused her to look at him.

"I won't hurt you, Gia. Can you please remember that?" he asked tenderly.

She touched his hand. "I'm sorry, Carter. I didn't mean any harm. I just edited ReTrac's manuscript, and the hero gave the heroine a gold bracelet with a Madeira Citrine gemstone. Anyway, that's not it. Those gemstones are my fave because on my tenth birthday, my parents gave me Madeira Citrine stud earrings. I'm planning to wear them tonight."

"Then, my gift is right on time?"

"Right," she replied self-consciously. "That's my bad."

"What am I going to do with you, my wife-to-be?"

He kissed her cheek softly. The electricity from his touch stirred her, and she tilted her head, desperate for his lips. Finally, he touched his lips briefly to hers.

No! No! No, her body screamed with disobedience.

Sensing her need, he ran his hand up and down her back to comfort her. "If we kiss like we did last night, we won't be able to honor our commitment to God."

Frustration mounting, her eyes rolled back, and she grumbled her displeasure before dumping her head on his chest.

He clasped her head with both hands and lifted it.

She gazed back at him and saw his love mushrooming. "I love—"

He kissed her before she could finish her sentence, and she accepted his kiss, her hand feverishly grabbing his head, his shoulders, his face to keep him in place.

After a moment or six, he tore his mouth from hers, then pecked her lips. Their parting felt more like an abandonment.

"I love you, too." His tone was serious. "I'm ready to get married when you are."

"Later this year would be okay if we can get it all together."

"I have no objections. We'll talk more after the party."

Anticipation bloomed in her heart when he leaned in.

He kissed her forehead.

He kissed her on the tip of her nose.

He kissed the corners of her mouth.

Finally, he kissed her mouth—lingering, coaxing, before his lips clung.

At the touch of his lips, she blossomed like a flower, kissing him back the same way he was kissing her. Submitting to the relentless pleasure, her hands gripped him… gripped him everywhere. Lost in his kisses, she could barely breathe when it was all over.

And just as quickly as he had appeared, Carter disappeared from the room.

Gianna closed the door, still tasting his delicious kisses.

CHAPTER 38

Gianna examined her fit-for-a-queen red evening gown in the full-length mirror near the dresser. The A-line metallic glitter gown had an overskirt that ran hip to hip but allowed the center of attention to be the long, fitted floor-length dress. The gown's sleeveless beaded bodice was supported by tank straps, and the slightly open back had a lattice design.

"You look beautiful, Ms. Gianna," Lissan said as she brushed Gianna's center-parted hair, which was hanging in sleek tresses down her back.

"Thanks, Lissan. That's a kind thing to say."

Gianna saw Lissan smiling at her in the mirror and couldn't help but notice the woman's white teeth against her cool bronze complexion.

She returned Lissan's smile. "I can't drink too many liquids this evening. This is not a dress to get out of in a hurry."

Lissan chortled softly. "Call me if you need help."

"I won't bother you during the function, but afterwards, I may need another pair of hands."

"Sure."

"Thank you."

A knock on the door caused Lissan to move away to answer. She returned with a radiant Nora, whose smile grew when she saw Gianna. She was holding a dusty pink attaché case in her hand.

"My dear, you look amazing," Nora said.

"Thanks, Nora."

"I was about to slip into my dress, then I wondered about your jewelry."

"I think I'm okay. I didn't wear a necklace because I have nothing that would match these earrings from my mom and my bracelet from Carter."

"I have just what you need." Nora turned, walked over to the bed, and placed the case on it.

Gianna and Lissan followed her.

Nora opened the case to reveal an assortment of jewelry. She lifted a gold necklace with Madeira Citrine gemstones. "This is a perfect match for your earrings and bracelet."

Gianna's eyes widened. "Nora—"

"It would be my pleasure if you wear it," Nora said.

Gianna relented. "I will give it back first thing in the morning."

"I know you would, but I'd rather you keep it. Think of it as an engagement gift."

"It's beautiful, but I couldn't. I'm satisfied just to help you celebrate tonight."

"Thanks, dear, but please accept it as a gift. I insist."

Nora made movements to put the necklace around her neck, and Gianna lifted her hair to grant access. When Nora completed her task, she smiled at Gianna. "My son will not be able to take his eyes off you."

Gianna grinned at her. "Thanks, Nora."

With a "See you later," Nora hurried away.

At ten past five o'clock, Gianna stood at the top of the grand curved double staircase to assess the scene before her. It was quiet except for three men who were decked out in black tuxedos and animatedly chatting with one another in the entryway. She held on to the railing and observed them—the McIntosh men, the McIntosh brothers.

As if sensing her presence, they all looked at her, and their flashes of smiles reached her. When she moved to descend the steps, Carter moved too, to the foot of the staircase. His smile lit the entryway, and she could tell he was waving off boyish jeers from his brothers.

Nevertheless, his starstruck gaze held hers.

Ignoring the inaudible comments and catcalls from the mischievous souls behind him, Carter's boyish whistle filled the air.

Gianna laughed, delighting in his open affection. She couldn't move any faster, though; the billowing fabric of her overskirt would not allow it. Instead, she enjoyed every moment. When she stood on the last step, he was giving her an ear to ear smile. She grinned back at him, touching his face.

"Woooman," he gushed, "you're an absolute vision."

"Thank you," Gianna said. She could feel her heart beating against the wall of her chest. "You look amazing," she managed to say.

"Thanks, beautiful lady." Carter moved slightly and offered his arm. "It's my pleasure to escort you to anywhere you like."

Before she could respond, one of his brothers yelled, "That would be to Mom's birthday party!"

"Says the joy-killer," Carter countered with a blank stare. His lips didn't move, but when the dimples in his cheeks became more noticeable, Gianna realized he was suppressing a smile. She laughed softly as Carter walked her towards his siblings.

"Let me introduce you to my brothers." Carter pointed to the taller man who was the spitting image of their father but a much younger version. "This is Paxton. We call him Pax. Pax, this is Gianna, my fiancée."

Paxton smiled and Gianna could see the signature McIntosh long dimples on his handsome face. He was obviously burning time at the gym. His caramel-colored complexion looked healthy and baby smooth. The edginess of his brush cut hairstyle was hard to miss. He seemed larger than life, and his warm smile immediately put Gianna at ease.

Smiling, Gianna extended her hand. "Nice to meet you, Pax."

"The pleasure is all mine, Gianna."

They exchanged a brief handshake.

"Welcome to the family and congrats on your engagement," Paxton told her.

"Thank you," Gianna said, turning to Rylan, whom she could tell was the troublemaker of the three. His handsome face would totally give actor Lance Gross a run for his money. He stood tall with his chest out. His tuxedo was custom-built for him, revealing his sculpted physique. He was easy on the eyes, his skin the color of smooth milk chocolate.

"This is Rylan, aka Ry," Carter said. "Thanks to him, some refer to us as two and a half men."

A gurgle popped from Gianna. "Carter, oh gosh. Just so shameful. I'm sorry, Ry, that was unexpected."

"That's alright." Rylan ran a hand over his wavy jet-black hair. "He's just jealous because I'm the most handsome and Mom's favorite."

They all laughed.

"Great to meet you, Gianna," Rylan said, smiling.

Gianna offered her hand, and he shook it. "Likewise, Ry." She noticed that his dimples were not as pronounced as those of the other men in the family.

Rylan released her hand. "Congrats on your engagement." His dark-brown eyes narrowed, drawing her attention to his strong jaw. "Call me if Carter messes up."

"Man, go sit down," Carter jumped in.

Laughter broke out again.

"Well, turn down the energy in here," a familiar voice said.

They all turned and witnessed Allison strutting like a peacock toward them. Her beaded royal-blue off-the-shoulder mermaid gown was so tight, little was left to the imagination. Knowing she was the center of attention, Allison took a turn as she neared them.

Gianna held back a gasp. The plunging back of her gown revealed the dimples just above her well-toned derriere.

Allison's eyes roamed the group. "I see you're all hiding your emotions deep down," she cooed.

Rylan had to be himself. "Alley, there you are! Can your lowly servant get you anything?"

Allison pierced him with her eyes and opened her mouth to speak, but Paxton raced to the rescue. "How are you, Alley?"

Allison pouted. She had the wilting daisy act down. "Ah, a little love at last. I'm doing well. Thanks for asking Pax. Wait, I didn't get the memo to wear red. I see red everywhere." Her eyebrow overarched. "Now I see Gigi in red, and you guys decked out in red bow ties."

"That's all, Mom," Rylan chipped in.

Allison eyed Gianna, then her gaze fell to the hand-to-hand connection between her and Carter. "Gigi, you look... nice. Wow, that necklace and matching bracelet. Gor-ge-ous!"

"Thanks," Gianna replied.

But Allison wasn't finished. "Madeira Citrine. Hmmm. Eighteen-karat?"

"Enough, Alley," Carter reprimanded her.

Oh, no. Gianna touched Carter's arm. She'd never seen him annoyed.

Allison eyed Carter for a moment, then turned to Paxton. "Olivia is here. I told her I would let you know."

"Livi is here. Yeah! Thanks, Alley," Paxton remarked with zeal. "See you all later. Alley, please show me—"

Allison cut him off. "I was planning to hang out—"

"Pax's girlfriend is here, and Carter's fiancée is with him. You can hang out with me and Lee-Ann, though," Rylan offered.

"Fiancée?" Allison blew out a breath, visibly shaken. Her head whipped in Carter's direction, and she eyed Gianna as if ready to take on the enemy. "You're engaged?" she asked.

"Yes. Gianna and I got engaged yesterday," Carter told her with exaggerated patience. "If you'll all excuse us."

Gianna witnessed many emotions flashing in Allison's eyes as they strode past her.

For all her tendency to exhibit cattish behavior, Allison's bravado didn't pan out. Even her veiled threat to Gianna in Nora's office came to naught, for when she'd arrived at the lunch table, Allison had been as meek as a lamb. Gianna surmised Nora might have put things in perspective for her.

CHAPTER 39

"Are you okay?" Carter asked Gianna when they were out of earshot.

"I'm fine, honey. Allison was just...." Gianna's voice trailed off when she couldn't come up with words to excuse Allison's behavior.

"I had to move you away because I sensed that Alley was about to be rude."

Gianna smiled up at him. "Thanks, love."

In silence, they moved forward, exiting the double doors that led to a circular entryway to the ballroom.

They greeted the two armed guards who opened the door to the estate's grand ballroom, elegantly decorated in gold, red, and ivory. Timeless elegance. It was obvious no stone had been left unturned in making the hall a one-of-a-kind experience for the festive occasion. Enthralled, Gianna gazed at the eye-catching setting—dome ceiling, floor-to-ceiling windows, huge screens displaying photos of Nora and her family, and a dance floor. Carter moved her through the ballroom, greeting relatives, A-list celebrities, and society elites.

At a table in the center of the room, Gianna was surprised to see the leaders of her church, Pastor Jeremiah Richardson and his wife, Elder Brenda Richardson. They were seated with Carter's pastor and his wife, Pastor Raymond McCallum and Elder Judy McCallum. Gianna and Carter made the introductions. After getting over the initial surprise, both pastors and their wives congratulated them on their engagement.

Soon, they moved on again.

The room was not too crowded even though many of the guests were on their feet, enjoying hors d'oeuvres and sipping aperitifs.

"Would you like hors d'oeuvres?" Carter asked.

"No. Thanks for asking."

The one-bite appetizers—shrimp cocktail, grilled scallops wrapped in prosciutto, fruit kebabs, smoked salmon rillettes, and crustless mini quiches—looked tasty. Still, Gianna didn't want to risk not being able to have dinner. As Carter moved them on, Gianna observed that the exquisitely decorated head table was in sight. However, shimmering lights in her peripheral vision made her turn her head. The musical instruments were glistening under the lights, and the band members were in place. Excitement lit her soul in the same way it had when she was a child and it was time to sing.

She tugged at Carter's arm, and he stopped and leaned in, all ears. Her temperature soared as she looked into the depth of his eyes. *Oh, God.*

"What's up, pretty lady?" he asked when she didn't speak.

She blushed, and her girlish giggle floated in the air. "I was excited to see the band."

He wriggled his eyebrows. "You should sing with us. You know that song."

"I do, but perhaps another time."

"And his heart palpitates in anticipation."

Chuckles escaped her.

"Well, aren't you two having fun!"

Gianna and Carter glanced up to see Brooklyn Morris and Phil Collier smiling at them, with an usher in tow.

After they greeted each other, Gianna offered Brooklyn a tentative smile and was a little surprised when she returned a wide smile.

"You look great, Gigi," Brooklyn said.

"Thanks! So do you." Gianna took in her black chiffon empire waist floor-length gown, perfected with gold rhinestone bling. *Talk about making a statement.*

"I'm glad we got a chance to see you both, before the party is in full swing," Carter said, his eyes sweeping Brooklyn and Phil, before turning to Gianna. "I saw Brooklyn before you came downstairs, and she introduced me to Phil."

Gianna beamed. "That's great."

"Congratulations, again," Brooklyn said, smiling at Gianna before her eyes shifted to Carter.

"Congrats! I heard the good news," Phil jumped in.

"Thanks!" Gianna responded as Carter hugged her to his side.

"Thanks, I feel blessed," Carter replied.

Just then, Michael Roman, the master of ceremonies, called for the guests to be seated as Queen Nora would be arriving shortly. His voice seemed to boom over the microphone.

As Brooklyn and Phil moved away, Rylan hurried towards them.

Carter and Gianna waited.

"We need a Plan B. Lee-Ann won't be here," Rylan said, looking at Carter.

"Is she alright?" Carter asked.

"Yes, she…." Rylan began, and then seemingly remembered that Gianna was there.

Carter waited, but Gianna could see he was working up Plan B.

"She wanted something I'm not prepared to give," Rylan said quietly.

Both Carter and Gianna's eyebrows climbed.

"I know, right?" Rylan added. "I'm willing to sing, but I can't hit those high notes. Let me do your part. I think you have a better chance of hitting those notes."

"Let's change the song," Carter suggested.

"I'll do it." It was out, followed by a gasp from Gianna.

Carter and Rylan gaped at her as if she had said something abominable.

Rylan recovered first. "You will?"

"No, Gia. I don't want to put you on the spot like that," Carter said.

She gazed at him with all the love she felt for him. "It's no trouble. I'll do it for Nora, and you."

Carter's eyes glazed over with tears. "Babes, don't make me cry."

Gianna rubbed his back lovingly.

"Do you need to practice?" Rylan asked, his eyes still holding a tinge of worry.

"No," Gianna reassured him. "I heard Carter sing the song, and he pretty much kept the original arrangement."

Once again, they looked at her and she hastened to calm them.

"I will sing it like the original, I'll do the female lead, and you do the male lead, and we can play with the chorus."

"Got it," Carter said. "Thanks, babes."

"Here's a thought," Rylan said, "I will take over from you at the keyboard once you feel the band is good with Gianna's range, and then you can join her out front."

"Sounds good," Carter replied. "Okay, let the band know what's going on, while I thank this lovely lady."

With that, Rylan took off.

"Babes, thank you!"

"Anything for you, hon," Gianna said. "And don't worry, I know the way you sing. I'm going to stay on top of you."

"Hmmm, I like that."

Gianna let out a loud chuckle. "Dirty old man."

"Just for you, babes, just for you."

Carter took her by the hand, and they moved towards the head table.

Gianna grinned all the way.

At the family table closest to the head table, Carter seated her and then sat beside her. He introduced her to Olivia Milner, who was seated with Paxton.

"Nice to meet you, Gianna," Olivia said in a warm and gracious tone. She was a chic, ethereal looking woman with steel-gray eyes and long blond hair. She looked to be in her early thirties, and the air around her said, *life is a blast.*

"Nice meeting you, too, Olivia." Gianna returned her smile just as Rylan joined them at the table.

"Ladies and gentlemen, please rise and welcome our honored guest, Mrs. Nora McIntosh, escorted by her husband, Dr. Henry McIntosh."

Thunderous applause and a chorus of "Cheers!" filled the room, and everyone was on their feet. Nora swept into the room on the arm of her husband and took the long walk towards the head table. Flashing lights and rising balloons supported their grand entrance. As the applause died down, instrumental music lifted the ambiance to another celebratory level.

Nora smiled and waved at her guests.

She looked beautiful in a long-sleeve, scoop neckline red velvet gown. An A-line maxi soft tulle skirt emphasized her surprisingly tiny waist and made her look angelic. It was hard to miss her stunning diamond necklace and the matching earrings that sparkled every time she moved.

Henry led Nora with grace and dignity. He was dressed in a black tux, suited for a king.

As soon as Nora and Henry were seated, the master of ceremonies called for the two pastors to pray—Pastor

McCallum to bless the occasion and Pastor Jeremiah Richardson to bless the meal.

Almost an hour and a half later, they had eaten dinner, and toasts were given by the McIntosh brothers, followed by Henry.

Finally, it was Nora's turn to speak. "Hello, everyone! Thank you for coming to celebrate with me. I am honored that you took time out of your schedule to rejoice with me. I'm grateful to be able to celebrate my life, sixty years on earth. That's a lot of years," she said with her eyes bulging.

The audience laughed loudly.

Nora continued. "Today, all I feel is gratitude. I'm thankful to my Lord and Savior Jesus Christ for just about everything. My husband, my sons, and my soon to be daughter-in-law, so many things." Her voice trailed off. "Can I just share something with you?"

Many responses filled the air from her captive audience.

"Go ahead!"

"Sure!"

"This is your night."

Delicate laughter left Nora. "I promise I'll make it short. We all need to hit the dance floor to burn off that food. Oh, it was delicious."

Pockets of laughter broke out all over the room.

"I want to thank God for my sons, Paxton, Carter, and Rylan, who are my everything. I loved them from when I first held them in my arms, and I love them even more today. They are my blessing from God. I must thank God for my husband. Henry has been a great husband and father. I love him more with each passing day." She looked coyly at Henry, who blew her a kiss.

Her blushing bride expression caused many "Awwws" to come from the guests.

"Yes, I adore my husband." Nora gave Henry a googly-eyed stare. "I thank God for giving him the patience to love me through thick and thin. I'll be the first to confess that I have not always played nice, but Henry would not give up on me, did not give up on me. The Word of God says whosoever finds a wife finds a good thing, and I strive daily to be that good thing for Henry. He makes me want to be better. I know that God has given me a man who loves me like He loves the church, and I am grateful. As you can tell, grateful is my new word. Thank you, dear Henry." She looked at her husband with her eyes brimming. "I-I love you with all-all my heart. You're my beloved."

The ballroom erupted with loud applause, and Henry leaped to his feet, walked swiftly to Nora, and kissed her cheek.

Plans afoot, Gianna and the McIntosh men left the table.

CHAPTER 40

In the dim light, at a spot behind the band, Gianna watched as Carter and Rylan sat at the keyboard. Paxton was on the drums. She inhaled and exhaled a few times when she heard the MC call Nora and Henry to the dance floor.

In silence, the guests waited for the couple to take their place. Gianna couldn't help but admire the caring, doting Henry. He reminded her so much of Carter. Earlier that day, at lunch, Henry did not hold back his fatherly affection for her. *Just the kind of father-figure I need. Thank You, Lord.*

"The next song you'll hear," Michael announced, "is 'Nobody Loves Me Like You do' and it's a duet which was performed by the late Whitney Houston and Jermaine Jackson. I understand there is a history between Dr. and Mrs. McIntosh concerning this song. Folks, don't ask, because I won't tell. Then again, maybe I should say."

The audience cracked up, then waited eagerly.

Michael cleared his throat as if he was going to let the cat out of the bag, then in the pregnant silence, he declared, "Some things are better left unsaid. Now, here to perform this tribute to Dr. and Mrs. McIntosh are her sons—Paxton, Carter, Rylan, and their friends."

As the guests whistled and clapped, the light dimmed further.

At Carter's smile and a nod, Gianna moved to a spot on the side of the stage that was not well lit. A tiny smile touched her lips. Even though she'd told Carter no razzmatazz at all, he'd insisted that a little mystery would help the performance.

Carter proceeded with the short introduction to the song, and Gianna inhaled and exhaled before lifting the microphone to her mouth. With joy in her heart, she sang the first line of the song.

Seamless.

Timeless.

Pristine.

Bell-clear tone.

She'd mirrored Whitney Houston's iconic voice.

Even she had to smile. And just as she did, the light revealed her side profile. She tried not to focus on the few loud gasps but instead concentrated on a stunned Carter, who was enthralled.

But she couldn't continue gazing at him for this performance was for Nora. She winked at him, and then allowed her eyes to float over the band members. With a trained nod and a smile reminiscent of yesteryear, she conveyed that they were doing a fabulous job.

They were all smiling in amazement.

Next, Gianna turned her attention to the queen of the evening, who was in the center of the dance floor, in the arms of her beloved. Only, they'd stopped dancing, and were gaping at her. Gianna lifted a hand and acknowledged them, and they broke out into smiles.

Mesmerized, the audience was mute.

When Gianna finished her lines, she turned slightly to smile at Carter.

It was his turn, and he was on it. His husky, intoxicating tenor voice—coolly endearing—rang out with effortless power.

Such passion. Gianna's smile popped all the way out.

His heart on his sleeve, Carter belted out the tune as he walked towards her.

Rylan had taken over the keyboard, and like all the band members, he was playing the masterpiece with his emotions on display.

Now Carter stood before her, his voice dripping with honey and his eyes displaying all the love he wanted to give to her. Gianna's response was spontaneous—an ear-to-ear smile. Her heart was on display. This man, her fiancé, could sing to her any day. His extraordinary range only fueled her boldness.

Carter reached for her hand, and they moved forward, singing the chorus to an audience who was either gawking or smiling at them. The collaboration of their vocal tones was masterful, but the beautiful chemistry between them made their expressions of love sentimental and infectious. Each time they sang the line— "Nobody loves me like you do."—they smiled at each other with the longings of their hearts written across their faces.

A moment like this was theirs to cherish.

As the song came to a close, Carter and Gianna smiled at each other and with passion declared, "Nobody loves me like you do."

There were seconds of silence, followed by deafening applause and beating of the tables. Their head-over-heels-in-love performance was a hit with the audience.

Misty-eyed, Gianna and Carter embraced.

"You're a vocal goddess," Carter whispered, kissing her cheek.

Gianna let out happy giggles. "Thanks, honey."

Smiling, he winked at her before they turned their attention to his parents.

Luckily.

Nora and Henry were heading towards them.

Instinctively, Carter held on to Gianna's hand, and they moved forward.

Group hug was the order of the moment, each echoing their sentiment. Not a dry eye was in the group when they lifted their heads.

As soon as they parted, the MC announced that the dance floor was open.

The guests cheered wildly.

"Ooooh yes!" Henry whelped in excitement.

Gianna was cracking up. She'd never seen this side of him.

"He gets this way when he hears music," Nora filled in with love.

Carter shook his head as if he'd seen this play out before.

"We'll see you all later," Henry said. "I've got to do this before my body realizes it's old."

Henry did not skip a beat; he smiled at his wife and offered his hand. She took it and they were off to get their groove on.

Gianna clutched Carter's arm and grinned as she watched them do their old-school dancing.

Soon, Carter and Gianna made their way back to the band and said their thank-yous. Next, Carter led Gianna to the dance floor.

They got down, dancing to several songs, sometimes even doing steps that made them cross the room. The line dances were Gianna's favorite. She loved to dance and was thrilled that Carter loved dancing as well.

Winded, she was glad when the DJ started "Unforgettable" by Nat King Cole and Natalie Cole. Carter pulled her into his arms, and they waltzed in sync, soaking in the words of the song. She was following his lead, when suddenly, he gently detached himself from her, turned her, and pulled her to him.

She had to smile.

When he swung her away from him, she turned and came back to him, and his arms were ready and waiting.

For a second time, he swung her away from him, and she laughed with glee and then kept twirling away, giving him the catch-me-if-you-can expression.

He threw his head back and laughed before watching her playfully.

When she wouldn't budge, he extended his hand.

She whirled back to him, and he was right on hand to catch her.

Winded and happy, she leaned against him, circling his waist with her hands. Her head pressed against his chest, she heard the feverish rhythm of his heart.

Her heart was beating fast, too. She expected that any minute it would burst from her chest. *I love you.*

And as if he had heard, he whispered, "I love you, too," his lips gently brushing her forehead.

CHAPTER 41

"Pitch-perfect," Brooklyn said, smiling. "I can't wait to chat." She waved goodbye to Gianna before sliding into the passenger seat of her black Mercedes-Benz.

Phil closed the car door, waved at Gianna, and dashed around the front of the car.

Gianna watched as he sat behind the wheel. *Can't wait to chat, indeed. I won't be the only one dreaming tonight.*

Gianna waited until the vehicle began to move away before making her way on the terracotta tiles to access the steps leading to the main door to the house. She'd left Carter in the ballroom, where the party was still in high gear, to go to the restroom. As she had made her way through the ballroom, she'd seen Brooklyn and Phil heading toward one of the exits and decided to see them off.

Nodding to the two armed guards, Gianna waited for one of them to open the door for her. She hurried through the entryway, recalling that her protector-in-chief would be meeting her at the double staircase in a few minutes.

Gianna scurried through the formal living room to access the passageway that led to the kitchen. She needed to find Lissan to help her with her dress. She knew that some of the house staff would be hanging out outside the sunroom. The party was a catered event, so that gave most of the house staff a well-deserved break.

As Gianna passed the first entrance to the formal dining room, she heard her name, followed by laughter. She recognized Allison's voice and halted.

"Not Carter. Ry, you know it was you that I wanted from day one," Allison cooed.

"Seriously, stop, Alley. Put your hands down," Rylan reprimanded her.

"You should be glad I want you."

"Glad? I'm everybody's type," Rylan shot back.

"Why are you rejecting me?" she murmured playfully.

Rylan gave a short laugh. "Why not? Isn't that the popular thing right now?"

"You know I'm standing here. Right? I should…."

"Alley, stop that."

Shuffling.

More shuffling.

Gianna was about to hurry along when Allison spoke again.

"Well, since Carter insists on being engaged to a nobody, I'm available, and I only have you."

"You're just mean and jealous. Stop doing that. I told you I have a girlfriend."

"I shouldn't be talking to you anyway."

"Zzzzz."

"Whatever. You took way too much pleasure in telling me that Carter has a *fiancée*. Which is a big fat lie. We *all* know Carter has one love, Kara. He's just using that poor girl."

Rylan chuckled softly. "All evidence to the contrary."

Gianna's stomach did an unsettling bounce, and she commanded her feet to move but they wouldn't. *Using me for what? Why didn't he ask using me for what?*

"We'll see who has the last laugh. Her illusion will die naturally," Allison stated sarcastically.

"Illusion?" Rylan questioned. "There will be a loud thud when *you* hit the floor."

"Oh, she'll find out about his little side hustle. One way or another."

"Best leave that alone," Rylan cautioned.

"That depends on you," Allison cooed.

Footsteps behind her made Gianna turn, and she took two steps and charged into a hard body.

"I'm sorry," she winced, backing up.

It was Paxton.

Concern lit his eyes. "Are you okay?"

"Ye-yes," Gianna replied, then wiped her eyes. They were brimming. She rushed past Paxton. "I have to go."

She heard his voice, but whatever Paxton was saying was lost on her for she was racing through the passageway, and then through the formal living room. She wiped her eyes in the entryway leading to the double staircase. Suddenly, the steps seemed impossible to climb, but she had to get to the top and fast. Using one hand, she gathered the skirt of her gown, and with the other hand, she held on to the railing. Eyes brimming again, she took the trek. With each step, a feeling of dread washed over her. Her thoughts were spiraling out of control, and she struggled to rein in the fury springing from her core.

Side hustle? Lying? To me?

This is a den of lions.

I have to get out of here.

Oh, God. Not another broken heart.

Help me not to crumble, Lord.

See, Gianna, you knew this was too good to be true.

But no, everybody said go for it. And you stupidly did.

When will this staircase end?

Finally, she arrived at the top of the stairs. Panting but driven, she hurried on, stumbling then catching her balance. Her bedroom door in sight, she speed-walked the rest of the way. After opening the door, she flipped on the light switch then slammed the door shut. Leaning against it, her heart swelled with sorrow, but before long, angry tears began to pour out.

Her bloodshot eyes stinging, Gianna rushed to the walk-in closet and came out with a few pairs of shoes on top of a pile of clothes. She threw them near the bottom of the bed, then rushed to the closet again. This time she came back with her suitcase and more shoes and clothes. Throwing her suitcase on the bed bench, she crammed the clothes and shoes in.

Hindered by her dress, she impatiently began the task of unzipping. Frustration mounted as the zipper refused to budge. She eased one strap off her shoulder, then the other strap, and finally managed to turn the dress around to the front and unzip it. Muttering to herself, she stepped out of the dress with speed, rolled it into a bundle, and dropped it in the suitcase.

She stared at the suitcase for a moment, tears streaming down her face.

Help me, Lord!

Next, she took off Nora's necklace, the bracelet from Carter, and finally her engagement ring, and placed them on the nightstand. She wiped her eyes then took her Kindle and word search book from the nightstand, but in the haste, both fell from her hand. She moaned and bent to pick them up. The pencil fell out of the book and rolled near the dresser. As she stooped to pick it up, she noticed that the yellow Post-it with the words she'd generated from Carter's name was lying nearby. She sucked a breath through her teeth at her foolishness. *Silly.* Just as she reached for the paper her hand froze in mid-air. The Post-it was upside-down, and Carter's name in all caps pulled on her eyes. Then in a bizarre magnetic pull, his name ran left to right. She blinked and blinked again. It couldn't be.

She grabbed the paper and glowered at it.

Carter, when spelled backwards, was R-E-T-R-A-C. ReTrac.

Oh, God. She was rubbing her chest without even realizing it. *I can't think about that now.* Heart pounding, she stood quickly and felt light-headed. Thankfully, the giddy feeling didn't last.

She dropped everything she had in her hand into her suitcase. Racing back to the closet, she came out dressed in a pair of black jeans, a white button-down shirt, and flip flops, pulling a black hanging garment bag on the floor. She swung the bag at the foot of the bed. Then she stared at it. *I should leave it.* Most of the clothes from her shopping expedition with Nora were in it.

Then everything began to click in place.

Meeting Nora....

Meeting Carter....

That was the greatest setup she'd ever seen.

Brooklyn was right, Nora....

Wait, Brooklyn is involved....

Confused, Gianna exhaled loudly and covered her face with both hands. Her world was crashing right before her eyes. She hobbled to the dresser and tried not to pay too much attention to the tears rolling down her cheeks as she took a scrunchy and tied her hair in a ponytail. Following that, she began putting her jewelry, which had been on the dresser, into a small pink cosmetic bag.

"Ms. Gianna, I knocked, but you didn't hear me," she heard Lissan say.

Stunned, Gianna wiped her eyes before throwing a glance over her shoulder. "That's alright." Tears began to run down her cheeks faster and faster, but she focused on packing her trinkets.

"Mr. Carter wanted me—"

"Since you're here," Gianna said, turning watery eyes to Lissan. "Please make sure Nora gets her necklace."

"Are you okay?"

Gianna pointed to the nightstand. "And please make sure Carter gets those."

"He's—"

"Thank you." Gianna concluded their conversation.

Knowing she was dismissed, Lissan backed away, doe-eyed.

Feeling apologetic, Gianna moved to call out to Lissan then changed her mind.

At the click of the door, she exhaled loudly.

After folding the travel bag, she dropped it near the suitcase and smoothed the bedcovers.

Knock! Knock! Knock!

Gianna refused to answer.

When she heard the door open, she stood akimbo waiting for the invader to come through the entryway. *I told you to go, Lissan.*

In walked Carter, breathing hard, his face creased with concern.

Gianna had to hold back from hissing her teeth. She turned her back to him and moved to retrieve her cosmetic bag from the dresser. *Go away! Just go away.*

"Gia, what's—?"

Her head snapped back. "Nobody loves me like you do." She threw the cosmetic bag into her suitcase and regarded him.

Carter seemingly tried for patience. "I saw Pax, and then I saw Lissan, and they told me that something is going on with you. What's the matter?"

"There's plenty wrong, *ReTrac*."

His eyebrows shot to his hairline, and he sucked in a breath.

"What a time to develop ignorance," she scoffed.

"Gia—"

"Don't speak to me, Carter." She crossed her arms in a protective manner. "You made me love you, but you're a liar. I hope you had a good time with me falling all over you and ReTrac. Your ring is on the nightstand."

He stood there wholly dismayed by her passionate outbreak. "I'm sorry I didn't tell—"

Her nostrils flared. "I bet you are now."

Gianna moved back to the dresser and dumped her hair accessories into a blue pouch that was nearby. She clutched the dresser as tears blinded her.

"Give me a minute to explain."

When she didn't respond, he touched her shoulder.

"Don't touch me!" Her voice was somewhere between frenzied and choking back tears. She swung away from him and began to hyperventilate. *Oh, God! Panic attack. Don't let him see me like this.* A sick feeling traveled up her throat and she wobbled a bit.

"Get out of my—" She could not get the words out. Heart racing, she threw out her hands, trying to grab the dresser.

Carter caught her, but she began to fight him.

He held her.

She quieted for a second then began to punch his shoulder, his neck, anywhere she could land her fist.

"Gia, stop."

She attempted a whack to his chest but was too faint to do so.

"Try to relax," Carter encouraged.

"I said... don't... touch—"

"Slow your breathing," he commanded.

Unable to help herself, she leaned against him, trembling as hot and cold flashes assailed her body.

He held her as he would a child, quietly repeating reassuring words.

Groaning, Gianna clung to him, feeling detached from her surroundings.

Carter lifted her, carried her to the bed, and placed her on it. He held her to his chest as he put one pillow on top of the other so that she would be elevated, then lay her against them.

As soon as her head hit the pillow, she turned away from him and folded herself in a fetal position. And when he touched her shoulder, she shrugged him off. Nevertheless, he removed her flip flops. When he began making rustling movements, she wondered what he was doing, but when the bed dipped, she knew he was sitting at the edge of it.

She rolled to face him then stared blankly at him. *I wish to God you would just go away. Leave me alone.* If she was sending him a telepathic message, he did not receive it.

The stillness of the room overwhelmed her and offered little mental relief from the weariness she was experiencing. She felt like she was moving closer and closer to the edge of nothingness.

"I'm sorry, Gia," he said softly.

"Whatever…." She paused, feeling nauseated.

"Can I get you something? Water?"

Carter's concerned voice reached her as she bolted upright. "Bathroom," she croaked.

No questions asked. He scooped her in his arms, and they were barely over the toilet bowl before bile rose in her throat and came rushing out. Carter held her as she poured out the unwanted contents of her stomach and then emptied it some more. The heaves she could handle, but the dry retching was the worse. It was like swimming towards the surface after a deep dive and unable to reach it. Her body begged to be free of the torment.

Eventually, the feelings subsided.

After she rinsed her mouth, Carter made her sit on the bathroom chair while he kneeled at her feet and used a small green hand towel to wipe sweat from her face and neck. When he finished, he scanned her body, seemingly to ensure he'd done an excellent job, but his gaze was intimate.

Self-consciously, her hand flew to her chest.

"Do I need to call Pax or Dad?"

Gianna shook her head quickly. *I don't need a doctor. I need to get out of here.*

"I don't want you to be dehydrated," he added.

She made a face then shook her head. "I'll be fine. Please take me back to bed."

"Gladly."

She landed him a blank stare. *I know you're not flirting with me.*

Under other circumstances, she would have found that funny, but she was mad at him. Still, she curled up in his arms as he walked with her into the bedroom.

"I'm going to get you water and tea," he told her.

She nodded, struggling to look at him.

He made a call to the kitchen for Lissan to take green tea and water to her room. After he hung up, he mentioned, "Lissan said that water is on the coffee table. I'll get it."

She watched as he walked around to the far side of the bed and took up two more pillows. He came to her and held her against his chest as he swung the pillows one at a time behind her.

A great caregiver, she thought, then mentally rebuked herself for thinking about him. It was then that she noticed he'd taken off his jacket, vest, and bow tie, exposing his broad, muscular shoulders and tapered narrow waist.

Infuriatingly handsome.

265

Oh gosh! I'm checking him out.
Oh gosh! He noticed.

Confirmed when she saw a smile curving his lips and his light-brown eyes twinkling before he moved towards the lounge area. Gianna grimaced and cut her eyes at his tight rear.

Carter returned shortly with bottled water and opened it. Snagging a few sheets of tissue from the box on the nightstand, he sat next to her and held the bottle against her lips.

She was too weak to protest. She moved her head, indicating that she was finished, and he took the bottle away.

"A little more," he encouraged, and at her nod, he gave her more water.

He was mopping her mouth when someone knocked on the door.

He tightened the cap on the water bottle and placed it on the nightstand before heading to the door.

He returned with a smiling Lissan.

"Hey, Lissan." Gianna tried for a smile.

"Oh, Ms. Gianna, I'm so sorry you're not feeling well. I brought you broth and tea and other goodies, which I'm sure you'll be able to eat."

"Thanks," Gianna said, as Carter wheeled the small cart with food to her bedside. "I'm sorry for being so sharp with you earlier."

"That's alright," Lissan responded. "Please let me know if you need anything else."

"Thank you. You've been—" Gianna paused for breath "—kind."

"Thanks, Lissan," Carter said, as she made her exit.

"You're welcome, Mr. Carter," Lissan replied, smiling.

Carter slipped around the cart, sat on the bed, and then pulled the cart closer. "Tea or soup?"

She frowned. "Soup. You know I can feed myself?"

He pinned her with his eyes. "You can, but I want to. You're still not strong enough."

"You must know that this is uncomfortable," Gianna grumbled.

He dipped the spoon into the small white bowl and placed the spoon near her mouth.

Her lips trembled as she took in the soup.

He was looking at her with an indefinable expression. "It doesn't have to be."

She couldn't look him in the eyes, so she concentrated on the spoon.

CHAPTER 42

Carter watched the streaks of morning sunlight streaming through the windows of the lounge area of Gianna's bedroom. He exhaled softly, not wanting to wake her as she rested peacefully in his arms. That was a great improvement; throughout the night, her body, exhausted from the ordeal, had shuddered as it attempted to regain balance. He tried to slip away a few times, but with each attempt, she buried herself deeper in his arms. Even now, her hand was hugging his waist, and her head was buried in his chest.

He loved the softness of her body against his, but he knew she would be mad as soon as she realized that she was cuddling with him.

Oh, God, what a pickle!

If only he'd waited until after his mother's birthday party to pop the question, as the Holy Spirit had instructed. Then, he and Gianna would have talked, and he would have thrown a party and proposed before their friends and family. But, no, he was eager to alleviate the fear and uncertainty in her eyes after their date. She didn't trust easily, and the last thing he wanted was for her not to trust what was happening between them. He had surmised she was a runner and he didn't want to lose her.

Last night after she had eaten, she kept having bile reflux, causing her heartburn. He had called Lissan and told her to let his father know that Gianna needed medical help. When his father arrived and checked her out, Gianna told him that she didn't usually have that kind of health issue. His father gave her medication and encouraged her to see her primary care doctor to ensure she wasn't developing Gastroesophageal Reflux Disease.

After his father had left, Gianna found it difficult to sleep, so Carter didn't want to leave her alone. He'd sat at her bedside and watched over her. He didn't realize he'd dozed off until he heard a gentle knocking at the door. Not wanting anything to disturb Gianna, he had raced to the door.

It was his mother.

He didn't let her into the room but instead, stepped out the door to speak with her. He hadn't started talking before Paxton and Rylan joined them. He briefly explained that Gianna wasn't feeling well and that his father had given her medication, and she was sleeping. Of course, they were all concerned and indicated that she would be in their prayers.

He had to level with them.

Carter ran a hand over his head, as he'd told them, "She found out I'm ReTrac, and she wants to end our engagement." He felt something squeezing his heart as he remembered seeing her engagement ring on the nightstand. But even as his heart began to flop back and forth, he had noticed their troubled expressions.

His mother recovered first.

"God will fix this, Carter," she said. "I know He will."

They encouraged him, and after they left, he went back to the spot he'd occupied at Gianna's bedside. He trained his gaze on her and tried not to pay too much attention to the shimmering of her engagement ring under the dim light from the lamp on the nightstand. He was happy that she was still sleeping peacefully.

He kneeled at her bedside and began to pray quietly.

He did not know when he fell asleep, but he awoke when he felt fingers urgently tugging his hand. It was Gianna, desperate for his attention to get her to the bathroom. He scooped her in his arms and quickly moved her. He watched as she tried to vomit, but nothing came. She was shaking so much, he had to hold her.

His eyes welled but he blinked rapidly because he didn't want her to think that he pitied her. It just broke his heart to see her like this. Eventually, he'd taken her back to bed, and propped her against the pillows. But as she slept, she would roll onto her side and start coughing. He was tired of seeing her suffering, so as soon as she fell asleep again, he'd sneaked into her bed and snaked his hand around her shoulders to hold her in place. Before long, she'd wrapped an arm around his torso.

The light pressing of her body against his and the sporadic soft moans that came from her lips made him realize she was relishing the warmth emanating from their bodies.

Dear God, the struggle had been real… all night long. With no heed to the storms raging within, he wished he could wave a white flag and surrender to the blossoming urges of nature. He needed a Plan B. Then he remembered his perpetual Plan A—prayer.

He prayed.

And prayed some more.

He didn't know when, but in the end, he too fell asleep.

But on this Sunday morning, he knew he had to come up with a game plan, or he would lose Gianna. That thought made him hold her tighter, and she reacted, mirroring his action. His heart rate quickened as her warm breath tickled his chest. *I can't*....

Just then, she lifted her head and stared at him.

He watched as several emotions crisscrossed her face.

"Hi," he said softly, noticing that her eyes were slightly red from last night's angry tears.

She didn't return his greeting but instead attempted to move away from him.

His hands held her in place. "Not until you thank me for being a great caregiver."

"Ca-Carter...."

She paused, and he knew she was distracted by the heat radiating between them.

She made a second attempt to detach herself from him, but he still held her. When her body grew pliant and limp, she looked at him with contempt and pushed out, "Thanks."

At his eyebrow lift, she added, "I appreciate what you did. I'm feeling better."

"I'm glad you're feeling better. My medical classes didn't go to waste."

The expression in her gaze was hard. Distant.

"I need to get going," she said.

"I want a little kiss as a gift."

Her body trembled. "Gift? I told you a kiss is not a *gift*."

"You're focusing on the wrong word. Kiss me before Lissan comes to check on you."

She frowned, then rolled her eyes. "You need to get out of my bed."

He refused to move.

"Have you lost your mind? I'm not kissing you. I don't even like you right now." Her expression iced over.

"That's not what your body is saying."

"Carter, please, I don't want Lissan to find us in this position."

"I don't mind."

She swallowed hard, assessed the situation, then moved towards his face.

His heart thudded with need as her mouth hovered above his. He watched as her lips came closer, then he felt her sweet peck.

She lifted her head, her eyes hoping he was satisfied.

He was. Almost.

He felt his brows draw together. "That was not a kiss. That was a peck." He pecked her lips, and she let out a sharp, aching gasp. "I'll show you the difference."

"Carter…."

He caressed her back, and she arched against him as if she wanted more of the delicious sensations she was feeling.

His chest heaved.

"We need to get up," she begged in a strained whisper.

But even as she spoke, he knew she didn't want to leave his arms.

She tried again. "Lissan could be here any—"

"You're right," he remarked. "Let's get ready."

Gianna blinked rapidly. "O-okay," she replied, her breath laboring.

Then as if claiming reality, she hastily slipped off his chest and glanced at him.

He couldn't read her expression, but her face was flushed and her hair disheveled.

He rose and picked up the jacket, vest, and bow tie from the bed bench. "I'll ask Lissan to set up breakfast for us in the upstairs nook. Is an hour good for you? We'll leave after breakfast."

"Yes, I'll be ready within the hour," she responded, looking acutely embarrassed before looking away.

"Gia," he called for her attention.

She looked at him, tears welling.

"I love you, and I want to marry you," he told her.

He didn't wait for a response, but he felt her eyes on his back as he left her room.

CHAPTER 43

An hour later, Gianna listened as Carter explained his lack of transparency while they ate breakfast. Neither one of them had eaten much of the delicious meal. She was ready to leave and he was bent on getting back in a right relationship with her.

"I intended to talk with you about ReTrac after Mom's party, but I got carried away. I wanted to reassure you of my love, and honestly, I didn't think the fact that I was ReTrac would have made much of a difference. ReTrac was birthed out of my ability to speak without stammering. As I told you, I was shy and withdrawn as a child so I would spend time reading, then I started writing. Around seven years ago, the Lord placed it in my spirit to write the Seven Brides series. I didn't want to write the series for many reasons, but I'm glad I did. The books released me to the possibility of loving again."

He looked at her to make sure she was listening.

She was.

"For me, writing is a ministry. I don't want to be in the spotlight. All my royalty checks go to my foundation, and that money is spent mainly on autoimmune disease research."

"That's all good, Carter, but what you did to me was not right."

"I'm sorry. I should have told you that I am ReTrac. I made a grave error in judgment, in keeping something so important from you, especially when it affects you directly. I hope you can find it in your heart to forgive me."

When she didn't immediately respond, he gazed at her. The sincerity in his eyes and the worry lines etched in his eyebrows pulled at her heartstrings, but she pushed on.

"To be blunt, you lied to me. And why did your mother have to visit Tallahassee when I was there? Was she

273

planning to threaten me? What if we didn't hit it off? I shudder to think about that." Her brows furrowed. "How did she manage to get a seat beside me on the airplane?"

"I hate to say this, but that's Mom for you. I didn't know of her plan."

"I see." Gianna's mouth thinned into a tight line. "It amazes me that betrayal always comes from those who are closest."

She heard his sharp intake of breath and watched a vein throbbing at his temple. And though he hadn't commented, she knew she'd hurt him. Somehow, she felt bad about that.

"I need time, Carter. I need to take a step back."

He didn't speak, but he was staring ahead.

That was okay with her, though; she needed to breathe.

Carter rose. "I'll move my stuff to the vehicle, and then I'll return for yours."

"Thanks," she replied stiffly.

Without another word, he exited the room.

Over an hour later, Carter pulled into Gianna's driveway, and she all but jumped out of the Navigator and kissed the earth. Relief was in sight.

While he took out her luggage, she disarmed the alarm from her cell phone.

In quietness, they walked to the porch and entered her home. Gianna put her purse, cell phone, and keys on the coffee table while Carter placed her luggage nearby.

They eyed each other, then she looked away.

"Thanks for bringing me home," Gianna said, feeling the need to break the uncomfortable silence.

"Gia—"

"Carter, please, I can't do this right now."

She moved towards the front door, in the hopes that he would follow.

He did.

She couldn't look at him when she opened the front door. "Take care of yourself, Carter."

He stalled.

Still, she didn't look at him.

"Take care of yourself, too," he said quietly, before walking through the door.

Gianna watched as he drove away from her home, then locked the door. She held on to the doorknob as a sense of loss shrouded her. *It's best to let go of this disaster*, she told herself.

The drive home with Carter had been uncomfortable. The silence in the vehicle bordered on oppressive after he got tired of her one-word responses to anything he had to say. He'd even dared to mention the heat that flared between them earlier that morning, before she'd chased him out of her bed.

Her mind might be troubled, but her body knew exactly what it wanted. Mentally, she scolded her body for betraying her. She had to admit that their little encounter begged many questions—questions she refused to acknowledge or, worse, answer.

Her body had better be under subjection.

Now, she was glad to be back in her zone.

She walked to the large sofa, and sat, staring mindlessly before her.

I can't believe I let myself trust those people.

All pretenders.

She rolled her eyes as she remembered their concerned faces—Henry, Nora, Paxton, Rylan, Celia, and Lissan—staring back at her and Carter as they left the estate. Nora had the nerve to hug her and whisper, "I'm sorry." It took the love of God not to push her away. *Hypocrite! Planning to use me to benefit your family.* Gianna had managed to keep her mouth shut.

No matter what they all said or communicated with their expressions, the McIntosh family could not be trusted, not one of them.

Without a doubt, she would be giving Carter back the engagement ring and bracelet. After they had breakfast, while Carter was moving their luggage to his vehicle, she'd called for Lissan and asked her to take Nora's necklace to her. Then, she decided that she would put herself aside and return the jewelry Carter had given her to him. To that end, she'd put the ring back in its case and dropped it along with the bracelet into a small black velvet bag.

When Carter had returned for her, she had attempted to give the jewelry back to him. He'd refused to take it.

"You shouldn't make important decisions when you're upset."

His words.

He wanted too much out of her.

She made sure he'd noticed her frustration before dropping the bag back into her purse.

Her eyes filled with tears as she reflected how happy she had been only hours ago.

I keep attracting the wrong sort.

Don't think like that.

You don't want those people in your life.

"Stop!" she thundered.

She had had enough. Things may not have gone according to plan, but she would live to fight again. She reached for her cell phone on the coffee table and selected the YouTube app to search for a fave, "This Is a Move." When she found it, she touched play and watched as Brandon Lake and Tasha Cobbs Leonard sang. A few minutes later, she placed the phone on the table.

She was meditating on the song when her doorbell sounded. She paused the video and headed for the front

276

door. She had texted Kamala before leaving the McIntosh's home. Though she hadn't mentioned exactly what was happening, her bestie had heard her silent cry for help. Kamala had said that she and Reyon had an engagement after church, but she would slip away as soon as she could.

Gianna was about to open the door when she sensed a check in her spirit. She looked through the peephole and pulled back.

Nora McIntosh was staring back at her, dabbing her eyes.

This is unexpected, and incredibly awkward.
Why is she here?
What's with the tears?

Gianna exhaled loudly and opened the door, but not enough to let her in. "Nora?"

"I'm sorry to visit without calling, but I was wondering if I could have a moment of your time."

"Now is not a good time."

"I know, but this won't take long. I was waiting for Carter to leave."

Gianna sighed. "Did you follow us here?"

"Actually, Dennis—you remember my chauffeur—he remembered where you lived."

Gianna looked to the left of Nora and saw her black Cadillac Escalade parked in the driveway. "I see."

"Please, can I come in? I'll be quick."

Gianna stepped back and allowed her in.

Nora waited until she closed the door.

Gianna waved her over to the sofa in the living room.

Nora perched on the edge of the small sofa with her burnt-orange purse on her lap while Gianna took a seat on the large sofa. She observed Nora as she prepared to speak. She looked classy in a pair of black pants and an orange blouse.

"I'm deeply sorry for not being upfront with you about who I am. I'm very fond of you." She laughed a little. "My entire family and house staff are fond of you. I was hoping you would find it in your heart to forgive me."

"Nora, I really don't know what to say. My life for the last few weeks or so has been a lie. I was on a temporary high, so I need to regroup and get me back."

A look of guilt gathered in Nora's eyes. "It was not a lie, Gianna. I'm sorry; I didn't mean to hurt you or Carter."

"Why did you feel the need to visit Tallahassee? To threaten me?" Gianna put up a hand as Nora opened her mouth. "Please don't deny it. I'm not sure why, though."

"I want to make excuses, but I won't. It's in my nature, Gianna. I wasn't planning to hurt you, I just wanted to talk with you."

"Talk? You mean to make sure I understand how connected you are in this city, so I would never hold another job if I didn't continue editing ReTrac's books."

Nora exhaled loudly. "Yes, but now I can see the folly of it all. I'm so sorry, Gianna. I'm deeply sorry, but please don't punish Carter for my mistake. He didn't know the plan because I manage that aspect of his book business. He was planning to be in Tallahassee the following week, but I played the mother card on him and got him to come earlier because you would be there. His love for you is real. He had already fallen for you before he discovered who you were."

"I don't know, Nora. He heard me going on and on about ReTrac and didn't say anything."

"He would have to explain that part to you, but please give him another chance."

"I forgive you all, but I'm afraid I won't be comfortable having a relationship with any of you."

A sob escaped Nora, and Gianna felt a pang of sympathy for her.

"I'm not trying to be difficult. I can't right now," Gianna hastened to say, making movements that their conversation was over. Then, she remembered something. "Can you hold on a minute?"

Nora nodded, then dabbed her eyes.

Gianna reached for her purse on the coffee table. She pulled out the small bag with the jewelry and handed it to Nora.

She took it.

"Please give that to Carter for me."

Nora's lips parted as realization dawned. "Is this what I think it is? You should give it back to him yourself."

"I tried. Please give it to him."

"Don't do that to him, Gianna. It will break his heart."

Gianna stood. "You mean like he broke mine."

"Gianna, please." Nora's eyes welled, and she stood, too. "Probably, I wouldn't beg for any of my other children, but Carter is my heartbeat. He has been through so much, but he's still standing. Carter's whole life is a miracle. His life led me to the Lord. I'm not perfect, but God knows I'm a far cry from where I started. I had nothing when Henry found me. When I look back, I see God at work in my life."

Found me, echoed loudly in Gianna's ear. *Oh, God, I need relief from this pressure.*

Nora sighed and tried again. "It has been a long time since I've seen two people in love with each other. You were in such sync when you both sang. It was beautiful. I cried, cried tears of joy. You both deserve happiness."

"Nora, I'm sorry. I need some time. Right now, I can't differentiate between the truth and the lies."

279

"Okay," Nora said, her eyes bouncing all over the room. "Thanks for seeing me."

"You're welcome."

They walked in silence to the front door, and Gianna pulled it open and stood back.

She felt Nora looking at her, but she didn't look in her direction.

"If you ever need to talk…." Nora offered.

"Goodbye, Nora."

"Bye," Nora said, moving through the door.

Gianna made sure she got to her chauffeur safely before closing the door.

CHAPTER 44

Lord, everything hurts, even breathing. Carter gulped several breaths on the sofa in his living room. As feelings of hopelessness consumed him, he wept, choking moans leaving his quivering lips. Half an hour later, his burst of grief came to an end. Eyes heavy, he stared ahead at nothing in particular. *Have I lost her?* He'd called and texted Gianna several times, but she did not respond.

Oddly unsettling.

On Monday, he'd call Rylan and Allena Young, his assistant, to let them know he was taking a few days off. He had to get his emotions in check before he faced the world. It had only been two days since news of his engagement broke in one of the city's newspapers—under the title "Another eligible bachelor off the market." He'd received many congratulatory texts, emails, and voicemails about his recent engagement. He hadn't looked online at the article, but from the messages, he surmised that there were a few pictures of him and Gianna at his mother's party. He didn't know where to begin to explain that his happily-ever-after had been short lived. That he had become an instant enemy to Gianna.

Painful.

The day he had driven away from her home, unrest raged in his splintered heart. He'd pulled off the road near her home for many reasons that day....

His heart was aching.

His eyes were burning.

Everything was a blur.

Mentally, he was losing control. Running around. Inwardly screaming. Panicking. He was having difficulty accepting that he'd come to the end of the beautiful journey....

As he sat in his vehicle, he'd felt his body being lifted off the ground and spiraling towards a black hole of humiliation that had opened just for him. His heart crushed; he had struggled hard to regain himself. He stared through the windshield, pondering and seeing the ugly shadows of yesteryear.

Unforgiveness.

Anger.

Sorrow.

Then, hollow laughter. The sounds came from everywhere.

Later at home, he tried to get a grip on his emotions. He had come too far with the Lord to turn back now. For sure, he'd shed one too many tears, and his sob-fest could not go on forever. He had to leave the darkness behind, even though uncertainty was beating at the door of his heart. He had to trust God to take him through this period of his life. He had to keep the faith, for God had been good to him. He had many testimonies to prove that.

Now, he needed to come up with a plan to get himself out of this rut.

His cell phone buzzed, and he located it on the sofa beside him and looked at the text message.

Mom: *Remember, you promised to come to dinner. If you don't, we'll be on your doorstep.*

A tiny smile curved his lips. His mother was bent on trying to fix everything, 'since it was all her fault.' Yet, he couldn't blame her because he should have done the right thing from day one when he'd found out who Gianna was. Plus, his mother had advised him several times to come clean with Gianna.

Carter texted back: *Yes, Mom, I'll be there.*

282

His mother had been the bearer of devastating news when she'd handed him the engagement ring and bracelet he'd given to Gianna. He could hardly bear to look at the jewelry after he'd taken such care in selecting them. He wanted to be big-mad, but when he saw the tears and anguish in his mother's eyes, he held his emotions in check and asked her to keep them until....

His voice had trailed off, and his mother had filled in, "I will, son."

His phone rang, pulling Carter back to the present. He dreaded hearing the phone ring, especially when the call was coming from family members because he knew what the call would be about—the breakup.

Insert blank stare.

The call was from Rylan. He hoped all was well at the office. Still, he cut the call off and texted Rylan.

Carter: *Not in the mood to talk, bro.*
Rylan: *Cut the crap. I'm at your door. Don't make me use my key.*

The muscles in Carter's back tightened. *Here we go.* He glanced around the living room for telltale signs of his mental agony.

Nothing.

He hadn't done much of anything since his relationship had crumbled. He wiped his eyes with the back of his hands. *No doubt, bloodshot.* He sighed. There's no bliss in being alone.

He texted back: *Use your key.*

Soon, Rylan sat across from him. Instead of asking about his red eyes, Rylan was eyeing him as if he was hiding something from him.

"What's up?" Carter asked, breaking the silence. The fragility of his voice surprised him, and he cleared his throat.

"You tell me. The woman you love walks out of your life, and you're silent."

Carter looked away. "What else is there to do, bro?"

"First thing, you can't hide away. The family supports you one hundred percent."

"Who's hiding?" Carter knew he sounded defensive. "I only need a moment to figure out my next step. Anyway, I'll be at dinner later."

"You don't need to have it all figured out, you know. Your heart is involved, so take your time." Rylan exhaled loudly. "You two are beautiful together, I can tell you that. On the night of Mom's party, I felt my zeal returning as I played. It was miraculous, bro. I hadn't played like that in forever." Excitement lit Rylan's gaze. "I can't wait for Saturday's rehearsal. Tell no one, but I started practicing 'So Will I.'"

"Now, that's a first." Carter tried to drum up joy. "Good for you."

"It's one of your favorite Hillsong songs, but if you don't mind, I will play while you sing."

Oh, man. Rehearsal. For the first time in forever, Carter wished he didn't have to attend. Worse, he had to be out front leading praise and worship on Sunday. He groaned mentally, but told Rylan, "You seem to have it all worked out."

"Thanks for the shouts of joy."

Rylan's voice snapped him back to the present. "What do you want, Ry? I'm glad your zest for music has returned."

"Now, hold up. I don't want a fight. I'm only trying to be there for you as you've been for me."

Carter remained silent.

"Don't start second-guessing what God has done," Rylan said. "I'm nowhere near your spirituality, but even I know that God pulled you both together. All I'm saying is keep the faith. God does not make mistakes, so let's not declare anything unless it is pure, true, and... er... whatsoever else the Scripture says?"

Carter chuckled softly. "Whatsoever things are true, honest, just, pure, lovely, and of good report."

"Right. If there be any virtue, and if there be any praise, think on these things."

"How are you coming here to minister to me and don't know your Scripture?" Carter teased.

"You got the essence of it."

"All jokes aside, thanks, bro. I appreciate you. Rough season, so I'm holding on to God's promises."

"It's the best thing to do," Rylan said quietly. "And I'm glad I got something right."

"What?"

"I pegged you as someone who would go the distance. I don't think you should give up on your relationship with Gianna. You're good for each other."

Carter let out a breath but said nothing.

"After Mom's party, I did a lot of thinking," Rylan said. He clasped his hand and rested his elbows on his legs.

"Thinking?" Carter's eyebrows climbed. "Careful. Don't hurt your brain."

"Whatever. I was thinking that I'm glad Lee-Ann left me."

"What? I'm sorry, bro."

"I was a little cut up because I like her a lot. I don't know if I love her, on some level. Anyway, I'm definitely not ready to be married. When I told her that, she said that

285

she wished I were standing before her so she could strangle me."

Carter's brow furrowed. "What? That's serious. Be careful."

"It gets worst. Strangle me with people watching. Yep, she didn't care."

"Whoa."

"That right there told me she wasn't right for me. A Christian woman. Anyway, that's that. I need to evaluate my choices in women. When I looked at the relationship that you and Gianna share, I know I'm not in love with her like that."

Carter knitted his brow. "Careful now. Love is not a look."

"Believe me, I know. I don't have that deep soul-connection that I sensed that you and Gianna have."

"That's a good description. I can't believe this is where we're at."

"It's not over until the Lord says so."

"Bro, she's carrying a lot. I don't know if I haven't added to it."

"God must have placed you in her life to help her heal. He knew you would be able to handle it. She's talented for sure. It's a shame to hide a talent like that."

"True."

Rylan chuckled. "Do you know my first thought when I saw the two of you together? You look alike." He snorted. "You know how they say couples look alike as they grow older in their relationship—you guys already look alike. You looked great together and so happy. Not to mention the joy your relationship brought to the family. I, for one, feel hopeful."

Carter released a blast of air from his mouth to release the pressure he was feeling in his heart.

They were both quiet for a moment.

"Thanks, man," Carter said.

Suddenly, Carter remembered that he'd glimpsed Savannah McKenzie in Tallahassee. For reasons he couldn't come up with, he'd never mentioned it to Rylan.

"Don't be upset when I ask this—did you feel a soul-connection to Savannah?"

Rylan considered for a moment. "That woman makes me mad every time I think about her."

"That we know, so answer the question."

"Yes."

"Thought so."

"Truth be told, I haven't felt that kind of love towards any woman since that woman disappeared with a piece of my heart."

"That woman. Her name is Savannah McKenzie. Maybe you still love her."

"The only thing I know is that it still makes me crazy when I hear her name. She just walked out of my life. Who does that?"

Carter was glad to take his mind off his own issue. "She's the reason you went rogue. Are you planning to break the heart of every woman who comes in contact with you?"

"Man, please. I keep thinking that Mom had something to do with her disappearance. She was way too heartbroken for me. We all know she hated Savannah."

"You said her name. Things are looking up."

"Whatever."

"Mom can be ruthless, but do you think she would go that far?"

"You know she could and would. She was not nice to anyone back in the day. She has changed somewhat, but she still has that ugly side as you saw with Gianna. But it seems she likes, and I would even say loves, Gianna. On the other hand, she has no love for Olivia."

"True, she loves Gianna. Livi is great. I'm not sure why Mom doesn't like her. Pax had that *talk* with Mom, so now she treats Livi cordially."

"Pax fixed that. *Quickly*." Rylan gave a short laugh. "I was trying to wait on Pax to say this, but I think he'll be okay with me telling you… you may be wondering how Gianna found out that you're ReTrac. I think that was my fault."

"It doesn't matter now. I should have told her. Anyway, what happened?"

"Me and Allison were in the formal dining room, chatting. You know Allison, always making her rounds with us men, depending on her mood. Since you're off the market, Allison decided she's crushing on me. Later in the conversation, she mentioned you and your side hustle. She didn't say ReTrac, but Gianna must have put it all together."

"Was Gia in the dining room with you guys?"

"No. Pax told me that he was heading to the kitchen while Mom's party was still in swing, when he saw Gianna standing near the dining room door. She must not have heard Pax coming down the passageway until he was near her, because he said that she turned and charged into him. After that, she was literally racing up the passageway."

"It doesn't matter now," Carter said, looking away.

"I'm sorry, man."

They both heard the rattling of a key in the front door and waited for Paxton to enter the living room.

As soon as he came into view, Rylan remarked, "You're going to lose the right to that key. You did not follow protocol."

Paxton gave him a blank stare as he walked forward. "Bro," he bumped fist with Carter, then rolled his eyes at Rylan before giving him a fist bump. "You're insisting on staying relevant in this brotherhood, I see."

Paxton dropped into the far corner of the sofa that Carter was sitting on.

Rylan rose swiftly. "Who you talking to?" His inner gangster was playfully on display as he beat his chest. "You don't want none of this."

Laughter erupted from Carter and Paxton.

"I'm good, I know," Rylan said, amidst the laughter, before plopping back on the sofa he'd occupied.

"You'll never change," Paxton goaded him. "Throwback thug."

"You mean wanna-be thug," Carter taunted.

"Y'all just jealous. Change? Only if I can improve on greatness." He pointed to Carter. "Some are born great." Next, he eyed Paxton. "Some achieve greatness." His eyes floated from Paxton to Carter and then back to Paxton before he sprawled deeply on the chair and pointed at his chest. "And some have greatness thrust upon them,"

Paxton responded in a monotone. "William Shakespeare would be proud that you're not afraid of the greatness that was thrust upon you."

"Don't hate," Rylan said, feigning hurt. "I own my greatness."

"That's abundantly clear." Carter shook his head. Cocky and arrogant. Rylan was good at what he did, and everyone knew it.

Rylan cleared his throat. "I've been thoughtful of everyone's position in the realm of the great, so I've kept my greatness under wraps. I'm basically a saint."

Laughter burst from Carter and Paxton.

"Humility looks good on you," Carter harassed him.

"Well, I give honor to God," Rylan said. "He's the greatest, and I take all my cues from Him."

"Amen. I like that," Paxton said, throwing Rylan a high-five.

"Amen to that," Carter responded. He stared at Rylan and observed that Paxton was doing the same. Whatever was going on with Rylan was good. *At least something good is happening around here.*

Paxton looked at Carter. "And speaking of The Great, that's why I'm here. We need to pray for you concerning Gianna. And we need to pray for Mom." He lifted a hand as Carter opened his mouth to speak. "I know you should have had a certain conversation with Gianna, but Mom needs to leave well enough alone and stop trying to get her way in everything. We need to break that chain over her life. And somehow, I don't feel an alarm in my spirit concerning all we need to pray about. In fact, I *hear* the chains falling."

"Amen," Carter and Rylan said in unison.

Carter's gaze swung between Paxton and Rylan; they were waiting for his agreement. Both of his brothers knew that he had a soft spot for their mother.

Carter nodded.

They moved to kneel at the coffee table and reached for each other's hands.

For a moment, Carter listened as his two brothers worshipped God. Then, his heart soared. He closed his eyes and prayed silently. *Jesus Christ—You are my rest, my peace, my dwelling place. God, You're the center of my joy, my delight. All that's good and perfect comes from You. Father, please forgive me for not listening when You said that I should wait on your guidance to propose to Gia. I know you're a God of second chances so I'm asking for another chance to get it right. I'm depending on You, Lord, because only you can fix this situation.*

Carter quieted his spirit as Paxton began to pray.

CHAPTER 45

Slouching against the sofa, Gianna hugged her knees tightly to her chest as she looked defiantly at Brooklyn. Brooklyn was watching her, annoyance in her gaze. Gianna had refused to take her calls, choosing instead to respond by text. She did the same for Kamala. Well, they were in a good position because she wasn't taking Nora's and Carter's calls or texts.

Not taking Kamala's calls was for a different reason—she didn't want her sorry situation to affect her best friend's wedding, which was four weeks away. She was hoping that Kamala would have turned up this past Sunday, but she'd called to say Reyon had plans for her. Gianna had faked her excitement so that her bestie would have a great time out with her fiancé.

Still, Brooklyn and Kamala knew something was wrong. When they had threatened to visit, she had texted to say she was fine but busy adjusting….

Kamala bought it, but Gianna knew it was more that she was busy with her wedding planning. To date, Kamala was dying to hear what had happened at Nora's party. She'd even texted the link to an article regarding Gianna's and Carter's engagement.

Brooklyn knew better, so she came knocking, and when Gianna did not respond to her doorbell, Brooklyn used the key that she'd given her for emergencies. When she opened the front door, Gianna's expression had her quickly declaring, "This is an emergency."

"Carter hurt your feelings, and this is what you do?" Brooklyn questioned. "Hide from the world?"

Gianna's aggravation rose to an all-time high. "He told you?"

"Yes, he's concerned about you. He wanted me to check on you. He said you were not responding to any of his calls or texts."

Gianna pushed air through her mouth. "What does he care? And for the record, I'm not hiding."

"Well, if this isn't hiding, then—"

"He lied to me!" Gianna exploded. "You of all people know how I hate that. How am I to feel comfortable with someone like that? What am I going to say when I introduce him to people? Oh, I get it." She jumped from the sofa, and in dramatic fashion, proclaimed, "Hello, everyone! It's my pleasure to introduce you to someone you all know in one way or another. He is the co-owner of McIntosh Homes and the son of Henry and Nora McIntosh of McIntosh Corporation. Ladies, this heartthrob with light-brown eyes is also the renowned international bestselling author ReTrac. Oh, and my fiancé. By the way, he's a liar." She plopped down on the sofa.

"Gigi," Brooklyn patiently called for her attention. "I'm speaking to you as your second mother and your friend. I've always looked out for your best interest."

"Best interest? I think you *all* played me."

Brooklyn's eyes blazed. "I'm ignoring that. Sometimes, I think you don't want to be happy. Maybe deep down, you think you shouldn't be loved, because of what happened to your parents. As I have told you many times, you were a child when the accident happened. You cannot go on punishing yourself for something you had no control over. With your current situation, as with the challenges of your past, you're lifting it, carrying it, and using it as a shield."

Gianna huffed.

"Let me finish. And the results are evident in your life—Isolation. Separation. Desolation. Every time someone gets close to you, you push them away."

"Really?" Gianna's brows furrowed deeply.

"You have to let someone in, Gigi."

"You mean like you're letting Phil in?" Gianna smirked.

"This is not about Phil and me. It's about your need to let go of your past hurt and trust God to lead you into your destiny. It's about you dreaming again and taking up your rightful position on this earth."

Brooklyn pulled to the edge of the sofa. "Don't you see you're a Rockstar? I was so excited to see you singing. You sang with Carter as if you were made to sing together. I cannot explain the beautiful sentiments that you guys sent into the audience. We were elated, but we knew we came up short, especially in the love department." She looked away, before quietly telling her, "You both helped me to make my decision concerning a relationship with Phil. We're keeping it quiet because we're still working out the details of his separation from BMP."

"I'm glad for you and Phil. But I'm disappointed that you didn't tell me that Carter was ReTrac. All this time, you knew and didn't say a word. You were only watching your bottom line."

"I'm sorry you're disappointed. I tried to warn you several times, but I was bound by his contract with BMP. As you well know, it has a non-disclosure clause. When I realized what occurred in Tallahassee, I spoke with Nora." Brooklyn looked to the ceiling before looking at Gianna. "That's putting it mildly. We had a blow-up. She assured me that Carter didn't know about her plan and that you two were already into each other before she could make the introduction."

Brooklyn eyed Gianna. "Even so, I had to be sure. I arranged a meeting with Carter after he came back from Tallahassee. He didn't divulge much but told me he had a growing interest in you. I asked him to talk with you about

ReTrac, and he said that he would. It was during that meeting that he told me that since you're taking on a new job, he would release you from the contract as his editor but to make sure that you recommend another editor for him."

Gianna's heartbeat gave a happy dance, but she still wasn't satisfied. "Why didn't he tell me he's ReTrac?"

"That he would have to explain himself. I surmised as with any man, he didn't want you to get him confused with his pseudonym. Now that you have both, shouldn't you be happy?"

"Happy to be in a lie? All this time, there was never a hint that you knew Carter."

"And I wouldn't say that I know him. I know of him for the business of ReTrac. The second time I saw Carter was when he'd come back from Seattle around two weeks after you guys were back from Tallahassee. That was the time he was trying to get back into your good graces. I asked Maya to help him. I also heard from him the other day when he was in Seattle. He called to let me know he intended to propose to you at some time in the week following Nora's party. This time he asked for my permission to marry you. I said yes, but I was mad at him for not telling you about ReTrac. Having been married, I knew the importance of starting right, so that's why I tried to pull you away. You're both headstrong, so I didn't have a fighting chance. I used my sources to find out about Carter's character, and I loved what I'd discovered. Yes, he has all his ducks in a row."

Gianna's eyes shifted to the ground.

"This is off the record," Brooklyn stated. "Carter is a true philanthropist. All of ReTrac's royalty checks go to Carter's private foundation. His foundation mainly gives donations to autoimmune disease research, especially lupus. As you know, his late fiancée died from lupus. Also, McIntosh Homes is in partnership with the University of

294

Central Florida to teach free courses in architecture to under-privileged students."

Okay-okay, so he's Mr. Perfect. A tiny gallop occurred in Gianna's heartbeat. "I see," was all she could come up with.

Brooklyn wasn't finished. "You've used your perceived role in the tragedy of your past to keep you alive, but I dare you to let *love* keep you alive. The love of God and the love of a good man. I dare you to dream again and live your dream."

Gianna's gaze bounced all over the living room, but when Brooklyn spoke again, she was forced to look at her.

"'There is no fear in love; but perfect love casts out fear, because fear involves torment. But he who fears has not been made perfect in love.'"

Gianna's eyes welled, for she remembered Carter quoting her the same Scripture the night he'd proposed. She dabbed her eyes with her fingertips.

"Love is a powerful emotion. That I can tell you." Brooklyn sounded like she was having an internal dialogue, only out loud. "I'm sure you can find billions of reasons to exit your relationship with Carter, but there is always that one reason that won't let you go."

"Sounds like you have a personal experience."

Brooklyn exhaled loudly, and her usually hardened facial expression softened. "You bet I do." But before Gianna could celebrate her victory, Brooklyn struck. "I'm not sure why Carter proposed before his mother's party; if he hadn't, you both wouldn't be in this position." She eyeballed Gianna. "I know you had a date. I can only presume that something special happened that night."

Something special? "Wha-what? No. Nooo," Gianna stammered when she realized what Brooklyn was hinting at.

"Don't sound so surprised. Unplanned activities can happen when two people are in love, especially when the two people are as in love with each other as you two are."

"Not that it's any of your business, but we're waiting until our wedding day."

"Thank you, Jesus! And when is the wedding?"

"I told him later this year," Gianna said quietly.

Brooklyn smiled at her. "I'm ready."

"I can't. I don't—"

"I've been praying for you but I'm going to suggest that you go before the Lord and lay it all at His feet. You should at least give Carter a chance to fully explain and also talk to him about what's on your heart. After that, whatever you decide, I'll still be your second mother."

Gianna laughed a little even though it didn't reach her eyes. "As if I'd let you abdicate your position."

"I like that, daughter," Brooklyn said, rising. Hands akimbo, she landed Gianna a pointed look. "And don't make me have to fight Nora McIntosh for your attention."

Gianna had to laugh.

CHAPTER 46

Gianna paced back and forth before the large sofa in her living room, excited about Carter's arrival. She was sure he would be earlier than she expected. Her eyes bounced around the room for no good reason. *Breathe,* she urged herself.

Yesterday, after Brooklyn had left her home, Gianna had come face-to-face with the vast wilderness in her heart, and she longed for peace. She had dubbed it her come-to-Jesus-moment. She had many reasons for not wanting to be in a relationship with Carter, but again, she had to accept the fact that she had trust issues and a need to protect herself, which was stemming from her childhood trauma.

As the memories of her childhood unfolded, she knew she had to resolve her challenges or risk losing the man she loved. The path before her became clearer, and she caught sight of a new vision—her hopes and dreams of having a family—and it was pleasing in her eyes. There, in the middle of the night, she mentally drew up a plan to reach out to those near and dear to her heart.

Aunt Dorette. Her aunt had been nothing but kind to her, but she'd been too busy missing her parents to see the phenomenal job that she and Uncle Reginald had done in raising her. Gianna knew she'd hurt her aunt's feelings when she left Chicago for college in Tallahassee. She'd had to leave the city that held unpleasant childhood memories. She recalled how her aunt would have the two dozen red roses ready for her to put on her parents' grave every time she was in Chicago.

Next on the list was Brooklyn—for her timely words of encouragement and helping her to stay on the right path.

Of course, the love of her life, Carter, aka ReTrac—the man who had refused to let her go....

She didn't want him to anyway.

Tired but filled with renewed hope, Gianna's mind had filled with images of Carter. Her head had fallen against the pillow, and she'd prayed that he would be hers again.

After putting her situation before the Lord, she had chronicled the things she loved about Carter.

Man of God.

Hard-working.

Talented.

Generous to a fault.

Kind-hearted.

Protective.

Physically fit.

Oh, his smile... gorgeous.

The way he makes my stomach flip when he's near....

Soon, her mind had slowed down, and within minutes, she had been asleep.

At the crack of dawn, Gianna had woken with a smile, ready for the day. She had called Brooklyn. After the initial 'has someone died?' from Brooklyn, Gianna had reassured her that all was well, but she wanted to thank her for being her third mother. Her Aunt Dorette had already filled the place of second mother. They had chit-chatted for a while, and Gianna had shared with her the revelations that the Lord had deposited in her spirit during the night. Brooklyn had been overjoyed.

After she had eaten breakfast, Gianna's call to her aunt had left her just as ecstatic as Brooklyn. Like Brooklyn, her aunt had brushed off her apology, but Gianna knew they were pleased. She'd promised her aunt she would spend more quality time with her and had told her she could visit whenever she liked.

Around nine o'clock, she'd made contact with Carter.

"Good morning, Gianna."

She had ignored his distant tone and the fact that he'd called her Gianna and not Gia. "Good morning, Carter. I was wondering if you're not too busy, later today, if we could talk."

"Sure. I should be available by six. Where do you want to meet?"

"We could meet here, I mean, my home."

A pregnant silence.

"I'll be there," he had finally said.

"Okay, thanks."

With that, he had disconnected the call.

Gianna had stared at the phone in disbelief.

She'd recovered quickly but had to test the temperature of their relationship. She had texted him a pic of them at Lake Ella, and indicated, *One of my faves.*

Carter texted backed, *OK.*

Since then, she knew she had to be ready for their meeting.

The chiming of the doorbell disturbed her thoughts, and she hastened to the door. Through the peephole she saw that it was Carter. Excitement swelled in her heart as she swung the door open.

"Hey! Please come in."

"Hey, Gianna." Carter came through the door and closed it behind him.

Gianna restrained a smile as she took in his navy-blue jeans and a navy button-down shirt that displayed red where the buttons were opened at his neck and at the cuffs, which were rolled up to his elbows.

"Let's talk in the living room," she said, when she realized he was looking at her.

"Sure."

In silence, they walked towards the sofa, and she noticed that he sat on the small sofa. He was mad, she surmised. She sat on the large sofa closest to the one he was sitting in.

"Everything okay?" she ventured, noting he was in professional mode.

"Yes, I'm good."

She eyed him, waiting for him to return the favor. He didn't.

"I'm sorry for not taking your calls or responding to any of your messages," Gianna said. "I had a lot on my mind."

"Okay."

Get to the point. She refused to. Mumbling irritably, "Why are you acting unfriendly, Carter?"

"Unfriendly? I'm not sure how to interpret that. You asked to see me, so here I am."

His voice was sharp. Curt.

Gianna pushed on, but what choice did she have? "I wanted to talk about us."

He frowned. "Us? What us? You ended our relationship."

She suppressed a sigh. "Carter—"

"I have a lot on my plate, so if that's it, I—"

"Carter, please stop being like that. I need clarity…."

"Clarity? About ReTrac?"

She nodded.

His face softened. "I'm going to repeat what I already told you. I'm assuming you were under stress, so you didn't hear me. I intended to talk with you about ReTrac after Mom's party, and before proposing, but I got carried away, wanting to reassure you of my love. I didn't think that me being ReTrac would have made such a difference to you. As I had said, ReTrac was birthed out of my ability to speak without stammering. When I was growing up, because I was embarrassed about my stuttering, I would spend time reading and writing. It was about seven years ago, that the Lord placed it in my spirit to write the Seven Brides series. So that's ReTrac." He looked at her, then admitted, "I knew how much you admired ReTrac, and I didn't want to come up short. I wanted you to love me for me."

"Thanks for sharing that, but for the record, I would have loved you anyway."

He eyed her for a moment. "Thanks. Please forgive my lack of transparency."

"Were you aware that I like Madeira Citrine gemstones?"

"No. I saw your comments at that scene in my manuscript and decided to get the bracelet for you."

"Thanks for that." She watched him gingerly before saying, "I saw you at Restwell Cemetery the other day."

His eyebrows climbed. "You did?"

"Yes. You were having a private moment, so I didn't want to disturb you. I had accompanied Kam to visit her parents' grave."

"I went to put flowers on Kara's grave. Rylan accompanied me. Truth is, I haven't been to Kara's grave since the burial. But I just felt the need to visit. It was time to do so."

"That's a good thing, Carter. I'm glad you were able to do that," she said tenderly.

"Anything else?"

"What about your comment—'I wanted to make sure that the Lord was still holding back the sea'?"

He watched her for a moment, and she could see that he was deliberating whether or not to tell her.

He rubbed a hand down the fabric of his jeans. "As you're aware, I didn't take Kara's death well, and that's putting it mildly. I thank God for my mother, who refused to let me give up on life. It was during that period that she became a Christian because she was beseeching heaven to save me. As I had told you, it took me a while to recover. One night, I was lying in bed, and I must have dozed off because I saw a vision of me singing as I walked through water. The water was clear, and it only covered my feet. I didn't feel afraid. I was singing and moving forward."

He paused to collect his thoughts.

"When I looked straight ahead, I couldn't make out a figure that was standing there, but I saw outstretched arms. That's when I looked to my right and then my left and saw that the Lord was holding back the sea so it wouldn't cover me."

"Praise the Lord," came from Gianna, instinctively.

"It was like the Lord was saying, you're going to make it; no matter what you face, no harm will come to you."

"That's beautiful."

"Thanks. Do you know the song 'Glorious Day' that features gospel artiste, Kristian Stanfill?"

"Yes, I love it."

Carter pulled to the edge of the sofa. "Every time I hear that song, I can't help but think how it mirrored my situation back then. God called my name and I sprung out of that watery grave and rededicated my life to Him. After that, I joined the praise team at church."

Gianna clapped excitedly. "Wow!"

"That was a great season. I felt rejuvenated and I was ready to walk in alignment with God's purpose for my life. I was ready to live again. To trust again. To dream

302

again. It wasn't easy, but I'm far from where I started. I can tell you this for sure—God is a way maker. He will give you peace in the middle of the storm."

"Oh, Carter, that's one of the reasons why I love you—you love the Lord."

"I do." His lips curved into a smile. "I feel like my life has been a series of miracles. It's as if each step I've made has been a strategic move of God. I still marvel when I think how God has lifted me time and time again out of situations and set my feet on solid ground."

"That's amazing," Gianna responded with a smile, gazing tenderly at him. "I apologize for the way I acted and for not giving you a chance to fully explain. Meeting you has had a transformative effect on my life. I can't ever remember feeling this alive. Your life story has given me the courage and tenacity that I need for the journey to overcome my past... and I have even begun to dream again."

She swallowed hard. "Our relationship didn't take long to form. Before I knew it, I was falling for you—and falling hard. That made me edgy, looking for something to go wrong. I couldn't understand our connection. I was becoming more attached to you every day, with every conversation, every smile, every embrace, and every kiss. I couldn't get enough of you. That scared me, and I wanted to run, yet I couldn't, until I learned about ReTrac."

She paused, clutching her hands to her chest, then admitted, "Maybe, subconsciously, I was looking for an excuse to leave our relationship because what we share was too good to be true. Finding out about ReTrac the way I did was overwhelming. I felt like you and your family played me, buttered me up to benefit yourselves. And I was mad at you for not telling me you are ReTrac, especially knowing I'm your editor. I felt you were deceptive." She let out a soft sigh. "I'm glad we have spoken about it though… and I believe I'm good now."

"I'm sorry you felt that way and I'm sorry for not coming clean with you. In retrospect, I should have," Carter said gently.

Her shoulders softened and so did her heart. "That's okay. I understand your perspective."

"Thanks."

They were quiet for a moment.

"Were you able to see your doctor?" Carter asked.

"Yes, earlier this week. I'm fine." She gave a half-smile. "Apparently, a traumatic event brought on the panic attack."

"Sorry about that. I never intended to cause you harm."

"No worries. It happened, and I'm okay."

"I'm glad you're okay," Carter said, rising.

"Where…?" Gianna jumped to her feet.

"I thought we were finished."

"What about our relationship?" she asked bluntly.

His gaze pierced hers. "I don't know. I'm waiting on the Lord."

"What?" Gianna took a step back in surprise.

He did not let up. "We got engaged pretty quickly; maybe it was too quick. I love you enough to let you know that maybe our timing was off."

Her heart dropped to her stomach. "Are you serious?"

"Yes," he replied, shoving his hands in his pants pockets. "Our unexpected connection might be the saving grace to let me know that I can love again and perhaps, what you need to move forward with your life. In this imperfect world, I was hoping that by the grace of God, we would build a family and a ministry. I love you, but I don't need to be with someone who will throw up arms or fall on a sword when trouble hits. Aside from that, I feel that you still have a few deep personal issues to deal with."

Tears blurred Gianna's vision, and she blinked rapidly.

Carter waited.

"Okay," she managed to squeeze out. *Don't do this.*

He pulled his hands from his pockets and moved towards the front door.

Her feet started following before she could process what had just happened.

A hand on the doorknob, he paused. "Are you going to be alright?"

His voice sounded strange.

Gianna nodded, then remembered his back was to her. "Yes, I'll be fine." Her voice sounded braver than she felt.

Carter turned and pulled her into an embrace. "Take care of yourself, Gia."

He released her, opened the door, and closed it behind him.

Dread filling her, Gianna gripped the doorknob and then halted as she felt their connection dissipating. She stared at the door willing Carter to return, but that was short-lived. The roar of the engine told her he was pulling away. Dazed, her legs folded, and she crumbled to her knees.

CHAPTER 47

On Sunday morning, Carter arrived at church earlier than usual. However, he parked in a secluded spot and did not get out of his vehicle. Instead, he spent more quiet time with the Lord. In ten minutes, he had to be in Pastor McCallum's office. The man of God had texted to say that they needed to meet privately before his meeting with the entire praise team.

When he had awoken this morning, Carter had spent some time in prayer concerning praise and worship, which he was slated to lead. He took his position on the praise and worship team as a calling from God, but he wished he didn't have to be out front this morning. He would forge ahead with the understanding that God had blessed him with all spiritual blessings. His parents gave him the middle name Levi, which meant joined in harmony. In the Old Testament, the priestly tribe of Levites descended from Levi, the third son of Leah and Jacob.

"I'm a worshipper," Carter declared boldly. "I'm here, Lord, use me." *Amp up! That's what I'm talking about.*

He'd also prayed for Gianna, even though he was still aching with the sense of loss. He was positive that she should be his wife, yet he felt a check in his spirit. That check told him to wait. Plus, he'd felt the Holy Spirit pressing on his heart to put on the whole armor of God and pray. That he had been doing, especially after reading Ephesians six verses eleven to eighteen, which gave full details about the armor of God.

Last Friday, he hadn't wanted to attend the meeting with her, but he'd had to put himself aside. His lips had twitched into a smile when she'd texted the photo of them at Lake Ella.

It had been hard seeing her again and not being able to relax in her presence or touch her. Seeing her tearing up when he was about to leave her home had torn his heart to pieces. She'd looked broken, shifty-eyed, and uncomfortable. Still, he hadn't wanted to do anything without God's leading. God's grace was on his life, and he would continue to trust God's timing. On his way home, he'd called Brooklyn to ask her to check on Gianna. Around an hour later, she'd texted back to say Gianna was okay. Relief had washed over him.

Carter took his Bible from the passenger seat, switched off the ignition, and exited his vehicle. While locking it, he took a cursory glance down the front of his red shirt, which was tucked into a pair of khaki stretch washed Chino pants. It was summer, so the praise team dressed in casual attire. Satisfied that everything was in place, he made the trek across the parking lot.

Suddenly, he slowed his steps, in his line of sight were his mother and...

"Alley?"

The word shock did not even express the emotions he was experiencing. He and his family had always invited Allison to church, but she hadn't shown up. He was glad that she'd made an effort, and he mentally thanked God.

In a split-second mental debate, Carter decided not to call out to them.

Yesterday, after rehearsal at his parents' home, he'd had that well-needed conversation with his mother and Allison concerning the business of ReTrac. Around the cherry oval oak conference room table in his mother's home office, he'd laid down some ground rules.

In anger, he'd opened his mouth to destroy Allison, and it took the grace of God to hold back the choice words he had wanted to say to her. Truth be told, he had intended to fire her, for she'd bordered on breaking the non-disclosure agreement she had signed relating to ReTrac.

Allison's perfectly sculpted brows had climbed. "My position as—"

He had cut her off and harshly told her, "I will tell you what your position is. You signed an agreement, and if you ever pull a stunt like that again, don't even wait for me to fire you. Resign."

Without another word, Allison had nodded and had begun writing notes.

"And if I find out that you treat Gianna with anything but respect…. Resign," he had added, looking at Allison.

His gaze had swung from Allison to his mother. "We will start holding biweekly meetings. I will send out a meeting invitation to both of you. I'm now going to be fully engaged in the ministry of ReTrac, as I should have been. Also, please copy me on all correspondence concerning ReTrac. We'll talk more at our meetings."

They'd both nodded like bobbleheads.

"Carter," Allison had called for his attention. "I didn't say anything to Gianna. You know this will be one of those she-said situations."

"Fall back in line, Alley," he had commanded. "All you need to do is the role outlined in your contract. Do not communicate with Gianna directly. For now, all correspondence concerning ReTrac should be sent to Brooklyn Morris."

Allison had bitten her lower lip. "Got it. And, for what it's worth, I'm sorry for my role in the… situation."

He'd stared at her for a moment. "Me, too. That's all I have to say. We'll pick up in our first meeting."

"Okay, son."

"Bye then," he'd said.

He had risen, kissed his mother's cheek, and left the room.

As his mother and Allison rounded the corner toward the front of the sanctuary, a smile lit Carter's face. *Thank You, Lord. This is a strong reminder that You're always at work... even when I can't see it.*

In Pastor McCallum's office, Carter sat before his desk listening to him. During the week, he'd shared with his pastor about the breakdown in his relationship with Gianna.

"This is what I hear in my spirit," Pastor McCallum said. "Everything is in place concerning you and Gianna. Trust God's heart. And as you wait, remember Psalm twenty-seven, verse fourteen—'Wait on the Lord: be of good courage, and He shall strengthen thine heart: wait, I say, on the Lord.' Also, be prepared for the moment when God brings you and Gianna together again."

"Thanks, Pastor."

"I know it's a difficult season for you, and you wish you didn't have to lead this morning. But God desires your praise, your *sacrifice* of praise. That means you will have to press past the temporary and reach for the eternal. As you may have sensed in your spirit, God is doing something in Gianna that requires your absence. Go out with a shout of praise as you lead this morning. Let your eyes remain fixed *not* on your situation but on our God, who can deliver you out of it, and work it out to your benefit."

Carter's spirit soared and he smiled at the man of God, whom he'd come to admire and respect. "Sure will, Pastor."

"Thank you." Pastor McCallum returned his smile.

Carter left the office, thanking God for having a Pastor with an on-time word that encouraged and blessed him. Immediately, he decided to switch to more lively songs for praise and worship. He'd sent out the list of songs on Friday night, so he prayed that the praise team and band would be on board with his new song choices.

Some twenty minutes later, microphone in hand, Carter walked to the podium with the praise team behind him.

"I will bless the Lord at all times, His praise shall continually be in my mouth," Carter declared, his voice booming throughout the sanctuary. "We're here to seek the presence of God. We have come to worship Him. We are here to praise him. Come on, church, let's go up with a shout of praise. Hallelujah!"

His excitement was contagious.

"Hallelujah!" the congregation roared.

"The Lord inhabits the praises of His people," Carter stated. "We announce even now that we want what God wants for us. This is a glorious day to praise our Savior."

The air was electrifying and filled with delightful expectation. Exhilaration.

Soaring to new heights, the band was ready, striking up the instrumental to "Glorious Day."

The congregation was eager to begin the lively song.

As Carter sang with passion, the praise team and congregation joined in, creating a jubilant atmosphere. And when the chorus came, cheers erupted as Carter and the praise team began to jump. Some members of the congregation followed suit while others ran from their seats and danced around, demonstrating the words of the song.

Triumphant yells of praise filled the sanctuary.

They celebrated.

"God is giving victory from the ashes of all our situations," Carter proclaimed. With that, he began dancing about. He paused to announce, "Praise is our weapon. Let's raise a hallelujah to the King of kings."

Screams of delight and shouts of adoration filled the sanctuary.

The band started the introduction to "Raise a Hallelujah" by Bethel Music, and the congregation began to holler "Hallelujah!" in what seemed like a crescendo.

Adrenaline pulsed from the praise team to the congregation before spiraling throughout the already splendid ambiance.

"Walls are falling down," Carter announced, lifting a hand in the air, while encouraging the congregation to put all their situations before the Lord. He allowed the congregation to worship for a few minutes before he started the song. Selina Minnott, a member of the praise team, sang the part done by the female lead, and then the entire team performed the chorus. By the time the song ended, he, too, had raised a hallelujah in the midst of his storm.

And as the band played Hillsong Worship's "So Will I," the atmosphere in the sanctuary became still.

Carter looked towards Pastor McCallum for permission before saying, "If you need to come to the altar, please come." His voice cracked into a whisper. "This is a move of God. Come. Come to the altar, people of God."

Pastor McCallum joined him, and they moved to the front of the altar along with other ministers and deacons.

Tears streaming down his face, Carter spoke to those who had gathered. "This morning, we walk by faith and not by sight. We come here not for a show but to meet with Jesus Christ, our Savior and Lord. The weapons of our warfare are not carnal, but mighty through God to the pulling down of strongholds. We serve a mighty God, a God who is able to deliver all that He has promised us."

With a nod of his head, Carter signaled to Pastor McCullum, who took over and began praying for those who were gathered. While Carter sang "So Will I," his eyes

311

wandered the group, which seemed to be growing in number. A smile lit his face when he saw his brother.

Rylan had come to the altar....

CHAPTER 48

Has he given up on us? Gianna's heart quivered at the thought and desperation rose inside her. For the last two days, she had been trying to reach Carter, but he had not replied to any of her calls, texts, or voice messages.

Terrified, she found herself on her knees.

When she rose, she decided to call Nora McIntosh.

"Hi, dear!" Nora answered, sounding like she'd been expecting her call.

Weren't you on my couch a few days ago? Have you forgotten what happened between us? Anyway. "Hi, Nora, I'm trying to reach Carter."

"He's in Seattle. When I spoke with him, he wasn't sure when he'd be back. Did you leave a voicemail?"

"Yes. I left him text messages, too."

"Okay. I'll let him know you need to make contact."

"Thanks, Nora."

"You're welcome, dear."

Silence ensued, and for once, Gianna didn't want to break the only contact she had with Carter.

"Call me tomorrow if you haven't heard from him."

"I don't want to trouble you."

"No trouble at all. Call me."

"Thanks, I will."

At that juncture, Gianna decided not to call Carter again but wait to see if he would make contact.

The next day, she was up staring at the screen of her phone, hoping for a text message from the man who had touched her heart. By eleven o'clock, she made a call to Nora.

"Hi, dear, good morning. Still no word from my son?"

"Good morning, Nora. No word from him. Is he okay?"

"Yes. He's not sure when he'll return, maybe a month's time."

Stunned, Gianna remained silent.

"Gianna—"

"So-sorry to bother you, Nora. Thanks for letting me know."

"Gianna, don't worry about it. You crushed his fragile ego, so you have a fight on your hands. I'm a firm believer though that love always triumphs."

"Nora, I—"

"Don't worry; it can be fixed. If you're not busy tomorrow, I can swing by around two. You know what, this is an emergency, I can be at your home at five o'clock today."

"Yes, I'll be home. Thanks, Nora. I'm sorry for how I treated you the other day."

"No need for an apology. I helped to create this misunderstanding, so let me help you fix it."

Gianna fought the sobs that were rising from her belly. "Thank you."

An hour later, Gianna was waiting for Elder Brenda Richardson in her office at Restoration Tabernacle of Faith Church. On Sunday, when she'd attended church, she had decided to get on Elder Richardson's schedule for some much-needed advice. True too, Elder Richardson already knew her childhood story.

Gianna admired Elder Richardson's sleeveless denim dress, which fit her perfectly. Her hair was pulled back in a ponytail highlighting her caramel-colored complexion. From all her testimonies, Gianna gathered that she was in her early fifties, but she could pass for a decade younger.

"Thanks for your patience while I took that call," Elder Richardson said.

"No problem, Elder," Gianna responded with a cheerfulness that sounded somewhat forced. She shifted to make herself more comfortable on the navy-blue chair before the mahogany desk.

"Okay, let's pray before we share," Elder Richardson said.

"Sure."

After Elder Richardson prayed, she smiled at Gianna. "I'm glad to see you. What's going on?"

Tears blurred Gianna's vision at the kindness in the woman's eyes, and she couldn't hold back the broken sob that came from her throat.

Elder Richardson raced to her side, sat on the arm of the chair that Gianna occupied, and patted her back.

Gianna hung on to the woman and wept. When her crying subsided, Elder Richardson gave her tissue from a box on her desk and Gianna mopped her eyes.

"I'm sorry," Gianna choked out.

"Not a problem. There's nothing wrong with a good cry. It releases stress." Elder Richardson gave Gianna space and sat in the matching chair next to her. "What's going on?"

"I broke off my engagement with Carter because I found out something about him."

"Tell me more. Was it a bad thing?"

"No, it's not a bad thing. Actually, it's good, but I wish he'd been upfront with me about it. I was mad when I found out, and I found out by the way—long story. He said that he had planned to mention it after his mother's party."

"Did he explain?"

"Yes, and I get what he's saying. I mean, I understand why he didn't mention it."

"I feel like I'm missing something."

"Before he explained, I had returned the engagement ring. We met after that and sorted it out, so I thought that we would get back together. Now he's not taking my calls or responding to my messages."

"So you feel like you've lost him?"

"Ye-yes," Gianna squeezed out, blinking rapidly.

"Second chances aren't easy. Try not to make a snap decision when you're in a tough spot, especially if that decision can wait."

"Harrrrrr," Gianna's moans broke free.

Elder Richardson smiled at her. "I doubt strongly that this is the end for both of you. Let's talk about you for a moment."

"Me?" Gianna avoided her gaze.

"What caused you to tighten the reins around your heart?"

Gianna felt her defenses climbing.

Elder Richardson held up a hand. "Don't forget, I saw you two at his mother's party. You both looked great together."

Gianna launched off. "I was living my life, and all was well. Enter Carter Levi McIntosh, whom I didn't see coming. Literally, I didn't." She laughed a little. "Suddenly, my life took a sharp right turn. I'd put up a resistance to the change in direction, but not my typical fierce opposition. But, in no time, Carter unraveled my defenses. He did it so subtly I didn't realize it was happening. He made me feel things that I longed for. I had even begun latching on to God's vision for my life. I was happy, but deep down, I was terrified. Then with my discovery, everything went up in smoke. Granted, before all of this, I had been praying and felt the peace of the Lord concerning a relationship with him."

Deep in thought, Gianna pursed her lips.

"I'm listening," Elder Richardson said quietly.

"At our meeting, Carter said that he didn't need to be with someone who would throw up arms or fall on a sword when trouble hits. He also felt that I have a few deep personal issues to deal with."

"Thanks for sharing that. You brought more clarity. Marriage is not easy. It's a complex road to travel, so I can understand Carter pulling back. Using First Peter four and verse eight, I will try to explain what is happening with Carter. That Scripture states, 'And above all things have fervent love for one another, for love will cover a multitude of sins.' Because you love Carter, he expected you to forgive him. Worst case scenario, hear him out."

Gianna took a deep breath and swallowed what she was going to say. She'd lashed out at Carter, but he'd still come to her rescue when the panic attack hit. He'd seen her at her best and worst. He'd witnessed it all. Her joys. Her sorrows. Her hurts. Her mistakes. Yet, he was relentless in his love.

"The best example of a love that covers sin is the sacrificial death of Jesus Christ on the cross," Elder Richardson said. "Jesus did it for you and me. Love covers sin, in that it is willing to forgive. Remember that in the future, when issues arise between you and Carter."

Gianna was wide-eyed.

"What else is on your heart?" Elder Richardson asked.

Gianna lapsed into contemplative silence for a few seconds before she spoke again. "I need immunity to thwart the plan of people who will hurt me. Things always seem right at first before they go horribly wrong."

"None of us is immune to that. The only difference is that as a child of God, you have the guidance of the Holy Spirit. You can put your faith and trust in God to lead you into all truths. He will help you to make decisions. Proverbs three verses five to six, 'Trust in the Lord with all your

317

heart and lean not on your own understanding; in all your ways acknowledge Him, and He shall direct your path.' So you must lean on the Lord, bring all matters to Him, no matter how big or small. That's where your trust should be—in God. He's got your back, and He will work it all out."

Gianna smiled at her. "Thanks. I remember Romans eight verse twenty-eight, 'And we know that all things work together for good to them that love God, to them who are the called according to His purpose.'"

"Perfect." Elder Richardson returned her smiled. "So tell me about that issue now, the secret one. The one that caused you to think your relationship was doomed from the start."

"Secret one?" Gianna's body stilled.

"The real reason you called off your engagement."

What in the world?

"That's the one we need to deal with Gianna, or you'll be going down this road again and again."

A sob erupted from Gianna's lips, and she used the back of her hands to wipe her eyes.

Elder Richardson waited.

Gianna stood and walked to stand near the window. A few seconds later, she turned to face Elder Richardson, who was now perching at the edge of her desk.

"I feel broken...."

"And?" Elder Richardson encouraged.

"I feel broken and he's so whole. His story is inspirational and full of hope. Which is great because it tells everyone that they can survive adversity and live out their dream." She paused and looked at Elder Richardson before her eyes hit the floor. "But he...."

"Go on."

"He feels like a man I shouldn't have."

Gianna held on to a cabinet nearby as tears flowed.

318

Elder Richardson was quiet as she gathered herself.

It was all or nothing, Gianna decided.

"I...I feel bad for thinking that about myself and about him because he has been through so much. His healing took time, but he recovered. I wonder if I look like a bird with a broken wing to him."

"There, you said it. It's okay. You're entitled to your feelings. Now, let me see you breathe in and out."

Relief washed over Gianna as she did as Elder Richardson suggested. She had never confessed those thoughts out aloud. She exhaled loudly, trying to settle her heart rate.

Following that, they both returned to the seats they'd occupied.

"I want you to give yourself kudos for voicing that," Elder Richardson said. "It takes a strong person to reach out for help and to say exactly what is on the heart. Now instead of thinking that you're broken, and Carter is whole, why don't you flip the coin and use Carter's life story as a hint from the Lord that He wants to make you whole?"

Gianna felt hopeful.

"You can think about your challenges in many ways but remember that all things are working for your good. Even the unpleasant and terrible things that happen to us, God will work out for our good."

She waited for Gianna to digest that.

"I have known Carter through church circles, so I have heard his testimonies. Yes, I know about Kara, which is why I'm sure he's in love with you. I doubt he would have proposed if he didn't genuinely love you and feel the Lord leading him in that direction."

Gianna's eyes bulged. "He shared about Kara?"

"Yes, but I'm thinking only when the Lord puts it on his heart to do so. That's what happens when you've passed through murky waters. You want to reach back and

319

pull someone out. You want to let them know that they, too, will survive. And it's a reminder of what God has done in your life."

"Indeed." Gianna nodded in agreement.

"You're absolutely gorgeous, Gianna, and you're precious in the sight of God. You went through a lot at a tender age; it was a lot for a child to bear. The whole world was against you, and nobody knew. Part of the pain you carry is that nobody knows what it's like to be you, pressed beyond measure, beyond your strength and ability. But look at you now; you've made it. You're still standing and that's something to celebrate. Something to tell the world about, not cover it and pretend it didn't happen or wish it away. You're still here because God wants it, so you have a lot to contribute to the world."

Gianna felt her spirit soaring.

"It's obvious that the enemy tried to kill your dreams at a tender age because he saw a glimpse of what you would become. There are many situations in our lives that we cannot fix or change. Nevertheless, we must press forward. I believe God wants to use you for His glory. There is an anointing in you that will bring forth the blessings of God, not only in your life but also in the lives of others. The question is, will you come out of the shadows and be the Gianna Giva Barrett that God created you to be?"

As the fog lifted, Gianna nodded with understanding.

She would not be standing in her own way.

CHAPTER 49

"Lord, You're the strength of my life. No good thing will You withhold from me if I walk uprightly," Gianna pushed out quietly, as she stood in the middle of her bedroom at home. "You have my whole life in your hands, Lord. You know all my situations and I'm confident that You're working them out for my good. Thank you, Lord, for reminding me that nothing is over until You say it is."

"Everything okay in there?" Kamala called out from Gianna's bathroom.

"Yes, I was talking with the Lord."

"That's a good thing."

Gianna nodded then remembered Kamala was not in sight. "Yes, it is."

"It's too quiet in there!" Kamala yelled. "I'm almost finished."

"I'm good. Take your time."

Gianna gazed at herself in the dresser mirror. Once again, Kamala had styled her hair—a curly, messy updo with long, soft tendrils draping her cheeks—the way that Carter liked it. She had to admit she looked stunning in her navy-blue cocktail dress with its V neckline, lace bodice, and floral appliqué on the fit and flare skirt. The hem fell a little below her knees, and the cap sleeves hugged her toned arms. Her jewelry—gold cascading twist drop earrings and the delicate gold necklace from her parents.

"Aren't you a sight for sore eyes?"

Kamala's voice caused Gianna to turn towards her.

"You're good for me," Gianna told her. "Oh, wow! You look gorgeous."

She admired Kamala's dusty pink one-shoulder dress that hit right below her knees. The long blouson sleeve was eye-catching.

"Thanks, bestie. Oh, those shoes," Kamala said, looking at Gianna's feet.

Gianna was wearing a pair of navy-blue three-inch evening slippers with ankle straps. The floral bow that was attached to the buckles made her feel like the cutest girl in the room.

"Thanks! Where are your shoes?" Gianna asked noticing Kamala's black flats.

"I have them in a bag near my purse. I will drive so you can breathe and relax."

"You don't—"

"I need to. We both need to make it safely."

"Oooo-kay."

A soft chuckle came from Kamala. "You'll thank me one day."

An hour later, Gianna and Kamala raced up the steps of Henry and Nora's home as Peter Nedran, a member of the household staff, drove away Kamala's CRV.

Covert operation "Give Me You" was in its initial stage.

"Hurry! Hurry!" Nora shrieked, her hands flailing in the air.

Gianna and Kamala rushed into her home, and she closed the front door.

"Sorry about that," Nora said, breathing a sigh of relief. "Carter is on the private road to get here."

"O-oh," came from Gianna, and she handed Kamala her purse and cell phone.

"You'll be great," Kamala encouraged her. "Just breathe."

"You ladies look absolutely stunning," Nora said, smiling.

"Thanks," Gianna replied, echoed by Kamala.

"Everything is as planned," Nora informed them. "Gianna, you can head to the ballroom, the guys are there and waiting for you. I have Celia on lookout duty. She'll fill you in shortly."

"Thanks, Nora. I appreciate—"

"You're welcome. I need you to get out of here. Kamala, you're coming with me."

"Off and running," Gianna said, walking quickly through the entryway and heading across the living room.

"Hello, beautiful lady!"

Gianna smiled widely as she came face-to-face with Celia.

"Thanks, Celia. I hear you're on lookout duty."

"Yes. Exciting times. I live for the thrill," Celia said dramatically.

Gianna grinned. "I can tell."

Celia snorted. "Let's go. I hear someone special is on the way."

They moved towards the door leading to the ballroom.

"Rylan will give you your cues. I will be in touch with him by phone, so as soon as Carter and Mrs. McIntosh are in the living room, Rylan will know. When they exit the door we just came through, I will let Rylan know."

She looked at Gianna with expectation as they entered the ballroom.

"Got it," Gianna told her.

"Here we go," Celia said, smiling. "See you later."

After Celia left, Rylan waved Gianna towards the band members who were standing in a sort of semi-circle.

Gianna moved through the ballroom, which was adorned in gold, red, and ivory. The stylish orchid centerpieces on the tables were delightful.

Tamping down the panic that filled her heart, Gianna picked up speed to get to the band members, who were looking expectantly in her direction. She didn't remember there being so many of them at the rehearsal, but she wasn't about to complain.

"Hi, guys," Gianna greeted them.

They returned her greeting.

Wide-eyed, Gianna looked at Rylan. "The band has increased."

They all chuckled.

"Yes," Rylan said. "I invited the whole gang. You'll meet them later. We have to get cracking."

"Yes, Carter is nearby," Gianna said, taking the microphone that Rylan was offering. "Thanks, Ry. Thanks, everybody. We'll meet later."

Some nodded, and others murmured "Yes" as they moved back to their respective instruments.

"We'll play the introduction twice," Rylan said, then added teasingly. "Just so you get your nerves under control."

Gianna smiled at him. "You feel me."

Rylan returned her smile, displaying even white teeth, a sharp contrast against his milk chocolate complexion. "I've got you. It's going to be alright."

"Wait for me!" a familiar voice called out.

Henry McIntosh rushed towards them from a side door in the ballroom. "Carter just pulled in the front yard."

"Dr. McIntosh," Gianna greeted him with a smile. "I didn't know you were involved."

"Gianna, you look lovely. Of course, I'm *involved*. These are exciting times," Henry said, giving her a brief hug. "Henry, remember."

"Henry, it is," Gianna told him.

Gianna watched as Henry took up his saxophone from a chair nearby, and just as she was about to turn away, he spoke. "As a matter a fact," Henry stroked his peppered gray beard, "just call me Dad. Don't tell the boys—" he said with a conspiratorial wink "—but I've wanted a daughter my whole adult life."

Gianna's eyes bulged and everyone cracked up. She laughed right alongside them.

Soon, silence descended as they took up their places.

Microphone in hand, Gianna took center stage and prepared to give the performance of a lifetime. She was hoping to do justice to Whitney Houston's popular song "I Have Nothing."

"The package is approaching the living room," Rylan said, causing soft laughter from some of the band members.

"Ry," Paxton said in a low tone, "you can make it plain. We all know the plan."

Rylan gave up an are-you-crazy expression, telling him, "This is a covert operation. No names."

That caused more low chuckles.

They waited.

The lights dimmed on the band.

Rylan started the countdown. Five… four… three… two…

CHAPTER 50

Nerves. Expectation. Gianna's pulse skyrocketed, and she could hear her heartbeat thundering in her ears. *Focus,* she cautioned herself.

The band started the introduction to the song, but Carter was nowhere in sight. She remembered that the band would play the intro twice before she started.

The ballroom door opened, and Carter strode in purposefully, then paused, looking around at the tables, before advancing again. His expression was almost somber, but he looked fashionable, his long bowlegs wrapped in a pair of black cargo jeans. His well-defined abs were on display in a relaxed fit, long-sleeved white shirt that lay perfectly against his body. A pair of black high-top sneakers completed his outfit.

As if realizing that something wasn't quite right, Carter slowed his paced while looking towards the band.

Just then, the light over the band brightened. Mic in hand, Gianna looked him in the eye and began to sing effortlessly and passionately.

Momentarily stunned, Carter's long stride stuttered as he caught sight of her. His eyes widened with confusion, a series of emotions rolling across his face.

Gianna kept focused, hearing the band in sync with her well-controlled angelic vocal range. She could tell that the band members were showing off their musical skills while enjoying every minute of her performance.

She locked eyes with Carter, and neither of them could look away.

Smiling, she conveyed her love for him in song, all the while making sure her eyes appreciated his superbly honed physical appearance.

Mesmerized, Carter watched, having eyes only for her. He walked forward as if in a trance as she wooed him with her voice. His piercing light-brown gaze fixed on her, Carter stopped, but his eyes displayed all the emotions he couldn't hide.

Gianna's heart lurched. He hadn't completely forgotten her. She smiled lovingly at him, her voice soaring at the chorus. And as their gaze grew intimate, she closed her eyes to keep singing. It still amazed her how in tune they were with each other's emotions.

When she opened her eyes, Carter was gazing steadily at her, with a half-smile, his eyes shining softly.

Her gut tightened, and she watched as his eyes searched her face, then admired her dress before moving back to her face. She was drowning in his gaze, but she couldn't stop smiling at him even if she tried.

She ignored the butterflies in her stomach as a surge of sensation hit her. Moving towards Carter, she continued to pour out her love for him in song. Directly in line with him, she stopped to sway gently, her powerful voice filling the ballroom.

He was thrilled.

Their deep, prolonged eye contact was magnetically pulling her towards him, but she couldn't be distracted because the high notes in the song were coming up. Oh, she was ready. *Effortless transition.* The lines rose triumphantly from her soul, just as someone flooded the ballroom with light, heightening the intense atmosphere.

Emotionally spent, Gianna walked and stood before Carter, the shrill notes coming out with great passion as she serenaded him. His smile widened and confident hope filled her heart, as she sang the last lines and ended with—"you, oh, ooh, ooh"—hauntingly sweet, sincere, and fervent.

Her eyes filled with longing, she told him, "The Word of God states, 'There is no fear in love; but perfect love casts out fear.' I love you, Carter Levi McIntosh." It came out in a whisper, displaying her desire and her love.

Seconds crawled by.

No response from Carter.

He couldn't hide his love for her. She saw it in his eyes.

In the silence, Gianna turned off her microphone. Helplessness seized her as she met his gaze.

Carter cocked a brow. "You're extraordinary, Gianna Giva Barrett. I'm a blessed man. I love you, too."

Happy thoughts twirled and danced across her mind. "I'm glad for that." She smiled widely; his words had left her floating with joy.

He was not making a move, but she had his undivided attention. She arched a brow. "Why didn't you answer my messages? I haven't seen you in six weeks and I prayed every day that you would return to me safely."

"Thanks. Maybe a brother needed more assurance that you wouldn't split his heart in two again."

Ouch! She had to be brave. "And now?" she asked, softly.

His voice was rough with emotions. "My heart doesn't want to walk away."

She grinned up at him.

His strong arm wrapped her waist and pulled her closer. She felt his erratic heartbeat as he stroked her cheek.

"Ca-Carter." The warmth he was evoking sent sparks flying through her body. She felt alive, and she loved it.

Mischief filled his gaze. "Why are you always calling my name in that breathless voice?"

Heat swamped her cheeks, and she placed her hands on his chest. "You know why," she mumbled. "You drive my emotions crazy."

"Is that so?"

He leaned closer, bringing with him the scent of Tom Ford Oud Wood cologne. He rubbed his nose against hers and then gently pecked her lips.

She clutched the front of his shirt. His mere touch was sending shivers down her spine. His mouth lingering above hers, he took his sweet time to bring his eyes back to hers. Face flushed, she whispered, "There are people watching us."

"And?" His eyes shone with amusement, yet they were full of loving promises. "That's what they get for putting us in this position."

"Their hearts were in the right place."

His eyes lingered on her face. "Luckily. For your sake…" he paused, his attention on her hands that were circling his neck. "I'm going to need my neck for my next task."

"Oh-oh." She didn't even know when she'd hugged his neck.

She released him, and he took the microphone from her hand and placed it on a table nearby. "You're going to need that," she mentioned, straightening her dress. "Remember, you have rehearsal…" She paused as loud cheers, whistling, and applause ricocheted in the room. *What?*

Carter was on his knees in front of her… for a second time.

Gianna twirled, joy immersing her soul in complete splendor.

He waited, soft laughter coming from his lips.

As she moved closer to give him her left hand, she glimpsed the smiling faces of the band members and all the people who loved and supported them—Carter's family, Kamala, Brooklyn, and Phil. Their pastors and their wives were also present. Gianna gaped when she saw Aunt Dorette. Hard to miss, were the tears streaming down

Nora's face as the group moved closer to get in on the action.

Gianna's gaze swung back to the man she loved.

Carter was smiling and holding her hand, waiting for her attention.

Mesmerized, she sank to her knees in front of him. "Yes. Yes." *Oh, a thousand yeses might just be enough.* She smiled until her cheeks hurt.

Carter flashed her an ear-to-ear smile, then confessed, "I don't have a ring right now."

"Disappointing," Gianna teased, grinning at him.

"I-I have the ring," an emotional Nora announced.

The room buzzed with excitement as everyone looked towards her. She walked forward and handed the ring to Carter.

"I had a feeling," Nora said, smiling widely.

Carter grinned at his mother. "Thanks, Mom."

"Awww, Nora!" Gianna cooed.

"You're both welcome. Just moving as the Sprit leads," Nora responded, winking at Gianna before moving away.

"Now, where were we?" Carter asked, playfully.

Gianna pointed to her left hand. "You were about to put a ring on it."

"You bet."

Chuckling, Carter slipped the engagement ring on her finger.

As cheers went up, Gianna threw herself against him and hugged him.

Carter held her closely, and she reveled in the warmth their bodies created.

She released him, and he stood and helped her up. Suddenly, he bent and lifted her in the air. At first, she was stunned, but when he started turning, she squealed exuberantly, causing laughter to explode from the onlookers.

But Carter had eyes only for her.

He deposited her on her feet.

Hands on his chest, she gazed at him.

She had heeded the alarm bells concerning men her entire life but had secretly wondered, "What if there's that one man...?" Her smile widened, for she had found the one whom her heart loved. Finally, she understood what it was like to experience a love so rare.

Her eyes welled, and she hugged Carter tightly. She smiled against his chest when she heard him say, "We need another minute, please," before holding her closely.

His hand rubbing circles on her back, her breathing stuttered in pleasure at his touch.

One touch...

And many more to come.

Their story which had seemed to be fading, was now brightened with delightful images and memories.

Soon, Gianna and Carter came out of their embrace and welcomed the hugs and congratulatory words from their loved ones.

In the midst of the celebration, Carter announced, "Everyone, I need to worship for this mighty move of God. I must give God thanks for bringing me and Gianna together again. We are grateful for your love and support. It is always a pleasure to be in the company of family, relatives, and friends. A big thank you to my parents and brothers, who left no stone unturned to get me here," he chuckled self-consciously, and some in the room sniggered, "to receive my great blessing from the Lord."

He looked at Gianna, who was hugging his waist. "Babes, I love you."

"I love you, too," she responded.

He pecked her lips, and she blushed as she buried her head in his chest.

A low rumble coursed from his throat as he held back laughter. "We'll eat and chat shortly. Now, let's worship," he told their captive audience.

Buzzing sounds of excitement filled the room as the band moved back to their respective places, and the others took seats at the tables in the ballroom.

Carter held Gianna's hand, and as they move towards the band, he picked up and turned on the microphone that she had used.

"Babes, are you okay?" Carter asked.

Her heart sang as she gazed up at him. "Never better, honey."

This season was bringing her many happy moments that would become her favorite memories.

When Carter placed the microphone near her mouth, she was ready.

"Praise the Lord! For the Lord *is* good!" Her shouts of adoration filled the room. "With God all things are possible. With just one word from our God, darkness flees, and His glory surrounds us. With just one word, He breaks chains and revives every dream. Our God is awesome!"

Smiling, Carter lifted the microphone to his mouth. "We will not forget Your mercy, Lord. We will not forget Your grace. We come to glorify You. We come to bless Your Holy name. We come...."

And as they moved forward to worship, Gianna had a vision of the new road ahead, and it was terrific. She never imagined her life would have taken such a turn. She couldn't wait to be married to her beloved, for his love knew no bounds.

It was heaven-sent.

Deep.

Intense.

She was looking forward to returning all his kisses during the day, and... All. Night. Long.

Aha, laughter bubbled from her lips, and she almost skipped the rest of the way to the band.

Carter stepped closer and wrapped an arm around her waist, bringing her closer to where she belonged... at his side... in his arms... in his heart. She hugged his waist, sealing their connection. It was amazing to have something this good, this right.

And as the band played the introduction to Brandon Lake and Tasha Cobbs Leonard's "This Is a Move," the atmosphere in the ballroom was charged with worship.

Gianna looked at her fiancé, standing slightly away from her. He was looking at her, and she smiled. Her desire was to worship with him.

The band elevated the musical notes and tempo to a heavenly sound, and with Carter's nod, Gianna sang from her soul. Soon, he joined her and there was no stopping their smiles.

They were in sync.

They were in harmony.

They were in awe of an Almighty God who still did wonders.

So they rejoiced as they worshipped. Thankful to serve a God who knew that they needed each other. A God who was focused on reviving, rebuilding, and realigning all that was once lost in their lives.

Their smiles grew as their eyes locked.

It was time.

To love again.

To trust again.

To dream again.

And with God their possibilities were endless.

READING GROUP GUIDE

01. With which of the characters in *Dream Again* did you identify most, and why?

02. How did the main characters change throughout the story? How did your opinion of them change?

03. What are your thoughts about Gianna's reaction when she first met Carter? Did her outlook on life affect her response?

04. Carter was deeply in love with Kara, his deceased fiancée. What do you think attracted him to Gianna?

05. In chapter 26, Gianna said, "It's like I'm allergic to happiness." Have you ever felt that way? If yes, why did you feel that way and what steps did you take to resolve the matter?

06. What aspects of Carter's life were used by God to help Gianna overcome the pain of her past?

07. In chapter 28, Gianna said to Carter, "I know your ministry was birthed out of your challenging circumstances, and it wasn't easy for you." Are you the steward of a ministry that was birthed out of a challenging situation?

08. Henry and Nora McIntosh kept their family together through music rehearsal, followed by dinner. What activities are you using to keep in touch with your family?

09. Do you think that Nora is overprotective of her sons?

10. Nora made it obvious that she did not like any of the women her sons dated or were dating. However, she liked Gianna. What drew her to Gianna?

11. Think about the supporting characters and the role that they played. What did they bring to the table?

12. Have you experienced a tragedy or loss? If yes, how did you recover?

13. Which scene moved you most in *Dream Again*?

14. If you were making a movie of this book, who would you cast?

15. The nature of God is love, and He gives second chances. Have you ever felt that God gave you a second chance?

SONGS MENTIONED IN THIS NOVEL

Nobody Loves Me Like You Do
By Whitney Houston and Jermaine Jackson
YouTube:
https://www.youtube.com/watch?v=eGl0e4GKOfI

This Is a Move
By Brandon Lake and Tasha Cobbs Leonard
YouTube:
https://www.youtube.com/watch?v=wLkHygFqQno

Passion - Glorious Day
By Kristian Stanfill
YouTube:
https://www.youtube.com/watch?v=LfzpfqrPUDo

Raise a Hallelujah
By Bethel Music
YouTube:
https://www.youtube.com/watch?v=e3RRU25dpPg

So Will I (100 Billion X)
By Hillsong Worship
YouTube:
https://www.youtube.com/watch?v=GfVd5x9W1Xc

I Have Nothing
By Whitney Houston
YouTube:
https://www.youtube.com/watch?v=FxYw0XPEoKE

A NOTE FROM THE AUTHOR

I enjoyed writing *Dream Again*, book 1 in the McIntosh Brothers series, a heartwarming story about two people who have experienced tragedy and loss and must learn to trust God to overcome.

In this novel, you witnessed the incredible transformative power of love in the lives of Carter McIntosh and Gianna Barrett as they lifted their faith and developed the courage and tenacity to leave the past behind. I pray that you caught a glimpse of God moving through time to secure the future of those He loves.

Do not forget to wear the whole armor of God and to pray. May God continue to bless you as you live your best life through Jesus Christ. Thanks for taking the time to read *Dream Again*, and for being a part of my writing journey.

Stay victorious!

With love,
Ann Marie

ABOUT THE AUTHOR

Ann Marie Bryan is a multi-talented leader with a passion for excellence. She is the CEO and Founder of Victorious By Design, an organization committed to providing top quality writing services, comprehensive author services, and exceptional performing arts services to meet the unique needs of individuals and organizations.

A Christian Fiction author, Ann Marie writes to educate, inspire, and empower others. She desires to tell great stories with fascinating characters to show the awesome power of God in the lives of people and places. Her celebrated bestselling Encounters of the Heart series blends faith and romance that test the resilience of love.

Ann Marie's greatest passion is to empower others to succeed by tapping into their God-given potential. She enjoys writing, reading, dancing, teaching, meeting people, and traveling. With all the knowledge and experiences with which God has so graciously blessed her, Ann Marie is determined to make her life a ministry for the Lord.

CONNECT WITH THE AUTHOR

I would love to hear from you. Let's stay connected!

Website: www.annmariebryan.com
Twitter: www.twitter.com/authorabryan
Pinterest: www.pinterest.com/authorabryan
Instagram: www.instagram.com/authorabryan
Newsletter: http://eepurl.com/bOw6sr
Facebook: www.facebook.com/authorannmariebryan
Email: abryan@victoriousbydesign.com

JOIN MY FACEBOOK READERS' GROUP

Ann Marie Bryan's Readers' Café

WRITE A REVIEW FOR DREAM AGAIN

Amazon

Goodreads

BookBub

AVAILABLE TITLES
BY ANN MARIE BRYAN

Unforgettable, My Love Has Come Along
A Circle of Love Novel

Two paths destined to cross. Friendship, faith, and love are intertwined in ways neither could have imagined. Can love conquer all things? Find out in the heartwarming and humorous pages of *Unforgettable, My Love Has Come Along*.

Mirrored Hearts
A Short Story

He is determined to keep his secret close to his heart. She is living under the crushing weight of her own secret. Will their marriage survive when mirrored secrets are exposed? Find out in the page-turner, *Mirrored Hearts*, a fascinating story about faith and love in the face of crushing secrets.

ENCOUNTERS OF THE HEART SERIES

Book 1 - Shades of the Heart

A fascinating story about the courage to love in the midst of broken promises, and ultimately about the healing power of forgiveness.

Book 2 - Mirrored Hearts: Sealed by Fire

When life takes unexpected twists and secrets are laid bare, remember to breathe. Two hearts. Mirrored secrets. The ultimate solution – a marriage sealed by fire.

Book 3 – A Place for My Heart

An emotionally gripping account of a most unexpected love, and a marvelous reflection of God's grace. Crushed by heartache and desperate for an escape, one man makes a life-changing choice.

Book 4 – Where My Heart Belongs

A heart-stirring story about love deferred and rediscovered under unforgettable circumstances. Love guided them to precisely what they needed—each other.

Book 5 – Hearts over the Line

A riveting story about rising from the ashes, unlocking love, and learning to create and maintain an atmosphere of faith.

MCINTOSH BROTHERS SERIES

Book 1 – Dream Again

A heartwarming story that brings together two people who've experienced tragedy and loss and must learn to trust God to overcome their past hurts. For all they ever wanted was to be loved.

COMING NEXT

Book 2 – Love Again

Book 3 – Trust Again

VICTORIOUS BY DESIGN
Lighting the path to your next level of success

You are one of a kind.

You are fearfully and wonderfully made.

Embrace your uniqueness, talents, and abilities.

You are designed for your purpose.

You are perfect for your purpose.

You are Victorious By Design.

Visit http://victoriousbydesign.com for more information.